Slippery when naked...

Saddled

When Bobby Blackhawk and Cale Yancey see a car slide off the highway and into an icy creek, they've got only minutes to get the beautiful driver out alive. And only one way to save her from hypothermia: take her to their isolated cabin, get naked...and hope like hell that when she wakes up, she doesn't scream the place down.

Katherine Duvall opens her eyes in a strange bed, and the tingles flooding her body aren't entirely due to restored circulation. She's snuggled between two handsome men, one a gruff, gentle giant, the other a sexy, playful Native American. Having just left her fiancé romping with another woman, she's not quite as shocked as she might have been.

In fact, these two lonesome cowboys could be the perfect bookends to satisfy her hunger for revenge and bolster her dented self esteem. It's not long before their raging hormones are melting the snow on the cabin roof.

To their surprise, they find something else is melting, too. Their hearts...

Warning: This title contains hot ménage scenes, man love, anal sex, double-dipping, and two sexy cowboys—double the heat to thaw one frozen woman—and the only toys a lonely girl needs!

Tough…or tender?
If she plays her cards right, she won't have to choose.

Unbridled

Dani Standifer arrives home at her West Texas family ranch a day early, ready to pick up where she left off with Rowe Ayers, her high school sweetheart. However, when she opens the door to their line-shack trysting place, it's clear she waited a day too long. Rowe's with someone else—another man.

And not just any other man—Justin Cruz, the bad boy with whom she shared one wild encounter, years ago.

Justin's waited a long time for this moment. He knows his reputation, but since he seduced Rowe, he's been a one-man cowboy—waiting for Dani to return and become the delicious fulfillment of his and Rowe's needs. If she's up to the challenge.

To her own surprise, Dani finds she's more than ready to have both men in her life—as soon as she and Rowe teach Justin a lesson or two about love.

Their small town may not be ready for their kind of relationship. And Dani's brother Cutter's mile-deep grudge against Justin throws in a complication that could break the foundation the three of them have built…

Warning: Hold on for the rodeo of your life with rough ridin' male-on-male action, blazing hot m/m/f scenes, and melt-your-panties lovin' as each of these sexy cowboys gives it the way they know best to turn their woman inside out.

How does a man get over a cheating woman?
Sweet revenge...

Unforgiven

For Cutter Standifer, the pretty little redhead who opened a café in Two Mule, Texas, was "the one". Until he caught her in a compromising position with the town's worst womanizer. To further strain his rigid code, his little sister just married the same damn bastard who shattered his world and she's living in sin with him and another man.

A year later, he still can't forgive his ex-girlfriend. And forget? Forget, hell. He's ready to kick his code into the nearest manure pile and take what he never had from her—full satisfaction.

That fateful morning, all Katie Grissom meant to do was use the bad boy's reputation to force Cutter to piss or get off the pot where their own relationship was concerned. But she went too far—deliciously too far—giving Cutter an eyeful she lived to regret.

When Cutter offers her a no-strings affair she jumps at the chance, hoping to either break through the rigid wall he's built around his heart...or get him out of her system for good.

Warning: When a hard-as-nails cowboy finally lets loose on the only woman he's ever loved expect the loving to get hot enough to melt a cold, cold, heart—toys, front and slammin' backdoor sex are only the beginning...

Look for these titles by *Delilah Devlin*

Now Available:

Saddled
Stone's Embrace

Lone Star Lovers series
Unbridled (Book 1)
Unforgiven (Book 2)
Four Sworn (Book 3)

Print Anthology
Captive Souls
Cowboy Fever

Cowboy Fever

Delilah Devlin

A Samhain Publishing, Ltd. publication.

Samhain Publishing, Ltd.
577 Mulberry Street, Suite 1520
Macon, GA 31201
www.samhainpublishing.com

Cowboy Fever
Print ISBN: 978-1-60504-932-8
Saddled Copyright © 2010 by Delilah Devlin
Unbridled Copyright © 2010 by Delilah Devlin
Unforgiven Copyright © 2010 by Delilah Devlin

Editing by Lindsey Faber
Cover by Mandy M. Roth

Saddled, ISBN 978-1-60504-478-1
First Samhain Publishing, Ltd. electronic publication: March 2009
Unbridled, ISBN 978-1-60504-835-2
First Samhain Publishing, Ltd. electronic publication: November 2009
Unforgiven, ISBN 978-1-60504-877-2
First Samhain Publishing, Ltd. electronic publication: January 2010
First Samhain Publishing, Ltd. print publication: November 2010

Contents

Saddled

Dedication

For every woman who ever lusted for a cowboy...or two.

Chapter One

Bobby Blackhawk shook his head as the taillights of the little Beemer just ahead flashed red again through the falling snow. Sure enough, as soon as the driver crunched the brakes, the tail end of the car began to slide on the snow-covered ice.

"She's gonna go right into the river if she keeps that up," Cale Yancey muttered beside him.

They'd been following the car for the last ten miles, inching down the lonely highway. They'd already figured out the car wasn't using snow chains, and the driver was too stupid to know she was skirting on the edge of real trouble.

"Why are you so sure it's a woman?" Bobby asked.

"Can't drive worth a damn."

"Love for you to tell Lacey J. that."

"Lacey's not like other women."

Now, that was an understatement that had them both sharing lopsided grins, considering how well Lacey had proven that point the previous weekend.

"Sure could use me a little of her lovin'," Cale said, sounding wistful.

The last trip into Wellesley, Colorado in anticipation of snow blocking the mountain pass had been a wild, lust-packed two days. With a lonely winter facing them, they'd both taken Lacey up on her offer of a threesome that was sure to keep the two men growling like hungry bears for the next two months, impatient for the thaw so they could get back down the mountain.

It was a good thing they'd discovered long ago that they were compatible in ways that would make most men blanch, otherwise the wait to make it back into town would have been unbearable. Neither was squeamish about helping the other out; however, both preferred emptying their passion inside the wet, snug passage of a woman. If the woman happened to be obliging, like Lacey often was, they didn't mind sharing.

Both vehicles climbed the last long hill right before the men's turnoff and another half-mile beyond to the highway, tire treads biting into fresh snow.

"She might make it," Cale said, sounding doubtful.

"Think we better follow to make sure?"

The car ahead made it to the top of the rise, and then the brake lights flashed again.

Cale cursed. "Wish she'd quit doing that."

Rental company plates on the back of the car explained a lot about the aptitude of the driver. "Doesn't know she should just gear down and take it slow."

They reached the top, and Bobby geared down. Sure enough, the driver up ahead hit the brakes again, and the rear of the car slid sideways. As though watching a movie in slow motion, both men held their breaths, hoping the woman would gain traction at the last moment, but one rear tire slid off the edge of the road and then the right front followed. With tires spinning and brake lights flaring bright, the car slipped slowly down the hill and into the creek.

"Not good," Cale said tightly as Bobby pulled into the snow bank at the side of the road and left his emergency lights flashing. Just a precaution since there wasn't much of a chance of anyone coming up on their rear end since the road crew had been taking the barriers off the truck when they'd passed.

Bobby slammed the car into park and climbed out, following Cale as he slid on his ass down the hill. They paused at the water's edge, staring at the vehicle, both knowing one of them was going to have to get wet.

Water was midway up the car door, and the driver had rolled down her window. Blonde hair peeked beneath a black knit hat. Terror-stricken blue eyes peered at them through the falling snow.

"Ma'am, can you get yourself out?" Cale shouted.

"I think so," she said, her voice tight and quavering.

"If you can crawl out your window, we can help you the rest of the way."

"I'm getting wet. It's cold."

"Gotta move now, sweetheart," Cale said, his tone gentling the same way it did when he worked with a fractious horse. "You wait another second, two of us are gonna be in trouble."

"My purse. I can't find it." She turned in her seat, reaching into the back of the car.

The car bobbed on the water, and for a moment, Bobby thought it might break free and start floating. "Lady, leave it," he shouted. "You don't have time to look."

"But my money—"

"Not gonna spend it if you're dead."

She bit her lip, and then her face screwed up as though she was going to start crying.

"Fuck sake," Bobby muttered, stepping past Cale and stripping off his coat. "I'll get her out. It's gonna be up to you to get us both up that goddamn hill."

And then he was plunging into water so cold his legs went instantly numb. He reached her door, stretched an arm inside her window and unbuckled her belt. Her skin was too pale, her body shaking violently. She was entering hypothermia, and he was fast on her heels.

"Sweetheart, you have to help me a little bit. *Please*." Then he reached inside and pulled her, dragging her out, using brute force and knowing he was banging her around the window frame, but he had to be quick because the cold was sapping his strength.

As soon as her legs cleared the window and fell back into the water, she moaned, but he turned with her, slung an arm around her waist and half-dragged her back to the edge of the bank.

15

Cale reached for them both, but Bobby shoved her at him. "Get her to the car first. I'll be right behind you."

Cale gave him a sharp glance but didn't argue. There wasn't time. He bent and heaved the woman over his shoulder and then clumsily made his way up the hill and out of sight.

Bobby took only two steps out of the water before his legs gave out, and he fell to the ground on his knees. Shivering with cold, he stuck his hands under his arms and huddled inside the coat he'd left behind, knowing he'd have to be hauled up the hill too.

It seemed only a moment later and Cale was kneeling beside him. "Your turn, buddy."

Bobby tried to give him a smile, but he was just too damn tired and his face felt frozen.

"Can't carry you. Dammit, you have to help."

"Gimme a minute. Too cold," Bobby managed to mumble, but Cale's hands were already under his arms and tugging him hard. "Just a minute. I'll...walk."

"You're in no condition, but this is gonna be slow. I'm not leaving you here."

"Woman...gotta get her warm."

"Just shut up," Cale bit out. "She's in the truck. Got the heat goin' full blast."

"'S good," Bobby said, trying to keep his mind clear, but he was tired. So goddamn tired, and he couldn't feel his arms and legs. One last moment of clarity and it struck him that he might die. "Leave me."

"No fucking way." The tone of his best friend's voice was rough, deeper than usual.

If he could have, Bobby would have smiled. The only time Cale got this shook up was when his cock was deep, his balls tightening and on the verge.

By the time Cale fell through the front door of the cabin

with his final burden, he was shivering hard.

Bobby hadn't spoken a word in too long. The woman was still unconscious, lying in the same spot he'd dropped her before he'd headed back to the truck for his friend.

Bed, he had to get them both into bed. He let Bobby slide to the floor and walked on wooden feet to his room, tore back the quilt, turned on the electric blanket and then began to strip as he headed back for them both.

The woman was in the worst shape, but he carried her to the bedroom, sat her on the edge of the bed and stripped her as fast as his frozen fingers could manage before drying her with his clothes, then scooting her to the far side of the mattress and covering her up.

Then it was back for Bobby, whom he had to drag by his arms. Once his friend was stripped and lying on the bed, Cale stoked the wood-burning furnace and crawled up between them, pulled the covers over them all and tried to still the shivers that racked his own body sandwiched between two frighteningly cold bodies.

He pulled them both close on either side of him and wondered as he drifted off to sleep if any of them would make it through the night.

Despite their dire circumstance, Cale couldn't help thinking that the girl they'd rescued was just the type the two of them would have rushed toward in a bar, crowding her between them as they both jockeyed for attention.

More often than not, Bobby would win the competition. With his glib tongue and darkly handsome face, he'd lead the woman away, grinning at him over his shoulder.

Cale might have been left a time or two with a hard-on he couldn't ease, but he hadn't really minded. Not much, anyway. He knew his limitations when it came to attracting a woman like this. He'd noted the lush pink and cream curves he'd uncovered when he'd stripped the woman raw. With pale, shimmering hair and a face so sweet and perfectly formed, he knew he'd have been left tongue-tied and staring.

That something as classy as this woman was lying right

beside him had him thinking that maybe this wasn't such a bad way to go.

Katherine Duvall awoke as sensation flooded her feet and hands—sharp prickling pinches that made her moan.

"Yeah, it's gonna hurt. But it's a good sign sweetheart," a man whispered against her hair. "And there's no frostbite. I checked."

He'd checked? One fact penetrated her pain-filled fog. He'd done a lot more than checked. She was naked. And his bare-naked body was pressed up against her back, a penis nudging her bottom.

"Where are my clothes?" she gasped, choking on outrage and fear.

"Had to shuck 'em. They were soaked."

She remembered the car sliding into the water. But why wasn't she in a hospital? "Where am I?"

"In my cabin. Couldn't chance taking you back to Wellesley. Snow's comin' down too hard."

Her fingers stung, and she pulled her hands from under the covers to peer at them in the inky darkness. "How long have I been here?"

"Maybe an hour. Was worried about you two. You both passed out."

"Both?"

"Bobby went into the creek after you. He's not in much better shape."

She edged carefully away from his body, instantly missing the warmth and rolled onto her back to get her first view of her "rescuer". What she saw didn't do a whole lot to alleviate her fears.

The man lying beside her was enormous—a broad-shouldered shadow. Her heartbeat thudded against her chest as her alarm grew, and she wondered what else he might have done while she'd been out.

"Let me get the lamp. You sound like you're about to freak out."

About to?

He leaned away. A light flickered on from a bedside table, and she got her first clear glimpse of the stranger in the bed beside her. He leaned on his elbows, his expression taut as she stared back. Shaggy, brown hair, thick dark brows over deep-set eyes. His skin was deeply tanned, his chest and abdomen a study in light and shadow as muscles rippled as he breathed. The thick fur covering his chest glinted with red and gold where the light struck it.

Then she caught a glimpse of another body outlined beneath the covers on his opposite side. "Just what the hell do you think you're doing?"

"It's not what it looks like," he said softly, a smile turning up the tips of his mouth. "Swear. I had to get you both warm."

She pulled the edge of the blanket higher over her chest and scooted away from him, caught by a hard shiver.

"You're still chilled. The electric blanket's set low. Didn't want to damage tissue as I heated you both up."

A groan sounded beyond the bear-like man. "Goddamn, would you both shut up? Fuck, everything hurts."

"Bobby, you need to wake up. We got a problem here."

The figure huddled under the blanket stirred and rolled toward them with a moan. When he came up on an elbow, air hissed through Kate's teeth. The man was even more attractive than the first, and she was wondering if she'd woken up on the wrong side of heaven. This one wasn't as large but was every bit as ripped. And his wide chest was hairless, his face austere, scraped clean over high cheekbones and a jutting jaw. An Indian by his bronze skin, even without seeing the long black hair that filtered around his shoulders.

Still, they were both naked. And sharing a bed with her. *And* she didn't know if she was safe or about to be molested. After all she'd felt an erection prodding her bottom.

19

She took a quick, silent inventory. The parts of her that weren't busy thawing didn't feel any different. She'd know, wouldn't she, if he'd already taken advantage of her?

"We're not going to hurt you, lady," Bobby said. "We saved your life. Get back under the covers and snuggle close. You'll warm up faster. Can't have you getting sick, seeing as how you'll be stuck here for a while."

Her heart stuttered, then began to race. "What? I can't stay here."

"Don't know if you noticed," Bobby replied, "but there's a storm outside. The roads are closed. No one's getting in or out."

She opened her mouth to make another protest, but she shivered again and moaned as the pain intensified in her fingertips.

"You're gonna have to trust us," the big guy said. "If something comes up between us, you'll just have to ignore it. My body's warmer than yours even though I've been stuck between two blocks of ice for an hour."

Color filled her cheeks. She shivered for another few moments and then gave in to the offer of warmth. Facing away, she settled on her side and held her breath as he snuggled close again. When his arm came over her waist, she jumped but calmed as he shushed her gently.

The embarrassment and fear was a small price to pay for the heat his body generated.

"Just go to sleep," he muttered. "This is as close as I'm gonna get."

It was close enough. Again, his cock was upright and poking at her bottom.

"Don't know how it's staying hard," he whispered. "Your ass is cold."

A gust of laughter surprised her. "Serves you right. Should have kept your underwear on."

"Lady, you always this grumpy?" came Bobby's slurred whisper.

"No. I'm just not used to waking up in bed beside

strangers."

Bobby grunted and slid closer to the bigger man's back. She knew because his hand reached right across the body between them to land on her hip. "Fuck, I'm cold."

Cale lifted his upper leg. He was relieved the woman hadn't starting screaming the house down, but he was embarrassed just the same that she'd noticed he was aroused. "Slide whatever you need to warm up between my legs." He slid his ankles forward, capturing the woman's feet between them.

She sighed and settled deeper against him. "Can't believe I'm doing this..."

He wondered if she'd really freak if two cocks poked at her when he felt Bobby's slip between his legs, nuzzling under his balls. His own gasp at the uncomfortable chill stirred thick, fragrant hair in front of his mouth. She smelled like strawberries. *Nice.*

Spooned front and back, and with his companions warming up nicely, he raised his eyes to the window beyond the bed, thinking it might be an interesting few days while they rode out the storm.

From the sound of the wind howling, shaking the glass and rustling thick drifts of snow over the roof, they might as well hunker down and stay warm inside. Cale tightened his grip on the woman's slender waist, slowly drawing her closer, and nestled his face against her soft hair. Yeah, the next few days might get hot as hell.

Chapter Two

Kate muttered a protest when the warm hand cuddling her breast slipped down to her hip.

"Sorry about that," came a low mutter.

Her eyes sprang open. She took note of the nipple that had tightened into a bud and hoped like hell the man hadn't noticed. But she thought it was already too late, because the cock digging into her back pulsed gently. It had to be killing him to hold her like this.

But he'd been a gentleman after all. Sharing his body heat, holding still to keep from disturbing her sleep. She hadn't been as careful. Her feet were snuggled between his legs. Her bottom snuggled even closer to his groin. Sweat had begun to pool between them.

Add the interesting extra factor of the other man included in their embrace, and she thought "The Bear" probably thought he'd died and gone to Hell. She smiled at his discomfort, amazed she'd woken so at ease inside his arms considering her initial reaction, but some of what had happened at the river had sunk into her mind. The two of them really had saved her life.

Objectively, she understood why he'd brought her here, stripped her to her skin and crawled into bed beside her. The man should get a medal.

However, she should have her head examined with the places her hazy waking dreams had taken her. It seemed forever since she'd woken inside a strong, sexy man's embrace. Her ex was slender and desk-soft, and never made her feel safe.

And her mind couldn't let go of what Bobby had said about her being "stuck" there for the next few days.

Around and around, thoughts swirled in her mind. Lusty, lewd images magnified by the heat surrounding her and the scents of the two men lying so close—the tang of wood smoke, the light, crisp smell of hay and horses, and male musk...

And her body was right there with her nasty thoughts, warming from the inside out, moistening, tingling...

The devil resting on her shoulder asked, *Why not see where circumstance and sheer desperation had landed her?* It was certainly a more pleasant prospect than she'd had before disaster struck.

She'd fled the ski resort in a fit of pique, devastated because all her plans for her bright, brilliant future had unraveled the moment she'd walked in on her fiancé's little afternoon tryst. Back early from her lessons on the bunny slope, she'd wanted to surprise him with a little of what he'd arranged the trip for—time alone to rekindle their sex life.

The months leading up to the wedding had been hectic, filled with parties and work as they prepared to take a month off to marry and honeymoon. As she'd boarded the flight from Sacramento to Denver, she'd complained about all the last minute details that still needed to be managed. David's angry reaction had taken her aback. His irritation had made him moody for the entire flight and for the drive up into the Rockies to the resort he'd booked.

She hadn't bothered waking him that morning before she left for the slopes, hoping sleep would ease his sour mood. Lately, he'd grown grumpier and more distant. When questioned, he'd remained taciturn, and they'd spent more nights than not on opposite sides of the bed. She'd thought that maybe he was as stressed out as she was even though he'd left all the arrangements for their nuptials in her hands.

Perhaps he felt neglected. Returning early, determined to repair the rift, she'd swiped her card key in the magnetic lock and gently pushed open the door leading into the suite. The sitting room had been empty, the curtains still closed. She'd dropped her jacket and gloves and unzipped the bodysuit and left it in a pile with her boots, walking in her underwear to the bedroom door.

The bathroom door had been ajar, towels heaped on the floor. He'd showered, so she thought he must have wakened and gone back to bed.

Then she'd heard a noise inside the bedroom. A sigh, followed by a thin, feminine moan.

Thinking he must have turned the television on, she opened the bedroom door and then hung onto the knob in shock for several agonizing moments as her mind wrapped around the sight that had greeted her.

A woman—no, the server who'd flirted with David at the bar the previous night—sat astride his hips, gliding up and down while his hands cradled her bottom, his fingers biting deep into her buttocks to quicken the strokes.

Her figure was rail thin, supple, her breasts slight but tipped with cone-like nipples. Her hair, long and dark, had fallen in a soft burnished cloud that bounced between her shoulder blades as she rocked up and down David's long cock.

Neither had noticed her standing there. David's eyes had been glued to the woman's pussy and his own dick. Hers had been squeezed shut.

No wonder he hadn't minded when she'd booked the lesson the previous night. He must have set up the liaison when she'd left to talk to the concierge.

Kate had backed away from the door and closed it.

She'd sat on the sofa in the sitting room, staring at the hands she cupped between her thighs, not because they were still cold, but because they shook. The plans they'd made, the life she'd dreamed of were gone. No doubt if she'd confronted him then and there, he'd have found a way to place the blame for his slip on her.

He'd made her feel guilty as hell the last time he'd cheated. And because she'd been impressed with his wealth, impressed with the people he knew and the places he took her, she'd come to believe she could live with that. That maybe the people who

24

lived in the upper stratosphere of society operated on a different ethical code.

She'd forgiven him and turned a blind eye to the late nights he spent at the office. When he'd insisted on the trip, part of her had been relieved that he seemed to be eager to spend time alone with her, loving only her.

Now she knew the truth—that any willing pussy would suffice, and that the fact his fiancé had been skiing on the slopes outside the resort only added to the thrill. For the rest of her life, she could expect him to fuck the maids, the secretaries, maybe even her friends—so long as she was willing to look the other way and shine on his arm when he needed to play the role of family man in public.

Kate had sat there shivering, glancing down at her lacy underwear, worn especially for him, and made up her mind from one heartbeat to the next that she deserved more.

She'd walked to the suitcase she hadn't had a chance to unpack the previous evening and pulled out a pair of jeans and a sweater, grabbed her jacket and purse, then went to the counter of the kitchenette, swiped up the keys to their rental car and left her diamond ring in their place. She wouldn't bother with the case, with her clothes. She just needed to get away fast.

The slamming of the hotel room door had gotten his attention. Dismayed, he'd followed her down the hallway. She'd stood in the elevator with a wide-eyed older couple as he'd pleaded, and her response had been to yank the towel from his waist and wave it as the doors slid closed.

She'd been stupid to think the sun rose and set in David Winter's lying blue eyes. She'd been shortsighted thinking that her life would be so much better with his money to console her when he travelled for business or worked extra hours. How long had she worn blinders, determinedly ignoring all the signs the man was a cheat and would never be satisfied with just one woman in his life?

On the drive down the mountain, as she'd slowed to a snail's crawl because she hadn't bothered to heed the bell staff's warnings about buying a set of snow chains, she'd had plenty of time to think. She'd known all along she'd never be happy with him. She'd let herself be swayed, comparing the heavily weighted "pro" side of the column against the single item in "con" side. There were so many qualities to admire about him that she'd wanted desperately to make their relationship work. As impressive as his good looks, wealth and connections were, she'd been turned inside out by his skill as a lover, and she knew she'd miss that. *Deeply.*

But now, fate had given her a chance to prove to herself that sex with David wasn't the best she'd ever have.

If the thick, blunt instrument denting her backside was any indication, she'd find plenty of proof that there were other men out there who could give her just as much pleasure as the smooth and confident man who'd swept her off her feet with his practiced moves.

But how could she broach the subject now after making such a fuss?

She pretended to murmur in her sleep and scooted closer.

Teeth ground; a muffled laugh from Bobby made the mattress quiver beneath her. And she wondered at the fact the two men seemed so comfortable snuggled up so close.

Maybe they were gay.

The thought arrested her rising excitement. Two beautiful men, a deserted cabin in the middle of a blizzard—and maybe she'd found the only two cowboys in Colorado who wouldn't be eager to share a little sexy heat. What a damn shame that would be.

Kate kept her eyes closed, trying to get a rein on her raging hormones. She didn't know who these guys were, what they were, but she'd been ready to risk everything for a little revenge sex. She was just as low as David, but at least he'd been honest about his needs.

Disappointed with herself, she held still as the man behind her began to move.

"Gotta put more logs in the furnace," Cale muttered. He had to get away.

He'd woken with his hand cupping a slice of heaven, a perky little nipple poking at his palm. He was as hard and horny as a man could get, and he needed some space to get control of himself before he gave the woman a damn good reason to be afraid.

Bobby mumbled a protest and pressed closer, not willing to lose the warm place he'd drifted in his sleep.

"Snuggle up to our guest while I'm gone." Cale extricated himself from his embrace and crawled down to the foot of the mattress.

The mattress rose. Footsteps padded away. Bobby cracked open one eye and looked across to the blonde still huddled at the far side of the mattress. Her breaths hadn't deepened, she hadn't made a single murmur, but instinct told him she was wide awake. Since she wasn't jumping up and screaming her head off, he wondered how far she'd let him get before making some noise.

He sighed as though he was annoyed and scooted across the mattress. When he carefully draped an arm around her waist, she rolled to her back, her eyes still closed tightly.

Her face was growing pink across her cheeks.

A smile tugged at his lips, and he closed his eyes too, peeking at her from beneath his lashes as he tightened his arm, which rode just beneath her breasts. A little quiver gave away her excitement. Coming closer, he pretended to sleepily nuzzle the corner of her shoulder and swept his thigh over her hip, bringing his cock up against her.

It twitched and hardened.

"Really think I'd sleep through that?" she whispered breathily.

He opened his eyes to find her baby blues staring back at him. "Who says I thought you were asleep?"

Her nose wrinkled. "Think he noticed?"

"I think he's a little preoccupied with the part of him that's hurting to know you've been playin' possum on us."

"You don't seem to mind."

One dark eyebrow arched in wicked delight. "Neither do you."

She sucked her lower lip between her teeth as though she was thinking hard about her decision. Then she gave him a coy look from beneath her gold-tipped lashes. "Think he'd be mad if we raised the stakes on the game?"

Bobby's lips twitched. "Gonna make him suffer a little longer?"

"Would he? I wasn't sure you two weren't...you know...together."

Bobby trailed a finger down her cheek. "Sometimes we are. But usually only out of necessity. Your being here is an unexpected blessing for us both."

Footsteps scraped outside the bedroom door. "He's coming," she whispered.

They both closed their eyes and scooted closer.

The soft scrapes neared the bed, and Cale muttered a curse under his breath.

Bobby nearly laughed, knowing Cale was regretting giving up his place beside her. But Cale surprised him, crawling onto the bed on the other side of the woman, squeezing up against the wall.

Bobby cracked his eyes open. "She's still asleep," he whispered, more for her sake than Cale's.

Cale stretched out on his side, facing them both. "Do you think she's gonna press charges if she wakes up between the two of us?"

"Maybe we should make goin' to jail worthwhile," he said with a wicked jag of his eyebrows.

Cale grinned and glanced at the woman lying quietly between them. His chest rose on a hopeful sigh. "She's mighty pretty."

"Maybe we should have a peek at the rest of her...while

she's sleeping." Bobby bit back a chuckle when her breaths stilled altogether. She wasn't telling them not to—that was close enough to permission for him.

"Maybe we're crossing a line here," Cale said.

"A peek. It's not like we're gonna molest her anything. Just seein' what we've been touchin' all along."

"Yeah," Cale muttered. "More than goddamn touchin'."

Before Cale's conscience put a halt to his play, Bobby slowly pulled back the edge of the covers, exposing her breasts to both their gazes.

"Nice," Cale whispered. "Much prettier when they're not blue."

"Look soft too. Maybe I should just make sure."

"Bobby..." Cale said shaking his head.

The woman had other ideas, sucking in a deep breath and muttering softly, then gliding her hand up her belly to rest atop one breast, her thumb and forefinger framing a nipple.

"Almost like she's offering us a taste..."

"Buddy," Cale said, warning in his voice. "We saved her life. Doesn't mean she owes us a thing."

"Maybe she just wants things to get a whole lot hotter. Ever think about that?"

Kate felt ready to scream the way the two men kept talking, staring at her, both of their cocks hardening against her sides, but not doing a damn thing to take the decision out of her hands. She wanted them to because she was basically a coward. Her plan was simple: let them get all worked up and begin some sexy little caresses, she'd wake up and be taken by surprise but already be so aroused she couldn't help but go along with it. At least that was her story, and she'd stick to it until the day she died.

But it seemed like the one "not Bobby" had some scruples about taking advantage of an unconscious woman. *Hell.*

She opened her eyes, her gaze swinging from one frozen face to the wicked gleam in Bobby's eyes. "Hi," she whispered, wanting to groan she sounded so lame.

"Hi yourself," the unnamed man said, grabbing the edge of the cover to pull it back up. But he tugged to no avail, because Bobby wouldn't let it go.

"It's okay. I'm a little warm," she said, her voice sounding high-pitched even to her own ears.

"It's not what it seems," he said, glaring at Bobby. "We just woke up and were getting ready to wake you and see how you felt."

"Right, we're all interested in how you feel," Bobby said.

"Uh huh," she murmured, narrowing her gaze on Bobby. Then she turned to The Bear. "I'm much better. All warm. Nothing stinging anymore. Thanks. You two saved my life."

"I went into the river after you," Bobby said, drawing her attention back.

Interesting that he thought he had to compete. "I remember. Thanks to you, too."

"I hauled your a—" the big guy cleared his throat. "I got you up the bank and into the car, drove you here and..."

"Stripped me naked. I know. It was necessary. I do understand."

"Guess, since you're warm and all, we should probably get dressed," he mumbled.

Not where she wanted this to go. "It's dark outside. Wouldn't you just have to get right back in bed?"

"There is another b—"

Bobby coughed, cutting off his friend. "You're right. Maybe we could just keep to our own sides."

"Seems you already have your own sides," she said softly.

Green eyes widened.

Bobby snickered. "Not a whole lot we can do from those sides."

"Really?" she said and stretched, arching her back and sighing with satisfaction when both males dropped their gazes to her breasts. She squeezed the hand still cupping a nipple. "I'm thinking there are two interesting places to start."

30

There, she'd said it. How much clearer did she have to be?

"Just to get this straight," the slow one said, his voice deepening. "You are awake, right? And I'm not dreamin'?"

"I'm thinking I'm still dreaming," she teased. "Two handsome men beside me in bed. Everyone warm and cozy. But you're right. It might feel more real if I actually had some names to attach to my dream men."

"I'm Bobby," Bobby said, lifting his hand as though they'd been introduced in church.

She took the hand warming her breast and placed it inside his palm. "Katherine, but you can call me Kate."

"I'm Cale," the other man said, leaning closer.

She glanced from one to the other and slowly smiled. "Since we know each other so well now, do you think we could dispense with manners? That or I'm going to have to ask you both to leave because something awfully embarrassing seems to be happening to me."

"What's that, sweetheart?" Bobby crooned.

"I'm wet," she whispered.

"*Dayum.*" Cale breathed deeply.

Bobby lifted one dark brow.

"Bobby," Cale said, swallowing hard. "Under the sink in the bathroom."

"Huh?" Bobby raised both eyebrows then met Cale's gaze. "Yeah, be right back." He rolled off the bed. "Fuck, the floor's cold."

Kate swung her gaze to Cale.

"We'll take care of you."

The way he said it, so solemnly, sent a shiver down her spine. His meaning finally sunk in. She hadn't given a single thought to protection. "It's weird, but I trust you."

"Don't trust that bastard."

She smiled. "He's your friend."

"Yeah, I know him best. And he tends to shoot first and then cuss."

Kate couldn't stop the giggle that erupted sharp and quick. "So you're the nice one?"

"Uhhhh...maybe just the one who thinks with more than his dick."

Her breath caught at the mention of the part of his body snuggled closest to her hip. "I've never done anything like this before."

"Don't have to explain a thing."

"I know. Just thought you might like to know a little about me. Besides the fact I don't look good blue."

"Oh you're pretty whatever color you are. Even red-cheeked like now."

Bobby padded back to the bedroom. "Didn't know how many we'd need. So I brought the box."

"Good for a start," Cale muttered.

"So, you're not nice," she drawled, "but you are pretty sure of yourself."

"We know our way around a lady's body," Cale said, in that same solemn tone. "Trust us not to scare you?"

"I'm not easily frightened. Not by anything you two might bring."

Bobby slipped under the covers and came in close, a hand sweeping over her belly under the covers. "Maybe I should check and see if you're about to make a mess of the sheets."

She wrinkled her nose. "That wasn't sexy."

"You're wrong, Kate," he said, his voice a smooth, whispering caress. Fingers trailed downward, slipping between her legs.

Her thighs clamped hard around his hand and then slowly eased as he gently slid between her folds.

"Relax. Just gettin' acquainted."

"Now that we're on a first name basis...?"

"First base, second. What's touching a wet pussy, Cale?"

"I'm not much into fucking baseball," Cale said, still holding back.

"But he is into fucking women," Bobby said, his fingers gliding deeper, touching the edges of her furled lips. "If you wondered about us."

"I thought you might be gay," she said, answering his teasing tone. "Until a couple somethings kept poking at me."

"Would it matter if we weren't all that particular about what we poked?"

Kate blinked. "I don't know. Um, are you talking each other or me, at the same time?"

"How 'bout both?"

Kate's body answered the question, releasing a gush of arousal that made Bobby moan as he dipped deeper into her. "She's okay with it. Now, let's stop talking circles around it and just fuck."

Cale grunted, giving her one last look that seemed to ask her permission.

Could she really do this? She was far, far away from home. No one would ever know.

She reached up, threaded her fingers into the thick hair at Cale's nape and dragged him down to her mouth.

His kiss was soft, exploring, lips molding hers in sexy circles. She parted her lips and then gasped into his mouth as Bobby dove under the covers and tunneled toward her legs. Hands pushed open her thighs and another set of lips smoothed over her mound and nipped the soft flesh. She opened wider.

Cale lifted his head, rolled the covers down to her waist and leaned over her to slide his mouth from her shoulder to the top of one breast. She cradled his head against her, and kept her eyes open, trained on the ceiling as sensations bombarded her. Hot and cold at the same time, rasping caresses, slick mouths...

She shivered.

"Cold?" Cale said softly.

"No. But can we lose the blanket? I want to move. Have to see," she said, gritting her teeth because Bobby had just plunged fingers deep inside her pussy.

"Sure thing, baby." He picked up the edge of the blanket and flung it toward the end of the bed, revealing Bobby who was kneeling between her legs.

His head came up and he gave them both a wink. "I think we can keep this heated up here."

Her laugh turned into a groan when Cale's mouth latched onto a nipple and sucked hard, his tongue stroking over the tip inside his mouth.

Bobby spread her with one hand, tugging her labia upward to expose her clit, then dove between her legs.

All coherent thought blew Kate's mind as the two men turned up the heat, sexy swirls of tongues and fingers going to work on her simultaneously. She widened her legs, raised her knees and stretched out her arms to grab fistfuls of the sheet beneath her to anchor her because she felt like she was flying apart.

Bobby withdrew and then slipped three fingers inside her, curving his hand upward to rub his fingertips against her G-spot. Cale released the breast he'd drawn into a point and slipped across her chest, his hand keeping the wet nipple warm as he suckled its twin.

Kate's thighs stiffened, widening more, and her hips began to dance upward, pumping to pull on the fingers twisting and rubbing inside her. When arousal began to tighten inside her womb, she moaned.

"Easy there," Bobby whispered. "Want to come this way? Want to come now?"

She wanted to shout "yes" because they had her wound so tight, but it had been so fast, so fierce that part of her was reluctant for it to end. "Too fast," she gasped.

Cale let go of her breast and shifted, coming up on his knees beside her and placing both hands over her breasts, continuing to massage her while he glanced back at Bobby.

Bobby's lips curved, and he pulled away his fingers. "Haven't even kissed you yet." He crawled up her body as Cale's hands slid away, and stretched out on top of her. His cock dug into her belly, thick and hard. His mouth stopped to scoop at both breasts, one at a time, but then he was above her, reaching out to enclose her hands and pluck them from the sheets. His fingers entwined with hers, and he brought them beside her head.

The play up to this point had been slightly impersonal—fast and fun—but now, staring into his taut face, free of any amusement, she swallowed, crashing back to earth with a lurch, knowing she was really doing this, really going let two men fuck her.

Her body was ripe for it, her pussy drenched, her nipples sensitized to the point of pain. When his mouth descended, she mewled because even the kiss felt more intimate, more of a commitment to their pleasure and their journey together than she'd ever felt with David. Which shook her.

"Want to change your mind?" Bobby asked softly. "You can. We won't hold it against you. Maybe you want to think about it some more."

She searched his gaze and found no recrimination, only the same sensual tension that kept her body hot and tight. Her gaze swung to Cale, who nodded sharply as though he was beyond the point of being verbal. She'd had a boyfriend like that once. He'd rutted like a goddamn animal, never gave her praise or sweet words, but had fucked like a god.

"I'm not changing my mind," she said, holding Cale's glance. The lifting of his chest, the unclenching of the fists resting on his knees was enough to convey his relief.

God, he wanted this as much as she did.

Bobby smoothed back her hair, tucking a lock behind her ear. "Want to try something? Might hurt a bit, but we can stop any time you want. You're in charge."

With her face so close to his she could see the excitement he tried to bank in his eyes. "What do you want to do?" she asked, nearly breathless herself.

"Let us take you at the same time. Share your pussy with us both."

"You think you'll both fit?" she asked, incredulous, because neither cock was small.

35

"You'll be surprised what arousal will let happen." His dark brows waggled. "And baby, I've been down there, you're plenty ready for it."

She wrinkled her nose. "I'm not sure I like you all that much. You're making fun of me again."

"Better than me crying, don't you think? Because, baby, I'm hurtin' bad."

A smile tugged at her lips. "We can try it, but you'll stop, right? If I say so?"

"You're in charge."

She nodded, taking a deep breath, and let them turn her on her side, facing Bobby. She thought she might have preferred staring into Cale's face, because he didn't make her feel so exposed, her desire so naked and openly lustful.

A foil wrapper landed on the side of Bobby's face, and he screwed up his expression in disgust. But he didn't hesitate, tearing the foil with his teeth and curving his torso to look down at himself as he rolled the latex circle down his cock.

From the noises behind her, Cale was doing the same, and Kate wished she could have had an eyeful of his cock as well. Bobby's made her mouth water. Thick, maybe seven inches long, it thrust from a sparse nest of black hair at his groin without a single curve or kink. A deeper bronze than the flesh of his belly, the tip was flushed and almost violet.

Bobby smoothed a palm over her hip while Cale stretched out behind her and came close, his cock once again prodding her bottom. Bobby brought his hips flush with hers, and lifted her thigh to drape over his. He reached between them, fit his cock at her entrance and then glanced up to catch her gaze. "Watch me come into you," he whispered.

Kate blew between her lips and dropped her gaze, trembling as his belly rippled and he curved it again to thrust inside her, sliding slowly up, then beginning a series of sexy little in and out glides to work his way deeper. The ridge around his crown rubbed just the right spot, and she opened her mouth to gasp. Satisfaction stretched his lips into a happy smile.

"Maybe you're nicer than I thought," she said softly.

"Don't mistake the fact your cunt pleases the hell out of me for nice, sweetheart. Cale's got that end all covered."

Yes he did. His hands cupped her ass, spreading her cheeks, and his cock glided right over her back entrance, pushing past her pussy.

"You're sliding under my balls," Bobby said, gritting his teeth. "Don't move for a second." His face flushed a deep red; his lips tightened against his teeth.

The pleasure flooding his expression leeched away his cocky self-assurance, and Kate could only stare as he struggled to maintain control.

When his breathing evened out a bit, he reached between their bodies and pulled open her labia, which were clasping him tight. "There you go, Cale. Push inside. Neither of us is gonna last long."

When Cale's cock slid back and pushed at the bottom of her pussy, she winced. "I don't think this is gonna work. Not enough room."

"Relax, sweetheart," Bobby said, bringing his head up to capture her lips in a swift, hot kiss.

Then Cale was prodding her again, his fingers slipping inside her, behind Bobby's cock, and opening her more, and, at last, the tip of his cock crammed inward.

Kate whimpered, stiffening between them, her frantic gaze meeting Bobby's. He ended the kiss and slid his cheek alongside hers. "Relax. Let him in."

And then they were both inside her pussy, both beginning to move—so thick they stretched her, burned her inner tissues. But fluid was washing down her channel, coating them both in warmth, lubricating her vagina as they churned in slow, short strokes as Cale crammed deeper.

"What does it feel like?" she whispered to Bobby. "Having him squeezing up against you?"

Bobby's mouth opened around a groan. "What does it feel like to you?"

"Tight, full...I'm not gonna last another second."

"Then come. We'll both be right there with you."

Both men gripped her body at the hips and waist and plunged upward, shoving deep, and Kate couldn't hold back. Her body quaked between them; her back bowed, slamming against Cale's chest. Her thigh clutched Bobby's hip hard, and her hands gripped his shoulders as the two moved in unison, fucking into her.

Kate felt caught between two rival storms, buffeted on both sides. When her orgasm exploded, she faintly heard the sharpening whimpers she made, and their muffled curses and grunting gasps.

When their bodies shuddered against her, deep groans soaring in the air around her, she had the random thought that she'd never felt so alive or filled with passion.

The men slowly settled, their cocks holding still inside her as their erections waned. The sweat dampening her front and back became chilled, and she must have shivered, because Bobby swore softly.

"Don't wanna come out," he muttered. "Not yet. You gettin' cold?"

She didn't want either to pull away any more than he did. With space, she might rethink what she'd let happen—no, what she'd asked to have done to her—and she wasn't ready for that. "Maybe if you came a little closer..."

"Baby, if I get any closer I'm gonna be breathing for you." But he did lift his hand to cup her shoulder while Cale slid his thigh over her hip.

Completely surrounded, she relaxed, closing her eyes.

"Kate, what the hell were you doin' on that road in a snowstorm?" Cale said, petting her hip.

She didn't want to talk. Didn't want to admit she hadn't given her flight from the lodge any thought for the conditions. "Escaping..."

Bobby's body stiffened against her. "Someone after you?"

"Maybe. Then again, he's probably just getting busy again with his little whore on the side," she muttered, glad her heart didn't ache even a little at the thought.

"You have a husband?" Cale asked. "Not cool, Kate."

"*Ex*-fiancé," she said softly, relieved when his tightening body relaxed behind her again.

"What'd he do to send you runnin'?" Bobby asked, his hand smoothing from her shoulder to cup her breast.

"Fucked another woman in our bed," she said, breathing deeply as he squeezed.

"I see," Bobby said, his tone neutral. "This a little revenge sex, then? I'm okay with that."

She couldn't stop a grin from tilting up the corners of her mouth. "I swear I don't think I've ever met a bigger smart ass than you."

"And to think, I get to spend my winters with that mouth," Cale mumbled.

"I don't know," Kate drawled. "I kind of like what he does with that mouth when he's not talking."

"You do?" Bobby asked with a crooked grin.

Both cocks locked deep inside her began to stir, flooding her pussy and her chest with warmth. "Mmmm-hmm. And if this is what getting a little revenge feels like, I gotta have me some more."

Chapter Three

Cale listened to his two companions trading quips and wished he was half as easy talking to women. Kate sounded so happy, nestling close to Bobby, that he felt a twinge of jealousy.

He didn't want to be eaten up with jealousy over some woman he barely knew. And he wished like hell he could figure out a way to have her all to himself for a little while, just so he could explore some of those other places Bobby had already test-driven. The thought of sliding his tongue inside her wet, juicy pussy, hearing her moans, all for him, made him restless.

"Maybe you should go check on the livestock," he said, lifting his gaze over her to glare at Bobby.

Bobby's lips twisted, then his gaze narrowed for just a second. "He's right," he said to Kate. "They have plenty of hay and water, but the snow's gonna get deeper before this is through." His forehead met hers for a moment and he groaned. "But I really don't want to come out of your sweet cunt, Katie."

"Do you always talk like that?" she said, half-gasping, half-laughing.

"Why be polite? You're goddamn hot. My cock knows it, and he's already complaining about having to go."

"I promise I'm not going anywhere."

Bobby sighed, then aimed another glare at Cale and slowly eased from her body, his fingers cupping the edges of his condom. Even before his bare feet hit the planked floor, Cale was easing his cock deeper inside her.

Cale smoothed his hand from her hip over the edge of her pelvis and spread his fingers to cup her sex and ring himself, holding the condom firmly in place as he dove deep.

His thumb toggled the knot at the top of her sex, but he held himself still inside her, waiting to see whether she was okay with a little one-on-one with him.

Her hand came over his, halting him.

His breath caught, disappointment twisting deep in his belly.

"Can I turn around?" she whispered. "I'd like to see your face."

Cale pressed his lips against the top of her shoulder and moved back, pulling out of her, waiting as she rolled to her back.

Then he was climbing on top, spreading her legs with his knees and lowering his body flush with hers. "Am I too heavy?"

"You're perfect," she moaned, a smile tipping up the corners of her full, soft mouth. Her hands cupped his chest, fingers threading into his chest hair and tugging. "I'm thinking it was a good thing you were the one to carry us up that hill."

Cale hadn't given it a thought. Bobby had been the one smart enough to think on his feet. Bobby would have managed if it had been the other way around, but maybe not as quickly. "It all worked out. That's all that matters."

"I agree. This whole trip could have been a disaster. Until now. Ever think that maybe things work out the way they're supposed to?"

"Like you were meant to be in my bed in the middle of a snow storm? That's more of a fantasy come true, just pure dumb luck."

"I mean it. I've had my head in the same sad place so long, wasting time on the wrong guy for all the wrong reasons. It's like my finding him that way, and then you finding me..."

"Don't paint rosy pictures around this."

She wrinkled her nose. "Don't get scared. It's not like I think I belong here or anything, but I guess what I'm saying is it's okay for us all to let go."

Letting go was all he could think about now that his cock was nudging into her moist, hot center. He braced his hands on the mattress and raised his chest from hers. Then he dug his knees into the mattress to leverage his hips and pushed upward, gliding easily through her slick walls until he was balls-deep at last. "Baby, you don't know how good this feels."

"Sure I do," she said, her thighs clutching his hips.

Cale began to rock, stroking in and out, loving the simple, basic motions that allowed him to set the cruise control while he watched the changes in her expression. At first, she smiled, almost politely, then her lips parted and rounded as her breathing deepened. Her nostrils flared, and her eyelids lowered, shuttering their expressive depths as though she could hide what she was feeling, what he was making her feel.

But taking his time gave him the advantage. Her arousal was winding up, causing her heels to dig into the backs of his thighs, her pussy to begin those delicious little quivers that worked their way up and down her channel, massaging his dick and urging him deeper.

Her hands moved from his chest to the corners of his shoulders like she needed something firm, something hard and immoveable to hold onto as the tension ratcheted up.

Stroking deep, keeping the rhythm even, he curled his hips just a little at the end of each thrust, just enough to chuff the hair at the base of his groin against her clit. He saw the way she jerked the first time he did it. Then he turned up the heat, grinding harder, deeper, until her eyes squeezed shut and her hips curved higher to meet his strokes.

Her fingers curled, her nails digging into his skin, and he knew she had to be close. Her sweet cunt was squeezing around him, liquefying, cream churning deep inside as he fucked in and out.

"*Jesus*, Cale," she gasped, biting her lower lip, her eyes opening, desperate, edgy heat flaring in her cheeks.

"Ready, baby?" he whispered.

"Please, oh please," she whimpered.

Cale came to his knees, pushed her thighs down and cupped her buttocks. Then he held them in his palms, his fingers spreading to dig into the tender flesh as he powered into her, slamming his cock, jerking her forward and back to meet his thrusts.

Her back arched off the bed, her breasts shivering with his powerful thrusts. When her breath hitched and a thin high-pitched wail burst from between her lips, he came, shouting as he blasted her with a furious flurry of short, deep strokes that emptied his balls, flooding the tip of the condom.

He fell over her, sliding skin on skin, nestling closer to her body as she wrapped arms and legs around him and kissed his cheek and shoulder. Her hands soothed his back, slipping over his damp skin, scooping into the small of his back and upward.

Cale lifted his head and glided his mouth across hers. Just a gentle press of lips before he leaned back to see how she was doing.

Her cheeks were a deep rose. Perspiration beaded on her forehead and the edge of her hair. Her eyes were half-closed, and she looked ready to drift into sleep.

"I should get rid of this thing," he said, slipping a hand between them to ring his dick and hold fast to the flooded condom.

"Do I have to move?"

He gave her a sheepish smile. "If you want, you don't have to lift a damn finger for next few days. We'll do all the work."

Her mouth stretched into a grin. "How'd I get so lucky?"

"Guess it was just meant to happen."

Bobby halted at the doorway, his eyes narrowing on Cale who was lying on top of Kate. Her knees were slightly bent, hugging his hips. Her arms were draped around his back. His buddy had gotten busy while he was outside tending to business.

From the look of the couple on the bed, they were both spent. He grunted and decided to let them have their little aftermath alone. In the meantime, he added more logs to the wood-burning furnace and started a bath for their guest, letting the water run until it warmed, then adding Epsom salts since they didn't have anything else to lace the water with that a lady might like.

Too bad her things were in her car. If he had her cell phone, he might have called the boyfriend to let him know she was "in good hands".

As the water gurgled, slowly filling the free-standing tub, he set the temperature in the house a few degrees warmer, wanting it hot enough that clothing would be an option rather than a necessity.

He had a hankering to watch Kate stride naked around the house, and he hoped between the two of them that he and Cale could manage to keep her so turned inside out that she never gave a thought to modesty.

That was the plan anyway. One of them had to be thinking. Cale couldn't get his mind past his dick when a pretty girl interested him. Not that he wasn't a good guy. He just operated on a very primal level with women, which was probably a good thing he worked on this lonely ranch for most of the time. If they had a woman underfoot all the time, they'd never get any work done.

The small ranch had been their dream since they were in high school. Neither had been born to the life, but they'd met in Ag class and dreamed about having their own place. They'd gone into the military together, saved their money and made their plans. When their time was up, they'd pooled resources to make their dreams come true. Everything they had was sunk into this property, not that either of them ever complained.

They were free.

Sure, winters left them stir-crazy, but they tended their animals, spent most of their days outside, sunshine, rain or snow. The work was hard, but they were young and healthy. Next year, they'd be in a place to buy more land. They weren't overly ambitious, but they did have plans to make the place pay, and eventually for them both to lay down deep roots and have families.

It would take a special woman to take either of them on now. The sweet, pampered thing in bed with Cale wasn't it.

That didn't mean they both couldn't enjoy the sweet gift of her company. He strolled back into the bedroom and cleared his throat.

Both heads swung his way. Both faces wore slightly dreamy expressions, and their skin flushed with embarrassment.

"Didn't know you were back, bro," Cale said, grimacing. He reached toward his feet and brought up the blanket to cover both their hips.

Kate's look of gratitude had Bobby tightening. She hadn't minded him looking before.

"I ran you a bath," he said quietly, waiting to see whether she'd made a choice and was sticking with it.

Her eyes widened, then came back to Cale. "I'd like that."

Was she waiting for his permission? Bobby's hands curled at his sides. "Cale, got a minute?"

Cale's mouth pressed into a thin line. He gave Kate an apologetic smile and scooted off the bed, his hand cupping his cock and his soggy damn condom. "What's up?" he asked, striding toward Bobby.

"Just need a word. Let the lady get into her bath in private."

"Sure."

Bobby walked into the living room, bent to the floor where Cale's jeans still lay and tossed them at his head.

"What's got into you?" Cale said, his voice gruff.

"I could ask the same thing. You two looked awful cozy."

"We were. She's sweet."

"And she's not staying past the storm. Don't get in too deep. I don't want you moping around here all winter long."

Cale's face reddened. "Buddy, I don't know what the fuck crawled up your ass, but I wasn't doing anything you wouldn't have if you'd had two minutes alone with her."

"I'd need a sight longer than two minutes."

The flush in Cale's cheeks deepened, then the corner of his lips twitched. "Got a little horny watching us, huh?"

"Didn't stay for the show, if that's what you wanted to know. But yeah," he muttered. "Didn't want you cuttin' me out."

"It's not up to me, buddy."

Bobby realized they'd squared off like two pit bulls. "Damn. We've never been this way with a woman before. Maybe it's not a good idea for either of us to get too deep."

Cale raked a hand through his hair. "You're right. Guess looking in her scared blue eyes when she was in the water got to me."

Bobby nodded. He'd felt the same tug at his heart strings, but he wasn't going to let himself forget for a minute this wouldn't last. "She's pretty. And she's got plenty of game. If we keep this light, neither of us will get hurt."

Cale nodded. "So you gonna help her with her bath?"

Bobby smiled, relieved they were back on track. "I was thinking about crawling right into the tub with her."

He left Cale chuckling as he pulled on his pants and let himself back into bedroom. The bed was empty, the bathroom door open only a narrow crack. Still, she hadn't shut it. Might mean she hoped for a little company.

Bobby eased it open, grinning when he saw her sitting in the deep tub with her head lying against a towel, eyes closed and her knees pulled up and folded to one side.

He ducked back out of the door and quickly stripped, then quietly opened the door again.

It wasn't until he slid his foot into the water and touched hers that her eyes shot open. "What are you doing?"

"Didn't take you for slow," he said, continuing to climb into the bath, facing her, as though she hadn't offered a single protest.

"I'm not," she huffed. "I just thought I might have a few minutes by myself."

"You don't want that. Too much time to think."

"I need to think. I have plans to make and *unmake*."

"Which you can do when you're on your way home," he said, sitting down in the water and sighing. "Right now, you need a whole lot of reasons to be happy you're not with asshole."

"His name's David."

"Like my name for him better."

"I don't know what you're thinking you're going to do in here," she said, her lips pouting. "I'm a little sore."

"I'm not here to fuck you, Kate. I thought you might like a little TLC. I'll bathe you if you like."

Her eyes narrowed. "Somehow you don't come across as the selfless one."

"I'm not. Just because my dick won't be getting anything nice sliding over it, doesn't mean I won't get pleasure from touching you. Come on. It's just a bath."

She swallowed, and her gaze locked with his. "I mean it. I'm feeling a little overwhelmed."

Bobby sighed. "And I'm sincere about this. Give yourself over to my care. You won't be disappointed."

Her frown eased, although her mouth was still crimped into a sullen moue. Then she rooted in the water with a hand, coming up with a wash cloth, which she flung at his chest.

Bobby leaned back, smiling, and eased his feet the length of the tub, enclosing her between his calves.

Her knees leaned upward, moving closer to her chest. "There's not enough room."

"Sure there is. We just have to share a little space. Why don't you give me a leg?" He patted his belly. "Put your foot here."

She stared at him, at his belly, then dropped her glance to the cock bobbing toward the surface. Her throat moved as she swallowed, but she timidly lifted one leg above the water and set her heel against his abdomen.

Bobby didn't comment, didn't dare tease her again. He smoothed his expression free of amusement and worked lather into the wash cloth then gently lifted her foot to wash it.

Slowly, as he passed the cloth over her foot, separating toes and being careful not to tickle, she began to relax. He scrubbed up her ankle, behind her knee and over it, then smoothed up the outside of her thigh.

She pretended unconcern with his direction, but two bright spots of color brightened her cheeks as he slid the cloth between her legs.

He halted just beneath her pussy and patted his belly again.

She was quicker this time to give him the other leg. This time he did smile, pleased with her eagerness for him to proceed.

When he'd finished with the leg, he placed it in the water between his legs. "Why don't you turn around and let me scrub your back?"

Kate sat up and wiped a hand on the towel where she'd rested her head, then reached back to twist her hair and hold it above her damp shoulders. Finally, she turned to give him her back.

"Come closer. I won't be able to reach all the interesting parts from here."

Her soft, disgruntled snort didn't faze him a bit. As soon as he began smoothing the cloth over her back, she leaned her elbow on the rim of the tub and sighed.

"So why don't you tell me what you were doing with a guy who cares so little about you he'd do another girl in the bed he shared with you?"

"I wish I knew."

"Come on, something about him attracted you."

"It's embarrassing."

"There's no one here but me. Who the hell am I gonna tell?" he said softly, continuing to scrub in soothing circles up and down her spine.

"David and I were introduced by a mutual friend. He's a junior partner in a prestigious law firm in Sacramento. I write copy for the newspaper. I guess I was flattered when he asked me out. He's got money, family money, and he knows everyone. My family didn't have a lot when I was growing up, and I let myself get impressed with everything he offered." Her head swiveled, and she gave him a look that had his gut tightening. "This wasn't the first time he cheated."

"You were willing to put up with that?"

"I thought I could. But when he brought it right inside our bedroom, something snapped. I grabbed his keys and ran."

"You deserve better than that."

"Maybe I deserved what I got."

Bobby dropped the cloth and began to massage her shoulders and back with his bare hands. "Maybe you just haven't figured out what's important to you yet."

"I thought the security he offered would be enough."

"Money's important," he murmured, more to keep her talking than in agreement.

"It didn't make me happy."

"Then take some time to figure out what does." He scooted a little closer and glided his hands around her waist, then reached for the bar of soap and worked up a lather before smoothing sudsy hands over her shoulders and the tops of her breasts.

Closer now, he brushed his lips along the side of her neck.

"You know, I've never shared a bath with a man," she said, sounding a little breathless.

"Then you've missed out on one of life's little pleasures."

She let go of her hair and settled her back against his chest, her hands cupping his knees. When he slipped down to palm her breasts, they jutted against his palms. "I didn't think I liked you very much."

"Don't pay my mouth any attention at all," he drawled. "I don't mean half the things I say."

"I think you try to keep people disarmed, at a distance, even when you're sunk deep inside a woman."

Bobby groaned. "Don't mention my dick. I'm trying to be a nice guy here."

"You are, you know. Nice. But if you'd like to be nicer, I can suggest another place for you to put your hands."

"Getting a little aroused?" he asked, then sucked on her earlobe.

Her head tilted toward him. "Mmm-hmm."

"I'm not nice, you know. I'm going to pleasure you with my fingers, but only because I want you thinking about it all morning long."

"Just your hands?"

"We weren't very gentle with you before. You need a little time to recover. You know I'm right." He smoothed over her mound and lifted the hood cloaking her clit.

Kate's legs opened wide, her knees resting on either side of the tub.

As he began to swirl on her clit, he ignored the strength of his erection and concentrated instead on her soft, sexy little moans. Yeah, he could be selfless in the short term, but he was dying to see her sweet mouth close around his cock.

Chapter Four

Cale scraped scrambled eggs from the pan straight onto Kate's plate. "That enough? Want more?"

She shook her head, grinning. "You two are going to spoil me."

"That's the plan," Bobby said, biting into a crisp slice of bacon with relish. "We figured we'd pamper you a bit—just to keep you happy so we can have our wicked way with you."

"Well, it's working."

She winked at Cale, and he felt a flush creep across his cheeks. Every teasing glance she gave him turned him on so much he couldn't sit comfortably. He set the pan on a trivet and stretched on the floor beside the couch, spreading his legs under the coffee table to give his cock and balls some room. The bare wooden floor was just cool enough to take away a little of the arousal that kept his brain lodged in his southern parts.

"So, why don't you two tell me what you're doing up here, all alone in the middle of nowhere."

Cale grunted. "Ma'am, this isn't the middle of nowhere. This is our own slice of heaven."

Bobby spread his arms over the back of the sofa, seeming not the least abashed at his nudity. "You're sitting in middle of eight hundred acres of our own personal kingdom. We can do whatever the hell we want out here."

Kate waved her fork. "You mentioned animals before. I take it this is a ranch?"

Cale shoveled in a spoon of eggs he'd drenched in Tabasco,

chewed twice and swallowed. "We're not very big, but we own it. And come next year, we'll be adding more acres and more animals."

"Sounds like quite an undertaking. Did you both grow up on ranches?"

"Nope. We were both raised in Colorado Springs. Air Force brats. Met in Ag class and started dreaming about a place like this."

"Again, what makes a man want to live way out in the middle of nowhere?"

Bobby reached down and slid his hand up and down his cock—a blatant cry for attention. "No rules but ours. Notice we're all naked as blue jays. Other than paying our taxes, we're free out here."

"Must be nice not to worry about dressing up every time you head out the door to work." Kate's glance went to Bobby's lap. "And convenient."

"Don't worry," Bobby said, lifting one dark brow. "Soon as we finish eating, the two of us have to head back to do our chores. You get a reprieve."

"That wasn't an invitation?" she said, her lips pouting.

"Whose idea was it to eat naked anyway?" Cale grumbled.

"Mine," Kate admitted. "Someone stole my clothes so it only seemed fair."

Bobby grinned. "You'll note neither of us is complaining about keeping the playing field equal."

"Seriously," Kate said around a bite of her eggs. "What made two city boys think they'd like this kind of work?"

Cale's glance went back to the fire. "The idea seemed...romantic, I guess. But then we both went into the Army together—"

"And we figured out real quick we didn't like taking orders from anyone else..." Bobby shrugged. "The idea just wouldn't let go."

Cale leaned back against the leather couch and the side of Kate's soft leg. "We pooled our money, saved every penny, and here we are."

"You don't ever get lonely out here?"

"Sure," Cale said. "But we've been so busy we haven't had time to do anything about it."

"See there?" Bobby said. "You're doing two lonely cowboys a public service."

Kate giggled, the tinkling of her soft laughter a refreshing sound.

Cale turned his head and kissed her knee. "Don't think for a moment we aren't happy as hell that you're here now."

"Will you miss me when I'm gone?" The teasing light in her eyes dimmed for a moment.

Cale's chest tightened. "You know I will."

Kate drew a long, trembling breath and placed her plate on the coffee table. "Well, maybe it's a good thing I won't be here long. You two could make a girl feel guilty about deserting you."

Bobby slid his plate beside hers, then pulled her over his lap to give her a quick, hard kiss. "We better get out there before we blow off our good intentions."

When they parted, Kate's face was flushed. "Sure you're going to be able to drag your Wranglers over that hard-on?"

"Gonna hurt like hell," Bobby growled.

Cale eyed his own erection and sighed. "I promise we won't be that long, but you might want to climb back under the covers."

"Boys, it's not any fun doing that alone."

Minutes later, the two men were bundled head to toe. Bobby had found her a robe and placed a blanket over her as she nestled into the couch, but as soon as they were out the door, she was too restless to stay there. She picked up the dishes and headed to the kitchen, enjoying the mundane task that freed her mind to think. But she was done worrying about the shambles of her life back in Sacramento. The two men filled her with plenty of fresh fodder. And again, her imagination wandered down lush, tawdry paths—filled with sexy possibilities.

Which might have given her old self pause because that Kate never obsessed over sex. Or over any man. Not even David. He'd only been a signpost in her life. Another step up the wrung of adulthood.

So what was this weekend all about? And where had the courage come that had her insisting on eating breakfast *au naturel*?

Her thoughts kept her moving and straightening their already orderly cabin while she admired the workmanship and care for detail they'd put into building their home. The log cabin's walls were smoothed planks on the interior walls and varnished. The furnishings were comfortable, masculine and colorful. Saddle leather sofas, bright throw rugs and Indian blankets. Photographs, not many, but offering slices of their shared lives were hung on the shining walls. She pored over them, sighing over the men in their dress uniforms and smiling at the photos where camouflage paint smudged their cheeks. The photographs of the ranch—Bobby, bareheaded and astride a galloping horse, Cale sitting on the porch holding a cup of coffee as he watched a blazing sunset—tugged at some deeper emotion she wasn't brave enough to face.

At last, wrapped inside the thick terrycloth robe while her clothes were in the wash, Kate sat on a leather sofa, her legs tucked under her and a cup of hot chocolate warming her belly while the fire she'd continued to feed in the hearth kept the chill from the living room.

Outside the picture window, the world was wrapped in a soft blanket of pristine snow. Just the sort of scene she'd imagined when David had suggested they head to the lodge for a break.

How different everything had turned out.

She was alone for the first time since her rescue. The telephone lying on a side table just within reach tempted her. But did she really want to call David? Or maybe the rental company instead, to let them know their car was floating down a stream? Only she didn't want reality to intrude on her little fantasy. Not yet.

Two sexy cowboys had set their minds on providing for her pleasure. Tomorrow, she'd be responsible. Today, she'd play and immerse herself in wanton delight.

Her body ached in interesting places. The muscles of her inner thighs felt tight and stretched. Her belly burned as though she'd done a hundred sit ups. Her skin felt as though a loofah had reinvigorated her surface, made her more sensitive to touch, flushed with heat—she thought the next time one of them smoothed his callused palm over her she might come from just a simple caress.

She tried hard not to think about the raw, wet state of her pussy. It pulsed and quivered, the sensations growing as footsteps climbed onto the porch outside the door, drawing nearer.

Would they be able to see the arousal slowly consuming her when they looked at her?

The front door opened and cold wind swept inside. Bobby and Cale entered, dropping the old-fashioned wooden latch to close them in. Their coats and legs were covered in snow, and they shed the jackets and boots next to the door and bent to brush away the snow clinging to their legs before walking deeper into the room.

Both their gazes honed in on her.

She lifted her cup and drank deeply, eyeing them over the rim.

"Warm enough in here?" Bobby asked, his voice sliding into a roughened purr.

Setting aside the cup, she wrapped her arms around her middle, just beneath her breasts to plump them up. "All cozy," she murmured.

Cale glanced at the couch and the fire and then walked stiffly toward the hearth, kneeling to open the fireguard and add another log.

Bobby showed no indecision, coming to the couch and easing down beside her, his long legs stretched in front of him.

He cupped her knee and gave it a squeeze.

He locked his gaze with hers and then reached for the tie at her waist and opened it with a tug.

Then his cold hand slipped inside and cupped her breast.

Her breath gasped.

His lips curved. "Can't think of a better way to warm up."

Cale glanced over his shoulder, his gaze dropping to where Bobby's hand had disappeared inside the robe. "Seems a shame to waste a fire," he said softly.

"It's plenty warm in here," Kate agreed, licking her lips, because she knew from the tension radiating from Cale's frame and the shortening breaths from Bobby beside her, that the boys had decided it was time to play again.

Cale rose swiftly and began to peel his clothing off. Bobby pulled his hand free from her robe and sat forward, scraping his sweater and T-shirt over his head and tossing them away. Then he leaned back again to unbutton his jeans.

She couldn't help staring at the vee of bronze skin he exposed as he slowly opened his pants. When his hand rooted inside and drew out his cock, she licked her lips.

"Damn, girl, don't do that."

"What?"

"Make me want that mouth."

She blinked, her cheeks flushing. He'd read her mind. She unfolded her legs and stood. Shrugging out of the robe, she let it puddle on the floor behind her and reached for a pillow on the sofa before walking slowly toward the fire.

Cale inhaled sharply, his hand gliding it up and down his shaft.

She turned away from the fire, dropped the pillow and knelt on it, bending her head to wait. Her pose was as submissive as she could manage since she'd taken up the reins. She knew the men sent each other silent messages above her head. And still she waited.

Bobby stood and shucked his jeans, then walked closer, standing beside her. Cale came around her. Now, both men stood side by side.

With the fire warming her backside, she waited until they both gripped their cocks and slid them alongside her cheeks.

She tilted her head, letting her eyelids drop and opened her mouth. The men guided the tips toward it, one rimming her lips, then the other.

Taking their silent direction, she reached up and gripped both sleek shafts in her hands and stuck out her tongue to glaze one head, then the other, as she slowly pumped her fists along their thick, hot cocks.

"*Dayum*," Cale whispered as his fingers sank into her hair, tugging hard to bring her closer.

Kate smiled, drawing in a deep breath, inhaling their mixed musks, rubbing her lips and tongues over them, alternating as she teased them both.

Then she followed Cale's insistent tugs and sank on his cock, pumping her hand harder on Bobby's as she bobbed forward, taking Cale's cock into her mouth, her tongue swirling and lapping along his shaft as it pressed over her tongue and deeper.

She backed away and turned to do the same to Bobby's, wetting his shaft and using the moisture to glide her hands freely up and down Cale's and Bobby's hard rods.

Her body shivered, not from the cold, but from the heady power she wielded over two virile men who patiently waited while she plied them both with succulent kisses and sucked on cocks that filled and stretched.

Both long, hard shafts expanded, skin tightening, feeling like warm satin sliding inside her mouth.

And then her hunger consumed her and she settled her cunt over one heel and rode it, while her mouth drew harder, greedy for the strokes they delivered, one after the other into her fists, into her mouth.

When she grew breathless, she pulled away, and rested her cheek against Cale's thigh, dragging in deep breaths.

His hand caressed her head and then tilted it back.

She opened her eyes and stared up at him. "Please," she said, not really sure what she wanted, but needing relief from her own rising arousal.

Cale's glance touched on Bobby, who nodded, a slow, tight smile splitting his face.

Bobby pulled her hands from their cocks, and Cale knelt, then stretched out on the rug in front of the hearth, raising his cock perpendicular from his body.

A condom landed on his chest. Cale quickly ripped the packet with his teeth and the rolled down the latex circle.

She knew what they wanted and accepted Bobby's hand on her elbow as she half rose and straddled Cale's body, sinking down on the cock he fit to her entrance. As her pussy consumed it in a steady rush of shallow pumps, she forgot about Bobby, using her thighs gripping Cale's narrow hips to raise and lower herself.

She forgot Bobby until a hand pressed between her shoulder blades, pushing her down to lie across Cale's chest.

Cale's hand cupped her head and drew her closer for a hard hot kiss that left her breathing hard.

Something slender and cold slipped into her asshole, and she moaned into Cale's mouth. Slippery gel flooded her back entrance, then wicked fingers spread it around the opening, a finger tip prodding then sinking into her ass to swirl and stretch the entrance.

She'd stopped moving on the cock her pussy had swallowed, stopped moving her lips against Cale's, breathing into his mouth as she hung above him, waiting...for the nudge of Bobby's blunt cockhead, rubbing and prodding her opening, then pushing.

Her head jerked back and air hissed between her teeth. Cale slid his hands between their bodies and palmed her breasts, massaging and molding them, exciting her enough that she relaxed the muscles resisting Bobby's invasion and he slid inside.

"*Godohgodohgod...*" she groaned.

"Hold onto Cale," Bobby said, whispering into her ear.

Her hands braced against Cale's shoulders and she hunched over him, trying to lift her bottom into Bobby's strokes without losing an inch of Cale's thick cock.

But she couldn't move, couldn't do anything but let Bobby's thrusts, teasing little forays that did more to frustrate than appease her arousal, move her forward and back, dragging her on Cale's cock.

Hot color filled Cale's cheeks, his mouth puckered around tense little puffs of air.

"Do you feel him?" she whispered.

Cale's eyelids drifted down, his green eyes locking with her gaze. "I feel him. I feel you squeezing around me. So goddamn tight. I gotta move."

"You can't," she yelped, just as Bobby thrust harder, deeper, his hands closing on the notches of her hips as he rode her, his strokes quickening.

"Goddamn tight," Bobby rasped. "You're chewin' up my dick."

"Do you need to stop?" she asked, her voice thinning to a soft wail.

"God no. Just don't move. Neither of you. I'm gonna come quick." He stroked again, a quick in and out. His fingers clutched her harder. "Oh fuck."

And then he was powering into her, jerking her on Cale's cock. The fullness in her pussy and her ass, the heat from the friction building against both inner walls, was too much.

Her body shuddered, her thighs tightened on Cale then loosened as she crammed her clit downward against the crinkly hairs at the base of his cock. It was just enough to excite her clit, just enough to send her over the edge.

She slammed forward and back, taking Cale and Bobby, ignoring the grinding grunts behind her and the desperate gasps from below.

Her body was on fire, her mind exploding as tension deep inside her core released in a powerful orgasm that left her shivering and shaking between them.

When she calmed, Bobby lay draped over her back. Cale's hands petted her hair, his fingers dragging slowly through it. His cock was still rigid. Bobby's was quickly flagging.

"Anytime you're ready, buddy," Cale said between gritted teeth.

"Right. Sorry," Bobby mumbled tiredly, then slowly pulled out.

When he'd moved away, Cale pushed at her shoulders. "On your knees, sweetheart."

"Jesus," she said, wondering if she had the strength for another round. But she climbed off him and went down on all fours, bracing her hands on the rug.

Cale caressed her bottom. His large hands cupping her as he slid his dick forward, nudging between her legs. "Wider," he growled.

She moved her knees apart, let her back sink lower and tilted her ass upward.

"That's it," he said, sliding inside her. "Christ, you're so damn hot."

His first inward glides were gentle, probing.

Her head sank between her shoulders. Her breaths slowed and deepened. Her body readying for what she knew he was going to deliver.

After another tentative thrust, he plunged harder, tunneling, cramming his huge cock through tissue already burning with friction.

Amazingly, she started the climb again, her channel convulsing slowly, caressing his long shaft as he drove into her.

His thrusts sharpened, strengthened. Her breasts shimmied with the force, her nipples drawing so tight they ached as they stretched forward and back, sending darts of arousal south.

Then hands smoothed under her belly, a finger circling her bellybutton, then more scraping downward, through the hair cloaking her mons and between the folds stretched taut at the

Saddled

top of her pussy. Wet fingertips glided around and around her clit.

She glanced to the side and caught Bobby's crooked grin. "Am I gettin' it?"

Was he what? She was beyond speech, her face contorting as her tension grew and tightened.

"That's it, baby," Bobby crooned. "Cale's gonna blow any minute now. You come first, then hold on."

His finger pressed harder on her swollen clit, rubbing, tapping, and at last, her body went rigid, her head flung back and she screamed.

Cale's hands cupped her hips and he hammered her, his sharp, short grunts growing louder, harsher, until at last his body erupted, his hips slapping hard into hers.

The sounds of their cries, the wet succulent sounds his cock made plunging into her juicy cunt were so delicious, so indescribably dirty, she shivered from head to toe.

Her arms quivered, then collapsed and she fell to the floor. Bobby's hands slipped from under her. Cale draped over her back.

With all three of them stretched out in front of the fire, so close there wasn't a part of her body that wasn't blanketed with heat, she dragged in a deep, shuddering breath. "I think you both killed me," she whispered.

Resting on his side, his head supported on a bent elbow, Bobby smiled. He plucked hair that stuck to the side of her sweaty face and smoothed it behind her ear. "Tell me we're not the best you ever had."

Suddenly, her eyes filled. It would be a lie. How sad was that? A man she'd been with for over four years, that she'd thought so talented, had never given her so much erotic pleasure as these two strangers had.

His grin slipped. "Hey, don't do that."

"I can cry if I want to," she muttered.

"Am I hurting you?" Cale asked sleepily, stirring at last above her.

61

"Don't move for a second," she said quickly, not wanting to lose the comfort of his crushing weight.

His torso lightened, as his hands pressed the floor on either side of her shoulders. "That better?"

"I can breathe." She sniffled, then closed her eyes to hide their expression from Bobby, whose face hovered closer than she wanted. The man seemed able to look right inside her.

"Let's get her back to the bed," Bobby whispered.

Cale grunted but pulled out. His glorious heat gone, she pressed her face against the carpet.

But the guys weren't going to let her play like a turtle. They rolled her to her back, and Bobby slipped his hands under her shoulders and knees and lifted her. With Cale trailing behind them, Bobby strode straight for the darkened bedroom.

Cale pulled down the covers. Bobby deposited her in the center. Then both men lay down beside her on their sides, facing her.

"What if I just want to be alone for little bit?" she said, hopeful they'd give her some privacy, because she was feeling vulnerable and embarrassed that she couldn't seem to control the emotions washing over her.

"Not happenin'," Bobby said softly.

Cale grunted his agreement.

"How about you tell us what happened back there."

Her eyes filled again, and she glanced up at the ceiling blinking away the moisture. "Can't you just let me have a girly moment?"

"We're not scared, you know," Bobby said. "And we've spent so much time alone up here that we actually want to experience some of those girly moments."

"You wanna rephrase that?" Cale said, rolling his eyes.

Bobby gave Cale a quick scowl, but when his gaze returned to Kate, his expression softened again. "All I'm saying is we've been through a lot together in a very short period of time. We're here for you. You can tell us anything. And if you want to cry..." He drew a deep breath. "You've got two shoulders to lean on."

The tears she'd been fighting spilled down the sides of her face, wetting her hair. "I don't know why I'm crying. Maybe it's because I don't recognize myself. I'm not like this."

"Not beautiful and sexy?" Bobby murmured, moving closer. His lips swept up the tears falling toward her hair.

Cale's warm mouth did the same. "I'm thinkin' I need to kick dickhead's ass."

"Whose?"

"Your fiancé."

"No. It's not all his fault. I knew what he was like. And I put up with it. I just didn't know *I* could be so...slutty. With you."

Bobby's breath stilled. Cale's body stiffened beside her.

"Sweetheart. Is that what we've made you feel like?" Bobby said, his tone even.

"Not you. But I didn't know I could be like this. With two men. The things you make me want..." She shook her head, knowing she wasn't making sense, and probably insulting the heck out of them both.

"You're just feeling a little raw," Cale said, his large hand clumsily petting her. "I am too."

She sniffed. "Raw?"

"I didn't expect to like you this much. To feel so much. I've been a walking hard-on since I stripped you out of your wet clothes."

"Maybe it's just because we survived something together," she said, wiping her nose with the back of her hand. "Maybe we wouldn't feel like this at all if we hadn't been forced together like this."

Bobby shook his head. "I don't think that's it at all, Kate. We like you. We both want you. We could have met at a grocery store, and I'd still have wanted to crawl all over your ass."

"It's us. Together," Cale said softly. "Don't you feel it, too? Bobby and I have shared women before. But it was only fun and games. A night here or there. Having you here, warming up my dick and knowing he's into you as well—hell, it's sexy."

"We don't think less of you for letting us have our way. But if you're feeling uncomfortable, maybe even a little scared, we'll back off."

Her face crumpled again. "That's the problem. I don't want it to end. And I want both of you lying so close, warming me inside and out. I never wanted that before. I used to spend days without thinking about sex with David, but I can't seem to last a moment without needing your touch."

"Baby, don't be ashamed," Bobby said, fingers curving around her cheek. "We'll love you right. Trust us, and we'll take care of you. All of you."

"You keep saying that."

"And I've meant it from the start. One glimpse of your pretty blue eyes from that car window, and I was ready to dive into an icy grave because I didn't want you hurting or scared."

"But this isn't going to last," she said, at last admitting the thing she feared the most.

His gaze softened. "Let's take it one day at a time. See what happens."

"Maybe we're just what you needed when you were down," Cale said behind her. "Or maybe it's just the start of something special."

She let Bobby rub his fingers under her eyes and her nose, watched his crooked smile as he did it, and her heart melted just a little more.

"Baby, give us a chance?"

Chapter Five

Bobby smothered a grin at the sight of Kate shoveling hay into a clean stall. She wore two layers of his sweats, ties knotted at the waist. She looked as shapeless as a bear, but he and Cale didn't have anything else she could fit into and didn't want her ruining her one set of clean clothing.

The snowstorm was waning. They'd had less than three inches last night. Tomorrow morning, the snow plows would have the roads cleared and she'd be able to leave.

So, it was a race for him and Cale. A race to convince her she had a place here...if she wanted it.

She'd called the rental company that morning and discovered that her fiancé had already requested another car be delivered. The bastard hadn't been in the least concerned about her whereabouts. The news had to have stung, but she'd simply stared at the phone at the conclusion of the call until Cale had reached for it. Then she'd squared her shoulders, set a smile on her face and asked them if she could help with chores. She'd said she was feeling a little lazy with all their pampering.

Bobby knew she just wanted to keep busy rather than think about all the problems that awaited her in the "real" world.

Because the thought annoyed him a little and because he was horny—a lot—he lifted his own forkful of hay and tossed it at her head.

She bent as the hay fell away from her, then aimed a scowl over his shoulder. "You know it's much too cold in here for anything to happen, so why start something you're not gonna finish?"

"Too cold? Depends on what stays covered," he said, sliding his hand down the front of his pants.

"Goddamn smartass," she replied, but her eyes sparkled at the challenge. She lunged for the door of the stall, but he was faster, sticking out a foot to trip her.

She tumbled into the pile of straw they'd been busy distributing. "Ow, I'm getting poked. Straw's not sexy."

Bobby lowered himself over her back. "This is my world. How about I teach you a thing or two about what's sexy?"

"God, I hate you sometimes," she said, her voice muffled and gruff.

"Why's that, sugarlips? I'm doin' my best to show you a really good time."

"Damn you. You make me want everything."

Bobby drew a deep breath, hearing the longing in her voice—longing that made his own body tighten in protest. "And that's bad? You wanting everything?" he said, tugging off his gloves.

"It's bad when I'm going to be walking away."

"Let's think about that later," he murmured, rubbing his tongue along the curve of her ear, peeking out from under her knit hat.

"Damn, damn, damn." She wriggled beneath him, but not because she was trying to escape, but because he'd slid the tip of his tongue into her ear and his hand was cupping a breast through layers of cotton.

"Not enough is it?" he murmured softly.

"I don't want to wait until we're out of these layers."

"Sometimes being a little hot and cold can be fun."

"Let me guess which parts are gonna be cold," she said, her tone wry.

"I promise I'll save your ass from frostbite."

She snickered beneath him and then groaned when he rolled off her then plucked up her hips. Braced on her elbows, he made quick work of the two sets of sweatpants, rolling them to the tops of her thighs.

"Cold, cold," she said, between tightly clenched teeth.

"Gimme a second," he said, scraping down his zipper. His cock met the chilly air in the barn and tried to retreat. "Oh no, you don't," he said to himself, leaning close to her ass and slipping it between her legs, holding it because it was losing firmness and he needed to get it someplace hot.

Her labia might have been slightly chilled, but her pussy oozed creamy heat. He purred as his cock sank into her, and he pressed deep until his bare groin and belly met her buttocks. Then he eased off his coat, tied the arms around her middle to cinch their bodies together.

"How's this gonna work? Neither of us can move."

Bobby frowned, realizing she was right. "Guess I didn't think it through."

"Duh, ya think?"

Bobby grinned and wrapped his arms around her, palming her breasts through her clothes. "Can't even give your pretty nipples a twist through all these layers."

"And there I thought you were some kind of sex god."

"Thought I had all the answers? Bet I can figure out a thing or two from here. How about giving me a squeeze?"

"That's not going to do much." Still she tightened up her inner muscles, giving him a sexy caress that went a long way toward heating his dick right up.

"Let's live a little dangerously," he growled, untying the arms of the jacket and letting it slide to the ground. Then he pulled out, sucking in air as his wet cock met the brisk air. He slammed back inside her slick heat and groaned.

"We're gonna have to make it quick," she said, her voice muffled against the straw.

"Quick, coming up. But I don't want to leave you behind." He thrust his fingers between her legs, felt for the top of her sweet folds and pressed a chilly finger against her distended clit.

Her breath hissed between her teeth. He plunged forward again, warming her clit with rapid rubs of the pads of two fingers. Because his ass was getting cold, and he didn't want to lose the delicious hardening, he plowed into her without grace or rhythm, stroking her with short, sharp rasps of his cock.

When her cunt clasped him hard, he breathed a sigh of relief that she was there with him. Together they pounded into each other in harsh, jarring thrusts. His fingers closed around her clit, pinching it, and she yelped but butted backwards, her cold cheeks slapping against his groin.

It was the funniest, clumsiest fuck he'd ever had, but no way in hell was he in the mood to laugh because he was so goddamn close his balls were drawing up against his groin, hardening to the point of pain. At last they erupted, and come spurted inside her, easing their movements, the scalding liquid heating them from the inside out.

Kate's gasping moans thinned and tightened, and then she wasn't moving anymore, suspended in the moment as he powered into her, giving her the last of his energetic thrusts before he too felt the need to hover.

The barn door opened and bitterly cold air blew inside, slapping his ass and making his cheeks tingle.

He shot a glare over his shoulder at Cale and met his bemused expression. "Yeah, not the smartest thing I've ever done." He pulled out of Kate, tugged up her pants and wrapped his coat around her hips. "Sorry, about that sweetheart. Want Cale to take you back inside and warm you up?"

A giggle escaped as she lay on the hay and rolled to her back. She sat up and started to pull hay from her hair and clothing. "I'm not even going to ask about what might be mixed in this hay."

"Better not think on it," he agreed.

Cale stepped closer, his head shaking as he reached down to give her a hand up. "You two are crazy. Even I have better sense than this."

"Couldn't help it. Her ass was right there in my face when she was shoveling," Bobby said, shrugging.

"Shut up," Kate deadpanned. "I know it looks wide as a barn in these clothes."

"It's attention-getting. My cock's living proof."

Cale clucked and pulled her by the hand toward the stall door. Then he tugged her coat down over her hips and zipped it up to her chin. "A bath. Then I'll see about what else needs warming up." He turned to Bobby. "You finished here?"

Bobby smiled, lifting one brow. "Just getting started."

Cale left Kate on her own in the bath after he'd made sure she had everything she needed. She'd still looked more than a little embarrassed after her tryst in the barn. He couldn't get over the sight of them, plush as polar bears above and bare-assed below. He was only sorry he'd missed the whole show.

Bobby entered the kitchen from the mudroom, blowing into his clasped hands. "Where's Kate?"

"In the tub. Thawing."

"Buddy, you know that wasn't planned," Bobby said with a sheepish grin.

"I hope you didn't have it in your mind. I'd think you were a complete idiot. Do you know how cold it is out there?"

Bobby grimaced. "My dick's still stinging."

Cale chuckled, shaking his head. "Serves you right." Cale settled his hips against the kitchen counter and locked his gaze with Bobby. "She talk about when she's gonna leave?"

Bobby's expression fell. "No. But I'm thinking it's probably going to be tomorrow."

Cale cleared his throat. He and Bobby hadn't talked much since Kate's arrival, and he wasn't sure how deep Bobby's feelings went with Kate. "I'm gonna miss having her here," he said, leading the conversation.

Bobby poured a cup of steaming coffee and wrapped both hands around the cup. He took a quick, tentative sip, then replied quietly, "Me too."

"Didn't think we could actually share a woman for longer than a one-nighter and not come to blows," Cale said, watching

Bobby's expression for a hint of what he really thought.

Bobby's lips quirked up. "Doesn't hurt she's a horny little thing."

"Bobby," Cale growled.

His buddy shrugged but still didn't meet his gaze. "I didn't mean any disrespect. It's pure compliment. Girl's got game."

Sounded like Bobby only wanted a bed partner. "She's kept us both satisfied," he muttered.

At last, Bobby lifted his head, his usual careless expression wiped clean. There was real yearning in his eyes. "Wonder what it would take to make her stay."

Cale's whole body tightened. "More money that either one of us has."

"Sonofabitch," Bobby sighed. "You're probably right. What the hell would she see in two cowboys in the middle of nowhere when she's used to caviar?"

"I don't think it's the money so much," Cale said softly. "She hasn't complained once about her things in the car. I think maybe she just liked the security."

"Still not something we can offer yet. We don't know from one year to the next whether we're gonna make it."

"Yeah, still, I'm gonna miss her."

Kate paused outside the kitchen, listening to the two men. They both sounded so forlorn she smiled sadly. They sounded like two boys about to have their favorite toy stolen out from beneath them.

She was going to miss them too. But this was just a tryst. A sexy little escape from all her problems. No way could she stay. She had a job back in Sacramento. A household to divvy up with her fiancé. Wedding gifts to return, arrangements to cancel. The list was endless.

Still, there was the vacation she'd arranged for her honeymoon. The tickets could be cancelled and the funds returned, but she could still take the time off. She wondered if the two men would be willing to put up with a houseguest for three weeks. She cleared her throat and sauntered inside, wearing the robe and a pair of Bobby's socks on her feet.

You'd have thought she was wearing Victoria's Secret lingerie by the way both their gazes lit up. "What's cookin', boys?" she drawled, giving them as simmering a look as she could muster.

Must have worked from the sharp breath Cale pulled and the smile that curved one corner of Bobby's sexy mouth.

"Did you hear us talking?" Bobby asked.

"Couldn't help but hear, the way both of you were moaning. Gonna miss me?" she whispered and rubbed up close to Bobby's chest.

"Like a toothache, sweetheart." But she thought the pain would be much lower going by the ridge rising against her belly.

"I could stay a little longer, if you like."

Bobby's smile widened, but a glance at Cale said he wasn't so keen on the idea. Disappointment stung harder than she thought it would. "Or not," she said quickly.

Cale shook his head. "It's not that I don't want you stayin', but I don't think it's a good idea. Not unless you think there's a chance for us."

Was he afraid he'd fall in love with her? Although disappointed, she knew it wasn't fair. "I get it. And it's okay. I'll go tomorrow."

Bobby's hands tightened on her ass. "Still got tonight."

She forced a smile and gazed at him from beneath her lashes. "Sure do. But since you two have been the ones doing all the thinking, I'm wanting a little quid pro quo."

Bobby snorted. "You wanna be in charge? What do you say, buddy? Should we let her give the orders?"

Cale's brows lifted in a very "Bobby-like" challenge. "I'm thinking she won't last long. She'll get breathless and weak-kneed and call uncle before either of us is winded."

She narrowed her eyes at both men, relieved they'd let her set a lighter tone. "I'm so gonna prove you two wrong."

"Supper first, boss?" Bobby said.

"Supper after."

Kate felt ready to scream. The men had taken her request to be in charge to ridiculous levels, both refusing to even remove a single sock without precise instructions. Then they'd embarrassed the hell out of her by requiring her to describe exactly which tongue and set of fingers had to do what as they gave her head. The result had left her frustrated and aroused, and they both knew it, sharing smirks across her body as she glared daggers at them both.

"Any time you wanna say uncle," Cale murmured.

She was close to throwing in the towel, but they'd pissed her off. She tapped a nipple and glared at Bobby. "I want your mouth here." She tapped the other and issued the same command to Cale.

Both mouths latched on but didn't move. She drew a deep breath, counted silently to ten and said, "Now suck until I tell you to stop."

Thank God, they didn't need more explicit instructions. They suckled enthusiastically, and she dug her fingers into both their scalps and closed her eyes at the delicious sensations while her mind thought of devious punishments.

"I'm remembering what you said," she murmured, "that first time about not being that particular about what you poked." That got their attention. While their mouths remained engaged, they shared a concerned glance between them. "I'm thinking I want to watch what you're not all that particular about poking."

Both mouths disengaged.

"Now, Kate," Cale said, a worried edge to his voice.

Bobby grinned wickedly.

"I am still in charge, aren't I?"

"Kate..." Cale started again.

Bobby shook his head, putting on a mournful expression.

"We did say she could call the shots, but she's gonna have to get specific."

This time, she didn't think she'd mind. Might be embarrassing as hell to direct, but she thought they'd be the ones squirming the most. "How about you two lie down side by side, facing each other."

Cale and Bobby shared another glance. Cale's lips tightened, but he sighed in resignation.

Bobby rolled away from her and waited as Cale climbed over them both to lie down beside Bobby.

Kate got up on her knees for a better view. "I don't think I've ever watched two men kiss each other, mouth to mouth, other than on television. Why not start there? And be sure to do it like you mean it. I want hands holding heads and a whole lot of tongue."

Cale's glare was blistering, but he didn't seem too terribly disturbed. They'd done this before.

The thought made Kate hot just watching as they stared at each other's lips and thought through what she'd demanded. "Anytime you're ready," she said softly.

Bobby, as always, made the first move, sliding his hand behind Cale's neck and leaning toward his friend, his mouth opening and pressing against Cale's thinned lips.

Rich hot color stained Cale's cheeks, but he returned the kiss, sliding his mouth over Bobby's. She didn't know whose tongue slipped inside first, but the heat between them escalated quickly until they were both leaning in, their heads circling.

"Nice start," she whispered, her own lips feeling dry. "How about you both slide your hands over the other's dick."

Again, she didn't have to get too specific. Hands reached across. Long fingers clasped rigid cocks and smoothed up and down long, thick shafts.

She was beginning to think she'd hoisted herself on her own petard because her body was heating up alongside theirs but they were the only ones having any fun.

"Bobby," she said.

He pulled his mouth away from Cale's and looked over his shoulder at her. Amusement was gone; his cheeks were just as hot, just as taut as Cale's.

She licked her dry lips, then did it again when his gaze dropped to her mouth. "Who usually goes down first?" she asked slowly.

His eyelids dipped, skimming her distended nipples and the way she clenched her thighs together. "Baby, you know it's me."

"Will you let me watch?"

"You're in charge," he crooned. "But you sure you don't want to join in?"

"You first," she said, her throat tightening as she swallowed hard.

Bobby came up to his knees and stepped over Cale who opened his legs to make room. He rested his head casually on one bent arm to look down his own body as Bobby's hair brushed forward and his mouth closed over the tip of his cock.

Kate had an inkling what Cale was feeling, having been the recipient of Bobby's talented mouth and tongue.

Cale reached down and gripped the base of his cock, holding it straight up for Bobby who began to bob on it, his cheeks hollowing as he sucked upward, billowing as he went back down.

Cale's narrowed glance locked with hers. Excitement seeped from inside her body, and Kate scrapped any plans for an extended viewing, pushing Bobby gently on the shoulder and bending down to join him, her tongue sweeping over Cale's shaft from the side as he swept the other.

When their mouths met for a brief hot kiss, Cale didn't seem to mind that they'd forgotten about the evidence of his arousal standing tall between them. His hands reached down and stroked both their heads, encouraging them silently to enjoy.

They shared tongues, wrapped their hands together around Cale's shaft and pumped. Kate learned a thing or two along the way, about how firmly Cale liked to be stroked, about how giving Bobby could be when he wasn't being a smartass. Their attention focused on Cale, their efforts quickening, deepening until Cale groaned and his come shot from his cock. Together they drank it down, rubbing it over their lips and sharing it in the sexiest kiss as they ate each other's lips.

When they'd finished, they lay their heads down on Cale's belly and grinned at each other.

"Don't suppose you have any more orders for me," Bobby drawled.

"I'm thinking I want you two to decide. My mind's blown."

Before she had time to catch her breath, Bobby had her on her knees. Cale turned and settled on his back, his feet against the headboard, his head between her legs. "Lay that pussy on my mouth."

"Jesus. Didn't know you could talk dirty," she said, but followed his order to the letter, lowering until his lips latched onto her cunt and suckled.

Bobby pushed between her shoulder blades until she lay over Cale's body, then used his fingers to find her entrance and guided his cock into her pussy, past Cale's tongue.

Cale laved her clit; Bobby stroked deep. And she buried her face against Cale's hard belly and moaned.

Bobby held off just until she squealed with the first burst of hot tension rippling up and down her channel. Then he powered into her, pushing her toward another, and another rippling orgasm before his come jetted deep.

"Damn, damn, damn," he said, holding her hips. "Forgot. Second time."

"On the pill," she mumbled.

"Not good enough," Cale said beneath her, his voice muffled.

She didn't give a rat's ass. She was boneless. Beyond content.

Cale and Bobby shifted her over, and they snuggled in close, one warming her front, the other her back. She thought she'd never felt more content in her life. Never felt so warm. She said so out loud.

Bobby kissed her shoulder.

"I'm right there with you," Cale mumbled.

Together, with both men's arms surrounding her, Kate felt her heart break.

Chapter Six

Spring came early to the mountains. Snow had melted weeks ago. Bright green leaves cloaked the aspens. The road up the mountain from Wellesley was unrecognizable from her previous trek and accomplished in merely forty-five minutes.

Kate pulled onto a graveled road and halted in front of the cabin that was the only thing she recognized from her previous visit.

She hadn't called. Cale had asked her not to. Bobby hadn't been as firm when she'd left with the man from the rental company. He'd pulled her into his arms for a quick hug and told her if ever she decided to come back...

Well, she was here and ready to see if the magic she'd experienced was real or something transient—a dream she couldn't help falling back into every time she closed her eyes to sleep.

The months had been awkward inside the apartment she'd shared with David until days ago. They'd had calls to make that he'd been surprisingly agreeable to divide up. They'd returned gifts, cancelled reservations. They'd slept in separate beds. And they never talked about what had happened in the lodge or where she'd been for those few lost days afterward.

When she'd gotten the last of her things packed and stored, he'd given her a hug and wished her well. She'd offered him the same. Any spark that had simmered between them long gone. All the anger and hurt over his betrayal had been swept away and replaced by a quiet hope that she'd nurtured as she'd planned her escape.

Quitting her job had been the hardest thing to do. A leap of faith into an unknown future. But it had felt right. She'd used her time in Sacramento to develop a portfolio of freelance work. She could write from anywhere, submit to any magazine or news rag. Maybe she'd even try her hand at writing a book. Her goal had been single-minded—to free herself and be free to start the next adventure of her life.

She closed the door to her new SUV and took the steps up the porch. A soft knock on the door went unanswered, and she tried the door handle. It was unlocked. They were somewhere here on their little ranch.

She contemplated going inside and waiting quietly for them to return, but she didn't want to meet them in a place that held so many memories. Didn't want her first sight of their expressions when they saw her to be colored with her hopes.

She set out for the barn behind the house, but it was empty, the doors open.

Sounds of cattle lowing in the distance, of horses whinnying, pulled her behind the barn to the pastures.

There she saw the two men, stringing wire along the top of a cedar post fence. Two tall, muscled bodies wearing long-sleeved T-shirts and blue jeans, cowboy hats covering their heads.

Bobby faced her and saw her first. He froze. His expression didn't give a thing away about what he felt, whether he was happy to see her or worried about what it meant.

His head turned to Cale, his lips moved, and Cale shot a glance over his shoulder and then slowly coiled the wire he'd been holding over the top of the post and turned.

Kate offered them both a lop-sided smile and walked toward them, her heart hammering against her chest. "Hi there," she said softly as she drew near.

Cale wiped his hands on his thighs, his gaze trailing down her body.

She'd dressed casually on purpose. Blue jeans and a paler

blue, short-sleeved sweater. She wore cowboy boots she'd been breaking in for a month—buffed but still showing a couple of scuffs at the toes. She'd pulled her hair into a ponytail. Nothing fancy, nothing too fussy. Hoping they'd get the message that she'd changed some things about herself. Hoping there was still a chance they might work.

"You sink a car in the creek again?" Bobby said.

She smiled and shook her head, reaching up to tuck a lock of hair that had escaped her rubber band. "I don't need rescuing this time."

"What do you need?" Cale asked, his voice gruff.

"Not a thing." Drawing a deep breath, she let her gaze slide away. "Since I'm officially self-employed, I just thought I'd take a little road trip. Visit friends." The words held the right casual note, but the fact she couldn't meet their gazes must have clued them in she was nervous.

Cale's hand reached over to grab the one fiddling with her hair. "I don't like repeating myself. And you've never been shy about telling us exactly what's on your mind."

"I'm not wearing a bra," she blurted out, then bit her lip.

Bobby's lips twitched. "We noticed."

"That the first thing that popped into your mind?" Cale said, his expression amused.

She shot them both a withering glance. "This was a mistake."

Cale tugged her hand, drawing her closer, then slipped his other arm around her waist.

When her head snuggled against his broad chest, she sighed.

"Been lonely on this mountain," he whispered.

"It was lonely back in California."

"You get things sorted out with your ex?"

"Yes. It's over. We parted...amicably."

His arms tightened, then he relaxed.

She drew back and lifted her gaze to him, then glanced at Bobby. "Guess you both know why I'm here."

"You pregnant?" Bobby asked, sounding oddly hopeful.

Her face heated. "No! That's not it. Although I did worry a little bit since we forgot something a time or two."

"I didn't forget a thing," he said, arching his brows. "Man's gotta do what he's gotta do."

She tilted her head to stare at him. "You really wouldn't have minded?"

Bobby shrugged, an endearingly familiar glint in his eyes. "Neither of us would have, sweetheart. If you haven't already figured it out, you're the only woman we've ever gone bareback with."

She shook her head, a smile tugging at her lips. "Still a smartass. I missed you."

He leaned over the fence and she met his mouth halfway, loving the gentle pressure of his lips.

"You're gonna stay this time, right?" he asked, as soon as he drew away.

"It's up to you both. But maybe we should wait to see if we still feel the same way. It was just a few days."

"Long enough," Cale said, his hand cupping her bottom and squeezing. "Now, if *you're* not sure..."

"I couldn't stop thinking about either of you," she said in a rush. "In the middle of all my friends, in the middle of work, I felt completely lost."

"Welcome to our world," Bobby muttered.

Still not sure if they felt as deeply as she did, she plowed forward. "You know I don't know a bull from heifer, but I thought I might set up an office in that bedroom we never used."

"It's yours," Bobby blurted. "I mean, it was mine, but I don't think we'll be needing it."

"That quick? Don't you need time to think about it?"

He stepped on the lowest strand of barbed wire and gripped the one just below the loosened strand they'd been stringing and swung over the fence to land on the ground beside her.

His gaze swept her again, and his throat worked around a

swallow. If the swiftness of his agreement hadn't been enough to convince her he was happy with her moving in on them, his dark, glittering eyes and straining jawline told her how deeply pleased he really was. "We were ready for a break anyway. Wanna celebrate?"

Kate relaxed inside Cale's embrace. His heart was thumping hard beneath her hand. "Depends on what kind of party you want to throw," she murmured.

"How about one that calls for us gettin' nekkid?" Bobby said with a lift of his brows.

"Going too fast for you?" Cale whispered.

She glanced up to meet his gaze and let a smile stretch her lips. "I'm way ahead. I'm not wearing panties either."

"Something I figured out too," he said, squeezing her ass again.

The living room was stifling hot, but perfect since they hadn't bothered with clothes the whole afternoon. Night was falling and the feeling of intimacy was enhanced, punctuated by the sounds of logs crackling and their softening breaths.

They stretched out, their toes toward the fire atop a new rug the boys had purchased, a thick creamy flokati. Something big enough for them all to share, warm enough in the winter to keep the cold from creeping across the floor and soft enough to cushion knees when the moment called for it. Or so Bobby said.

The men had kept her firmly planted between them. And they'd shared some of their wildest "nekkid Kate fantasies" they'd been storing up over the lean winter months.

Her body was relaxed, her mind eased beyond simple satisfaction. Both men lay on their sides, heads raised and resting on one hand, their hands roaming her body. Bobby plucked at nipple. Cale had fingers teasing between her damp folds.

"Happy?" Bobby asked.

She smiled and turned to meet his dark gaze. "I'm so far beyond happy, I'm feeling smug."

"Smug's good," Cale said. "But I need to hear more sweet whimpers."

"I don't whimper."

"Sure you do. And you moan and groan and grunt. It's all good, sweetheart."

She blushed, a smile tugging at her mouth. "You guys sure like being in charge."

Bobby's dark brows waggled. "Cale gets nervous when you give the orders."

"Don't think I won't ever make demands. I like it when you're both a little embarrassed. Brings you down a peg or two. And it makes me hot as hell knowing you'll do anything to make me happy."

"All worries gone, baby?" Bobby asked, pinching her nipple. "Do you think this will work?"

"It does for me," she said, swallowing hard, because she was trying to work up the courage to tell them she loved them. She didn't want to be the first. Didn't want to make things awkward, or have them feeling like she was pushing for more than they could give. They'd already showered her in enough lusty, happy affection she knew she could be content.

Cale and Bobby shared a glance, then returned their stares to her. "Someone's gonna have to marry you, you know," Bobby said. "Make you a permanent part of this family."

Shock held her still, and she hoped like hell she wasn't going to cry. Had he read her mind again? "We don't have to decide right now," she said, wanting to reassure them. "And I don't want to choose. I can honestly say I love you both."

Both steady gazes softened. Bobby cleared his throat. "Just what do you love about us, sweetheart?"

"I love you both," she repeated for emphasis. "And I don't think I could be fully happy unless you both loved me back. Bobby, you make me smile and know just how to make me squirm and beg. But I love it best when you let me see the warm, loving man behind the smartass. He makes me melt." She turned. "Cale, you're the rock we both lean on. The one I want when I'm scared. And there's nothing sweeter than spending time with my arms and legs wrapped tight around you. I couldn't choose one of you. And I'd prefer never having to."

"We'll let things lie for now," Cale said. "The two of us will figure out what happens next."

Kate lay between them, holding her breath still because she'd just laid her heart out on a platter. She wanted the words back. "Well?" she blurted, then bit her lip. Her face heated because she didn't like practically begging them to return the sentiment.

Bobby palmed her breast, caressing it gently. "Sweetheart, I've loved you since I saw your face in the window of that car. I went into the river, ready to sacrifice myself for you. If neither of us made it, I didn't want you to be alone."

Her eyes filled slowly.

Cale edged closer, his head coming closer. His lips grazed her cheek. "And I've loved you ever since you played possum in the bed while the two of us got all worked up over how pretty you were. You were willing to share the pleasure of being with you with both of us."

She nodded, satisfied at last. "I thought I was rebounding. That's why I couldn't commit before I left. What I felt happened so fast, I thought my emotions were clouded with lust. It wasn't until I got away and thought about how you both seduced me, so gently, so thoroughly, that I knew I didn't want to be without either of you."

Both men released deep sighs. She smiled, blinking back the tears. They shared sheepish smiles.

"You okay with letting us be in charge for a while?" Cale growled.

"We were kinda quick before," Bobby said, nudging her nipple with his nose. "It was damn embarrassing how fast we came."

"You didn't see me minding," she said, her smile widening.

Two thickening cocks pressed against her hips.

"We can do better," Bobby drawled. He bent and gave her nipple a kiss, then sat up, coming to his knees. "Come here," he said, patting his bent thighs.

Cale gave her a wink, and Kate rose, straddling Bobby and scooting so close his cock was trapped between their two bellies. His arms encircled her, their heads drew close. His kiss was warm and sweet, but it was the hard ridge pulsing against her that had her core melting.

Cale's hands cupped her buttocks from behind and lifted her. Bobby rooted at the breast hovering in front of his mouth, and Kate reached down between them and centered the head of his cock between her slick lips.

Slowly, she sank, dragging Bobby's lips from her breast. His hands cupped her head and this time their kiss was carnal, voracious, lips sucking, teeth tugging, tongues lashing. Below, she began to rock, up and down, with Cale's support, as he pressed into her back and kissed her shoulder and the back of her neck.

Bobby leaned back, lifting his hips slightly, letting her use his cock to fuck herself, which she did with gusto, slamming on him, driving down, while she leaned back against Cale who cupped and molded her breasts, twisting nipples until she came unglued.

Bobby snuck two fingers between her legs and pressed them against her clit, circling hard and she came down one last time, rocking shallowly on his cock, grinding and moaning, shudders running up and down her body.

Then Cale soothed her, his hands and lips smoothing over her flesh, waiting while she caught her breath, only to realize the cock still sunk deep inside her was rigid and Bobby's face was tight, his expression a little wild.

Without breaking their connection, he eased his legs from under him and lay flat. Cale pressed her over Bobby's chest, and she moaned again, knowing what they were going to do. They'd been here before and she'd been left as limp as a noodle buffeted between them both.

"God, I don't know," she said, half laughing.

"You don't have to do a thing," Bobby said, cupping her face.

Her nipples mashed against his smooth chest, she began to rock slowly forward and back, even as Cale began to finger her asshole.

She could do this. Take them both. But she thought she wanted it the other way, both of them stroking her pussy, filling her so tightly it hurt.

"Not my ass," she whispered.

"Can we share your cunt?" said Bobby who was never shy with words.

"Fuck," Cale said, apparently losing the last of his reserve as well. "Gonna be tight," he rasped. "I'm already so hard from watching the two of you." But he didn't wait for her to change her mind; he pushed her harder against Bobby. "Move your knees back a bit, you're too stretched this way."

She slid them back. Cale reached for a pillow and waited while Bobby shoved it under his ass.

Then Cale slipped a finger between Bobby's cock and the back of her entrance, sliding it in her moisture and pulling to stretch her.

It wasn't uncomfortable, not yet, but Bobby's cock was pulsating and her vagina was beginning to ripple again. When Cale came over her, his cock prodded, and fingers tugged at her to make room for him to press inside. She buried her head against Bobby's chest.

"It's okay, baby," Bobby whispered. "We're both gonna fit. Relax while he comes inside." But he gritted his teeth and groaned as Cale shoved inward, sliding up in shallow little drives that had both Bobby and Kate quivering together.

When Cale was seated, she couldn't catch her breath. Her pussy burned.

"Don't know how you managed it, buddy, but I can't move," Bobby gritted out. "Again."

Cale laughed behind her. "I get to do all the work. Just

close your eyes and feel."

"It's like having a tree trunk shoved up inside me," Kate groaned.

"Your idea, sweetheart,"

"Must have had something to do with the cold," she said feeling desperate. "We don't fit."

"Sure we do," Cale crooned. "I just gotta move slow."

Sweet hot cream released in a gush, drenching both cocks. The men groaned and Kate gave a pained laugh.

"See?"Cale whispered. "I'm moving easier now.

"Shit, your balls are rubbing on mine," Bobby said, his face screwing tight.

"Do you mind?" Cale muttered.

"Fuck no. Jesus, don't stop."

Cale rutted slowly deeper, stroking her inner walls and Bobby's cock.

"Guys?" she said, her voice thinning.

"Yeah," came two rumbled grunts.

"I'm coming," she said and her body went rigid between them as her orgasm sent quivers up and down her channel, caressing them both in liquid heat.

Bobby's thighs rose and he gave shallow jerks of his pelvis.

Cale crammed in and out and then slowed as Bobby cursed and his head thrashed.

At last, with Bobby's erection softening, Cale slammed inward, rocking them all until he came.

Kate rested, sandwiched between two hard, sweaty bodies, her pussy pulsing and filled with come and cocks—the nastiest, most fantastic feeling she could have imagined sweeping through her. This was what she had to look forward to. Two inventive, fearless lovers. Her body and her life filled with happiness. With love.

"Imagine how much easier this will be when you start popping out babies?" Cale said, sliding his mouth across her shoulder.

Kate felt her chest jerk, and then a laugh gusted, shaking through them all. Bobby grinned beneath her, his eyebrows arching.

Cale tightened up his arms, still braced around her waist. "What'd I say?" He pulled out and rolled to his back beside them, his face red, but a crooked smile gleaming.

Kate gave Bobby a smile and shook her head. "I'm not moving. If you have to breathe, tough."

His arms looped around her back, and he heaved a deep sigh. "I'm fine. Everything's fine. My dick's limp but gloved in the sweetest little cunt."

She bit his shoulder. "Behave." She reached out and clasped Cale's hand, settling her face on Bobby's chest but staring at Cale. "I love you."

"We know," he said. "Good thing, too. Because we were both set to take a trip to Sacramento and haul your ass back."

She closed her eyes, her lips still curved. She was sleepy, her body wonderfully warm.

"Do you think she's gonna get mad when she realizes we left off the condoms again?" Bobby murmured.

She nuzzled against him, drifting off. She hadn't forgotten. Didn't give a damn. In fact she hoped that by the next snow's fall she'd be filled with more than love.

Unbridled

Chapter One

There are moments that can change the course of a woman's life from one heartbeat to the next. For Dani Standifer, this was that moment.

She'd returned to Two Mule, Texas, a day earlier than she'd planned, intending to surprise her boyfriend. But the surprise was definitely on her. Rowan Ayers's body, hardening with arousal, demonstrated more poignantly than any "Dear Jane" letter that she'd been gone far too long. He'd moved on.

Everything she'd ever dreamed of for her future evaporated like the sweat glistening on his naked chest.

As well, it hurt that he'd chosen this place to bring another woman. The isolated, ramshackle line shack had been their favorite place, their secret love nest. The cabin sat nestled in a thicket of scrubby cedar, a tall live oak providing the structure shade from the late afternoon sun. The shack was situated inside the Ayers fence line, equidistant from both of their ranch houses. Perfect for the trysts they'd shared throughout high school and during summer breaks from university. Here, they'd explored their young bodies, talked about their dreams for the future...and made plans.

Just moments ago when she saw his horse and realized he was here, emotions had welled up, threatening to overspill— gratitude for his friendship, uncertainty because he'd been so aloof of late, and certainly lust since this place had been their special sanctuary from the world.

She'd squared her shoulders, preparing to climb up the steps, but then she'd heard the soft nicker of another horse.

Peering around the corner, she'd spied a tall, gelded bay, and a leaden weight settled in her middle. But she hadn't wanted to jump to conclusions. There could have been a simpler, more innocent explanation for why two horses were hitched to the rails outside the cabin.

She had to know the truth.

Dani had crept silently onto the wooden porch and edged toward the window to take a glimpse inside. Two cowboy hats lay on the table. The twin mattress from the bed in the corner had been pulled to the center of the floor—just as it always had whenever they'd met for a little afternoon delight.

Rowe stood naked, a hand roaming his taut, flat belly, another gliding up and down his straining cock. But he was alone.

No fire burned in the hearth, but the cabin had to be hot from the amount of sweat gleaming on his long, lean frame. She stood frozen, noting that his light brown hair was longer than it had been at Christmas, and he hadn't shaved. A couple days' worth of bristles dusted his rugged, square jaw. He'd always been scrupulous about his appearance, but she liked the slightly scruffy look and wondered grumpily if his new girlfriend did too.

Which reminded her she needed to get moving or she'd really embarrass herself. And him. Although why she worried about his feelings when he hadn't had the *cajones* to tell her the truth, she couldn't say. With only one room in the cabin, she knew whomever he was meeting had to be outside.

Still, she stayed there for another long moment, staring, lust and anger curling inside her as she watched his ice blue eyes slide shut while he touched himself.

He was readying himself for another lover. Stoking his arousal. Something she'd often watched him do, sometimes sneaking up on him, like now, to spy on him and let her own desire climb. Sometimes, she'd lain on the mattress in front of him, pleasuring herself, both of them staring as their hands and fingers played while their mouths curved into slow, sultry smiles.

Heartsick, she edged backward, trying to decide if she should storm inside to confront him or slink away. One option might leave her feeling foolish; the other would save her a bit of pride while she regrouped her emotions. But did she even have a right to feel hurt? He hadn't betrayed her. Not really. She'd been the one reluctant to make any lasting promises, sure she could pick right up where they'd left off when she returned.

Maybe she'd waited too long. The extra year and a half she'd lingered in Austin while she worked on her graduate degree had been something she'd wanted. He hadn't complained. Not once. The last time they'd been together, he'd still been full of plans for their future. As soon as she said yes, they'd announce their engagement and give her brother the chance to provide the wedding her mother and father would have wanted. They'd do things right.

Liar, liar, liar!

Suppressing the sob threatening to shudder through her, she backed up another step and came up against something solid.

Strong arms wrapped around her, and she froze. The scent of horse and clean male sweat engulfed her.

"Easy there," came a low, familiar drawl.

Shock rendered her mute and rigid.

"Not what you expected?" he whispered into her ear.

Not what she'd expected? Did Justin Cruz know about Rowan's new lover? Did he also know that she and Rowan had been seeing each other before she left Two Mule? *Couldn't be.* She and Rowe had taken a perverse pleasure in keeping everyone guessing for years.

Still, Justin had a bird's eye view of everything that happened on the Ayers spread since he'd taken over as the ranch's foreman. Was he here to gloat?

"I don't know what you're talking about," she said tightly. "And you can let me go now."

"Not a chance. Don't want you slinking away. Things just got interestin'."

"How's that?" she asked breathlessly while squirming inside his tight embrace. "Seems Rowe's busy."

Justin's steamy breath blew against her ear and she remembered the last time he'd been behind her, hot breaths gusting. She closed her eyes and ruthlessly pushed aside the disturbing memories.

"Disappointed?" he drawled.

"Course not. It's not anything to me."

"Liar."

Something wet slid along the edge of her ear. "Did you just lick me?" she said, her voice rising, although she really had to work hard at outrage.

The one time she'd stepped out on Rowe had been with this man—just after she'd graduated from high school, when sex with a grown man seemed like the ultimate rite of passage into adulthood. Something she'd never admitted to Rowe, but still felt horribly guilty about. The fact Justin had scared her into monogamy with Rowe had made her feel only slightly less like a complete slut.

But she'd never forgotten her one and only encounter with Two Mule's resident bad boy. Late at night, just as she slipped into her dreams, Justin would saunter into her mind, tempting her to slip back into the dark, erotic fantasy he'd woven for her that long-ago afternoon.

"And if I did have a little taste, what are you gonna do about it, Dani-girl? Gonna scream the place down and let Rowe know you've been spyin' on him?"

"I didn't mean to spy."

"But you didn't exactly back up the second you realized he was expectin' company, did you?"

"I shouldn't have lingered. But I was...surprised." An extreme understatement of how she really felt. Cold, numbing shock was more like it.

"No, you shouldn't have stayed. Why are you here,

sweetheart?"

"I just wanted to say hi. I saw his horse..."

"Nothin' stoppin' you now," he said, pushing her toward the door.

"Stop it, Justin," she whispered harshly, dragging her feet. "Quit playing around—"

He reached around her and pushed open the door.

"I started without you," Rowe said, without turning around.

"Did I tell you that you could?" Justin said coldly.

Dani blinked, then drew in a deep, sharp breath. "You were expecting *him*?" She shrugged out of Justin's embrace and stared from one man to the other.

Rowe's head swiveled toward her. "*Jesus*, Dani, what are you doing here?" he said, color flooding his cheeks. His gaze went guiltily from her to Justin.

Justin's lips curved into a bitter smile.

"I'm back early," she said, her voice thickening. "I thought...when I saw your horse..." *What the fuck? Rowe and Justin!* She couldn't get her head around it. Well, at least not around the fact Rowe was involved with Justin. Justin was another matter altogether. She wouldn't put any form of perversity past him with his reputation.

"You didn't think it odd there were two horses here?" Justin casually leaned a shoulder against the doorframe. One dark brow arched in a wicked challenge.

Dani stiffened. "I thought he might have another girl. I wondered who she was."

"Jesus Christ." Rowe bent to grab his blue jeans from the floor, then held them in front of his gleaming cock.

"A little late now," Justin said. "I think she's already jumped to the correct conclusion."

Rowe's fist clenched around his jeans, then he dropped them to the floor and straightened his shoulders. A look of resignation entered his face; a silent plea for understanding glittered in his pale eyes as he returned her stare.

"I didn't know you were gay," Dani blurted out, ignoring

Justin's smirk.

Rowe's crimson face tightened. "I'm...it's complicated."

"You're naked, obviously aroused. What could be more simple?" she asked, trying to gather anger around her, but mostly feeling confused. How could she not have known?

"She's got it *almost* right," Justin murmured.

"Shut up," Rowe bit out.

"Yeah, what'd I miss?" Dani snarled at Justin, hating him at this moment for rubbing her nose in her own naiveté.

"The fact I knew you were comin'," he said, his voice dropping to a sexy purr. "This is your homecomin' present, baby."

"Justin, you bastard!" Rowe said heatedly.

The larger, more rugged man shrugged. "She needed to know. She has choices to make here."

"I would have broken the news more gently."

"Doesn't look like she needs you to sugarcoat it." Justin's gaze pinned her. "She's not exactly looking ready to bolt or puke. Fact is, the thought of it, of watching us, turns her on."

"Does not," Dani denied hotly, heat filling her face.

"Your nipples always poke holes in your shirt?"

"You're a jerk." And yet, she barely resisted the urge to cross her arms over her breasts. She tilted her chin in defiance while heat crept deeper into her cheeks. She met his narrowed gaze, while images flashed through her mind. Since she knew what both men looked like naked, she couldn't help the raw, nasty pictures that flashed one after the other.

And yes, they aroused her.

"Prove me wrong," Justin murmured. "Leave now."

Dani shot Rowe a hot glare. "You gonna let him talk to me like that?"

Rowe's jaw flexed, but he didn't offer any response.

"He doesn't let me do anything," Justin said slowly. "He obeys me. In all things—here, at least. Rowan, your cock's flagging." Justin's gaze dropped, drawing all their glances to Rowe's sex, which pulsed and lifted again.

Rowe groaned.

"Get it ready for me," Justin growled.

Rowe's eyes closed briefly, then a look Dani had never seen slid across Rowe's face—something vulnerable and needy. "Justin, not now."

"Not now, what?" Justin said, his voice dead even.

"Please," Rowan whispered, his strong jaw flexing.

"Uh-unh." Justin shook his head. "You've carried around this picture of your innocent little sweetheart for years. But I don't think you really know her at all."

"And you think you do?" Dani bit out, hoping like hell the bastard wasn't getting ready to drop the other shoe that she'd succumbed to his bad boy charm herself. Rowe didn't deserve finding out that the two people he'd taken as lovers had a history of their own.

"The things you asked him to do, Dani," Justin said, his tone dropping to a raspy rumble. "The sexy little spankings, the special bonds you left underneath the bed... It's not in him to do that to you, but he did because he cares."

Dani's jaw dropped and her embarrassment caused her to tremble. "Rowe, you told him about that?"

Again, a muscle flexed along Rowe's square jaw. "I wasn't gossiping. It just slipped out. He found your things and asked. He's a friend."

"Friend?" Justin straightened away from the doorframe. "I'm a little more than that, aren't I? You don't keep any secrets from me."

But Rowe had kept one big goddamn secret from her. Dani's shoulders slumped.

"Don't take it so hard, Dani," Justin said, all traces of mockery gone now. "He loves you...almost as much as he loves me. But every time he was with you, every time he spanked that pretty little ass of yours, he was denying his own nature. Rowe's submissive. Just like you. He's just finally figured out he's not finicky about which gender offers him the kind of sex he craves."

"How the hell did you figure that out?" she bit out. "I've known him all my life."

"Because I watched him...with you. When you dared him into spanking you, he didn't get off on the act. He only got hard when you told him what it did to you, what it made you feel."

Her mouth suddenly went dry. The thought of Justin's dark, hungry glance raking her body as he watched her with Rowe caused another distressing wash of arousal to dampen her panties. She licked her lips. "You watched us?"

"Sometimes," he said softly. "You weren't as careful as you thought. Had to run interference a time or two with your big brother."

"Cutter knows?" she asked, her voice rising. "About Rowe and me?"

"He suspects. But he never got close enough to the cabin to ever know for sure. You have me to thank. And if I happened to catch a glimpse or two of your...sessions...well, I think I earned the right."

"Pervert!"

"Who's the pervert? Me for watching, or you for wanting his hands to leave your ass pink?" He lifted his chin toward Rowe. "Or him for needing the same damn thing from another man?"

"I don't believe you. Not about Rowe. This..." she said, gazing at the mattress in the middle of the floor, "...is just him experimenting a little. But I'm back now." Her gaze locked with Rowe's, pleading with him. "It doesn't mean anything. Not to us."

Rowe's glance fell away from hers, and her stomach dropped. What he had with Justin was important. Special enough that he hadn't bothered dressing because Justin didn't want him to.

"Dani, I never wanted to hurt you." Rowe's tone was low, aching.

Like the lump filling the back of her throat.

"Tell yourself whatever lies you need to stay in happy land, Dani. But we're about to get busy." Justin opened his belt and stripped back one side then locked gazes with her. "Now's your chance. You can run out the door. You don't have to see anything that might *traumatize* you."

Why was Justin being so cruel? He'd won. He didn't have to rub her nose in this mess. "I'm not a scared little virgin," she said, her voice shaking.

"But you're also not faithful to your boyfriend here either, are you?"

Dani stared at Justin's hard face through shimmering tears. "Justin...don't."

"He can't fulfill you," he said softly. "Not those dirty needs that keep you restless even after he's fucked you."

"Shut up," she said, tears filling her eyes.

Justin pulled apart the snaps of his shirt, letting it fall open to expose the dark fur of his broad, muscular chest. Then he unsnapped the top button of his pants. "Last warning..."

She stood rooted, unable to move as he scraped his zipper down.

"Rowe, take out my dick," he said, never looking away from her. "Now."

"*Fuck.*" Rowe's tone was agonized, but his cock bobbed eagerly between his legs. "Dani, get out."

But she couldn't. Part of her died a little in that moment. But another part, one only Justin had ever touched, caught fire.

"Rowe, don't disappoint me," Justin said, his gaze never leaving Dani's.

Rowe's naked feet dragged across the floor. His expression was taut, his cheeks a brighter red than they'd been moments ago.

Justin firmed his jaw. "Can't turn back now. She knows. Let her see what it's like. If she hates you afterward, she isn't worth cryin' over."

Dani narrowed her eyes, knowing he expected her to bolt. She braced apart her feet and lifted her chin higher, even while she questioned whether she really could do this—watch the only two men she'd ever known intimately have sex.

Rowe didn't glance her way, but his chest rose sharply. Then he slipped his hand inside Justin's pants and slowly drew out his cock. His fingers clasped the shaft gingerly, but his thumb rubbed slowly over the smooth cap. Justin's cock thickened.

"Push down my pants," Justin said, his voice tighter than it had been before.

Both of Rowe's hands slid over Justin's narrow hips and shoved down the faded jeans.

Dani hated to admit it, even to herself, but watching Rowe do such an intimate thing to another man, knowing how the scrape of his rough palms felt on her own bottom, caused her sex to melt.

"Get on your knees and take me in your mouth," Justin rasped.

Rowe groaned, and Dani understood the feeling. Shame and arousal roiled together. Her own body was hot, moisture seeping into the crotch of the lacy undies she'd worn just for Rowe.

Rowe knelt, his hand shaking as he gripped Justin's cock and brought it to his mouth.

Justin cupped the back of Rowe's head with one hand, his fingers threading through Rowe's honey brown hair with surprising tenderness. For long moments, he stared as the other man's lips closed around the tip of his cock and sucked.

Rowe's cheeks hollowed, his eyes closed tightly, but his hesitation ended there. Surrendering, he groaned and opened wide his jaws, gliding along the thick, veined shaft.

"That's it," Justin said softly. "Take me deeper," he said, stroking his hips forward, his cock disappearing into Rowe's eager mouth. Then his gaze rose. For a moment, something almost haunted entered his expression. That wicked brow rose again. "He does it because he knows the rewards. But so do you, don't you, sweetheart?"

Dani didn't answer. She couldn't have pushed a word through her tightening throat if a rattler had slithered over her boot. Watching both men, engaged in such a carnal act, caused unexpected emotions to rise inside her.

Sadness, because she'd never guessed Rowe wasn't fully satisfied with her. Jealousy, because Rowe never made those hungry sounds when he went down on her. And shame, because she wished she were brave enough to approach them and sink to her knees beside Rowe.

How she wished Justin would command her to, take the choice away from her. The hard edge of his voice when he'd cut through Rowe's objections had caused her own body to react with an instant, juicy response.

Justin braced his legs apart, and his face darkened as Rowe's strokes, forward and back along his shaft, picked up the pace. The slippery suctioning sounds and choked excitement gurgling in Rowe's throat caused Dani's whole body to vibrate.

Forgotten for the moment by both men, she wet her lips with her tongue as she imagined how Justin might taste. Moisture flooded her channel as her inner muscles clenched hard.

When Justin flung back his long, black-brown hair, her breath hitched. Starkly masculine elation softened his expression for just a second before his head lowered and his hard gaze met hers, issuing a wordless challenge.

Only Dani wasn't ready to accept. She lost her nerve, turned and fled through the door of the cabin, stumbling down the steps in her haste, before catching herself on the rail and bolting toward her horse.

Booted heels bit into the wood porch, but she didn't look back. With the sun sliding below the horizon, she nudged her heels into her mare's sides, kicking up dust behind her and leaving both men in her wake.

A zipper scraped behind Justin.

"I should follow her," Rowe said, coming up behind him.

Justin leaned against the doorframe, holding his cock in his hand and stroking it absently. "She's not heading toward her ranch."

"She's going to the creek. She goes there to think when she's upset."

"And she knows you know that. She expects you to follow her."

Rowe nodded. "I always do. When she gets into a snit about something, she just needs a little time to vent."

"This isn't something little. I was rough on her."

Rowe's hand swept up Justin's back and curled around his shoulder. "I wish she hadn't found out this way. But I can't say I'm not relieved."

Wet lips brushed his skin, whiskers scraped deliciously, and Justin shivered. If he actually had planned it, things couldn't have worked out any better. Rowe was upset, but not wallowing in shame. The clothed cock snuggling close to his backside told him that while Rowe's feelings might be conflicted, he wasn't about to end their relationship. Which only left Dani's response as the missing side of the equation.

Justin turned and hooked a hand behind Rowe's neck, pulling him forward.

Rowe's mouth opened eagerly beneath his. Firm lips met firm lips, tongues tangled. Breath intermixed, and both men swayed closer, their cocks grinding.

Something this wickedly good couldn't be wrong. And Justin never questioned where his instincts took him—not when it came to sex. "Give me some time alone with Dani. I'll bring her around."

"Should I be jealous?" Rowe said between suctioning sips against his mouth.

Justin snorted. "Sure you want me and not her?"

Rowe's steady gaze locked with his. "Can't I have both?"

Since Justin seconded that sentiment, he simply smiled. He stepped back and unspooled his belt from the waist of his sagging jeans.

Rowe's expression grew rigid with excitement, but he drew an inward breath between his teeth. "I should follow her. Make sure she's okay."

"I said I'd handle her." Justin wound the belt around his fist, leaving a foot-long strip of leather dangling. "You know what I want."

Rowe hung his head, pretending shame and resignation, but the eagerness of his steps as he reentered the cabin betrayed his true feelings.

Justin glanced once over his shoulder, listening to the hoofbeats that faded in the distance. "Yeah, I'll handle her," he promised himself. He'd have everything he'd ever dreamed of if he didn't let a little thing like the fact he was in love with Dani Standifer get in the way.

Chapter Two

Justin stared at the silent house, taking in the understated wealth it represented. The Standifers were old money in these parts. Old money—and spoiled and unappreciative of their advantages.

Eyeing the pristine white Victorian, he thought about the crummy apartment in town that he'd kept after his mother had died—the only thing he could afford with the odd jobs he'd worked until he'd landed the job as a wrangler at the Ayers ranch.

He'd have liked to go to school, just like Dani and Rowe. He'd had the grades. Could have ridden a football scholarship, but his sister had needed him to provide a roof over her head until she'd finished school. Now that she was attending a community college in San Angelo, he was free at last to pursue his own path.

Funny how he'd always thought he'd leave Two Mule in the rearview mirror of his pickup truck first chance he got, but things hadn't worked out that way. When he'd hired on as a wrangler on Rowe's family ranch after high school, he'd been happy for the employment. He'd discovered an affinity for working with horses and cattle, skills that had quickly gotten him noticed by Rowe's father, who took him under his wing and groomed him to assume more responsibility. Over the years, he'd thrived on the attention, enjoying the respect he earned that didn't have a thing to do with how well he tossed a football or how popular he was with women.

When he'd been asked to step in as foreman when the ranch foreman retired and moved to Florida with his daughter, the promotion had been a mixed blessing. He'd liked the authority, the trust invested in him, but he'd felt bound to stay, especially after Rowe's father died. He'd managed everything, moved into the house, so that Rowe could finish his education. After he'd returned, Rowe asked him to stay, saying his house was too big and lonely without the company.

When Rowe had snagged his lustful attention after taking over the ranch, no one would have been more shocked than he was. Justin had never known he could be aroused by a man, had run through a string of girls in high school and an equally impressive list of women afterward, but other than his very brief fling with Dani, no woman had ever held his attention long.

Catching his boss skinny dipping in a newly dug cattle pond on a particularly hot summer day had opened his eyes to whole new world of sensual pleasure.

Not that Rowe had intended to attract him. He'd grinned when he'd been caught, then motioned for him to join. Just a couple of guys cooling down after a hot day's work.

When Justin had stripped to his skin, his cock had betrayed him in an embarrassing way. He'd tried to make a joke of it, but Rowe's expression as he'd tried not to stare at Justin's cock had inspired that pesky little devil who sat securely on Justin's shoulder—the whoring side of his nature that was ready to fuck at the slightest invitation. The side that never knew approval unless he saw it in the happiness of a lover's face at orgasm.

Justin had ignored his dick, knowing all the while that Rowe couldn't keep his eyes off him. Rowe had been careful, too careful, to keep the edge of the water at his waist.

But Justin had known, just as he always did whenever a girl was interested. The air heated around them, and his heart reacted predictably, slowing into a steady, expectant thrum. He'd accepted his attraction, accepted that something was going to happen that would change his world.

The two men had swum, talking about football, plans to

move the herd, anything but the fact they were naked and enjoying the unexpected freedom. They'd sat afterward at water's edge as the sun dried their hair and skin, talking about women. Doing their manly best to lay the blame for the thickness of their cocks on their increasingly raunchy conversation.

Justin had carefully turned the conversation toward kinkier topics, ending with the very acts he knew were foremost on Rowe's forbidden pleasures list. Without ever betraying the fact he'd watched Rowe and Dani a time or two, he'd said, "Ever tie a woman up?"

Rowe's pained smile and quick shake of the head didn't fool him.

"Come on. Never wanted to know what it was like to be in total control?"

Rowe cleared his throat before saying, "Have you...done that to a woman?"

Justin grinned, letting his eyelids drift down. "There's nothing sweeter than bringin' a woman along slowly, tying her up and making her feel helpless and a little scared, then watching as she comes apart."

Rowe stared down as his hand skimmed the top of the water. "How do you know they like it...that you're doing it right? I mean, without asking them outright."

"Orgasms are easy for women to fake, but arousal's not. Their nipples and cunts swell. Honey coats your fingers every time you dip inside to test how far along they are..." Justin leaned back on his elbows, uncaring that his cock was bobbing against his belly. His cock ached for a set of warm, wet lips to engulf him, and he was damn close to not caring whether the lips belonged to a man or a woman.

Rowe looked away. "I've done it a time or two. Didn't think to check. But she told me when she'd had enough."

"You see, there's your mistake. You don't ask. A woman that far along, you can push her farther, make her really beg. Make her cry. When you finally do let her come, she's so grateful she'll do anything for you."

Rowe's jaw tightened. "They don't hate you afterward?"

"Not if you're careful. Not if you aren't mean about it. Have to make sure they know it's all about their pleasure. That you're only doing it, prolonging the sweet torture, to make it the best they've ever had."

"I think Da—she'd like that."

Justin had known instinctively that Rowe wasn't really talking about Dani and her pleasure, but was imagining his own. "I could teach you how," Justin had said casually, watching Rowe from the corner of his eye.

Rowe sat straighter, winding an arm around his bent knee. His growing arousal must have been threatening to peek above the water's edge.

Justin suppressed the sly smile tightening his mouth. "Ever been with a man?"

Rowe choked and looked away. "No," he said, so softly, Justin barely heard him.

Still, he hadn't gotten all bent out of shape by the question.

"Me neither." A long awkward pause followed, then Justin drew in a deep breath. "Ever been tied up?"

"What?" Rowe's eyes were a little wild, like the conversation was going too fast for him to think what the right answer might be and not betray himself.

But Justin didn't care whether Rowe was comfortable with the pace. He pushed, sensing Rowe needed someone to take command. "Ever let anyone bind you so you couldn't move?"

A frown pulled Rowe's brown brows together, but he stared straight ahead. Justin wondered if it was because he wanted to watch Justin from the corner of his eye too.

Excitement drew Justin's balls closer to his groin, and he didn't resist the urge to wrap his hand around his cock and slowly stroke it, just once, before he let it go and lay on his back, closing his eyes against the bright sun. He peeked between his slitted lids while Rowe gave him a hungry once-over, his gaze resting on his cock.

Justin liked the way the man's strong jaw ground tightly

when he stared, was growing excited simply by letting his own gaze rove over Rowe's masculine frame. The more he let his imagination fly, the more sure he was that this could work, that he had something to give in this relationship, something Rowe wouldn't be able to resist.

Rowe eased up the bank, at last exposing his cock to Justin's view, his chest rising and falling faster as he settled back on his elbows. His cheeks billowed around a long exhalation.

Justin rolled his head to the side, raking Rowe's cock with a glance. Thick and long, it curved slightly toward his belly. The cap was tapered, like a single-sided arrow.

Rowe's cock pleased him, intrigued him, but so did the rest of the other man's body. Long and lean, strong arms and thighs, light brown fur stretching between flat brown nipples then arrowing down...

"Have you ever...?" Rowe asked, his voice thick and guttural.

Justin forced his gaze upward and wondered which question Rowe was really asking, but decided that for his purposes, he should keep up the ambiguity. "Last time I was with a woman, I tied her face down. All that pale skin faced my way made my palms itch."

"For what?"

"To leave a mark or two. Hear her squeal."

Rowe licked his lips. "Sounds...dangerous."

"Coulda been if she hadn't been creaming after I told her what I wanted to do. Always have to ask first, you know. I paddled her ass until she came."

Rowe swallowed hard, but by then, he wasn't looking away. His eyes glittered with excitement. "Not something I've ever experienced. That can really happen?"

Justin gave up the coy innuendo. "Only if *the partner* wants it bad enough. And if you're good. Rowe, I'm very good."

"*Shit,*" Rowe said under his breath.

Justin stroked his shaft again, squeezing the tip as he

came off, forcing a drop of pre-come to bead in the tiny slit. He dipped his pinky finger into the bead and smeared it on his lips. Justin knew Rowe couldn't think of the line shack without associating it with sex, so drawled, "I'm headin' to the line shack to make sure it's stocked up for the winter."

"You should do that," Rowe said, his voice rasping.

Justin had given him a slow smile and rose, standing close enough his cock bobbed in front of Rowe's face. Then he'd slowly dressed and left, confident that Rowe wouldn't be able to resist the invitation.

Rowe strode into the cabin half an hour later, looking nervous and ready to puke.

"You don't have to do this," Justin said so casually no one would have known by looking at him that a knot of cold terror sat in his belly. Hands steady, he opened his belt and unsnapped his jeans.

Rowe's gaze locked on Justin's hands as he eased the zipper down and shoved his pants over his hips. His mouth pursed around a slow exhalation as Justin's cock sprang free. Rowe's wild gaze went to the door, but then he glanced back and his expression hardened. He took another deep breath and met Justin's steady gaze, his own unwavering.

Justin had known how Rowe felt. And he'd known exactly what he needed. "I'll say it again. You don't have to do anything you don't want to. But I'm thinkin' you might like the decision taken right out of your hands."

Rowe's eyelids had flickered. He licked his lips. "You want me to fight you?"

"Only if you feel you need to."

Rowe cleared his throat. "What if I want you to stop? For real."

"Then you have to make me believe it." Justin hadn't given him any more warning than that, springing for Rowe and wrestling him easily—too easily—to the floor.

Face down, his knees under him, Rowe breathed harshly as Justin pushed his cock against his clothed backside.

With his forearm pressing the side of Rowe's face against the planked floor, Justin gritted out, "I'm gonna let you up, just a little. Get one hand under you and open your pants."

Rowe bucked against him. "Can't breathe, you bastard."

"Do you really need to?" Justin arched his back, just enough for Rowe to bow his back and get a hand between him and the floor. Then he waited.

Rowe shuddered beneath him; his breaths came in soft, ragged exhalations. But his jeans unsnapped, and his zipper scratched.

Justin smiled. He hadn't asked for that, but now he knew how eager Rowe really was. He tugged down Rowe's pants until his buttocks were bare.

Air escaped through Rowe's tight lips as Justin's cock grazed his backside.

"Never thought I'd be sayin' this to a man," Justin growled, "but my cock wants to sink right inside your ass."

Rowe shook his head violently. "Can't. Never done that before."

"What do you want from me?"

"What you talked about...before."

Justin's lips twitched. "Want me to beat your lilywhite ass?"

Rowe grunted, but his body shivered underneath him.

Good enough for Justin. Backing away, he smoothed a hand over Rowe's tight buttocks. Not so different from a very athletic girl's. That he got a peek of a velvety ball sac only increased the tension winding like a spring deep in his belly. He lifted his hand and struck.

Rowe's head turned, his forehead tilting against the floor. But he didn't say a word or make a sound.

An ugly anger bubbled up inside Justin, directed at Rowe for tempting him but not having the guts to admit it out loud, at Rowe for having Dani at his beck and call, for having all the advantages and still not being satisfied...

Justin slapped Rowe's ass until his hand burned and

Rowe's ass glowed a bright pink.

"Stop," Rowe groaned.

Justin couldn't stop, not to think anyway, he reached around Rowe and clutched his cock, ringing the base. "You can't come until I'm damn well through with you."

"Jesus," Rowe hissed. "*Fuck.*"

"That's what I want to do. Fuck your ass. Gonna let me?"

Rowe shook beneath him, but his head rocked up and down.

Justin leaned away, stripping open his own pants and shoving them down. A second's hesitation was all he allowed as he donned a condom. Then he spread Rowe's ass cheeks, and set the blunt tip of his cock against Rowe's tight little virgin hole.

When he pushed, Rowe groaned. "*Jesus*, too much."

Justin knew he'd never breach him without a little help. He spit into his palm and rubbed the moisture over the crown of his dick, then pointed it at Rowe again. This time, he didn't relent until he was squeezing inside.

Rowe's asshole was agonizingly tight. But slowly, the sphincter's tight grip eased, letting his cap slip inside. When he was there, he paused, shocked to find himself buried in a man's ass.

Rowe must have been equally as taken aback. "Shouldn't be doing this," he whispered.

"Can't stop," Justin ground out.

"God help us."

"He doesn't have a thing to do with it." With a final, stubborn push, Justin glided deep. Where the strength came from he didn't know, but he didn't spill instantly even though his balls throbbed. The feeling was too indescribable and he didn't want to lose it too quickly.

Triumph mingled with a tight-chested pain. He'd done something he'd never thought himself capable of, something he'd never be able to take back.

He hammered Rowe's ass, holding the other man's cock,

until it swelled to bursting, but still he didn't let him come. When his own release washed over him, he pulled free, turned Rowe and bent over him. His mouth opened, swallowing Rowe's cock down, and then he eased the press of his fingers, and Rowe exploded inside his mouth.

He drank the hot, salty streams as Rowe pulsed helplessly against him, moaning—a jagged, torn edge to his voice. Justin felt the same. Like he'd taken a step off a cliff and was free-falling into a dark abyss.

Only the thought that somehow he'd make this work for them, make Rowe need him as much as he needed to breathe, kept him sane.

Today had been the first big test their shaky relationship had weathered. Having Dani stumble into the truth could have been a very bad thing, but it hadn't stopped Rowe from begging Justin for release.

"Why don't you ever let me fuck you?" Rowe had asked quietly after Justin had taken them to hell and back again. "Do you see me as a woman?"

Justin grunted. "As if." Rowe lay inside Justin's arms, back against his belly. Justin didn't know the answer to that one. But then again, maybe he did. Maybe the fact he'd never let himself be fucked kept him feeling above the gnawing need. "Maybe I'll let you fuck Dani's ass. While I watch."

Rowe had stiffened inside his arms. "Shit. We can't do this anymore. She might not be able to handle it."

"Think she'll tell?"

"No. She's not like that. But I hate hurting her."

"I don't think she's hurting—not the way you think," Justin drawled.

"You see something I didn't? She looked like she'd swallowed poison."

Justin smoothed his hand over Rowe from his belly to his chest. "You're looking from a place of guilt. I'm not."

"Because this doesn't mean anything to you?"

Justin clasped Rowe's shoulder and kissed the back of his

neck. "Because I don't happen to think we're wrong. Just because this isn't what everyone expects of you doesn't make it so."

Rowe sighed and edged away. "I'm going to see her in the morning."

Justin came up on an elbow. "Won't you just let it rest? Let her come around to you?"

"Might work better for her but I can't stand her being angry with me." Rowe sat on the edge of the mattress and raked a hand through his hair. "We've been friends a long time."

Justin grunted. *Friends.* He'd never been friends with a woman. What was the point? "Do what you have to." He'd do what he had to do.

Which is how he found himself outside her home as the lights inside blinked out one by one. With too much time on his hands and memories swirling in his head. He'd already figured out which bedroom on the second floor was hers. A light had blazed behind lacy curtains while her brother Cutter checked the horses in the barn then ambled back through the kitchen.

Justin watched in the dark like a thief, waiting for the house to quiet. Waiting for big brother to fall asleep. Then he leaned the ladder he'd scoped out in the shed against the upper floor balcony and silently climbed upwards.

Standing outside the French doors to her bedroom, he tried the handle, but found it locked. He knocked softly.

The curtains inched to the side. A wide-eyed gaze stared back. Then Dani's face screwed into a fierce scowl.

He couldn't help it—he chuckled.

The door flew open, a hand reached out and closed around his forearm and she pulled him inside. "Are you insane?" she whispered harshly. "If Cutter catches you out here, he'll pepper your ass with buckshot!"

"Worried about my ass?" he asked, closing the doors behind him.

"No, just how I'll break the news to Rowe that you got yourself killed trying to sneak into my bedroom. What are you

113

doing here?"

"Thought we might talk."

Dani crossed her arms over her chest. Had she just now noticed how thin her cotton camisole was? "You and I have never had a conversation. Why start now?"

Justin took a step toward her. "Want me to get down to business?"

Her eyes nearly crossed, and she placed a hand against his chest to halt him. "You're crazy. Crazy and a pervert."

Justin grinned. "Which turns you on more?"

She gave a high-pitched squeal of frustration, but Justin cut it short, covering her mouth with his hand and forcing her against the wall beside the door. "Hush now. I really did come just to talk." Although her eyes glared daggers at him, her body stopped wriggling. "That's better," he whispered, slipping his hand slowly from her mouth and letting her slide down the wall.

Dani swallowed. "We can't talk here. This is my bedroom, but it's my brother's house. Doesn't feel right."

Well, well... Little Missy wasn't exactly telling him to get the hell out. "Wanna shimmy down the ladder with me?" he asked, dropping his voice to a sexy purr.

Her hand shot to her blonde hair, which pulled thin cotton taut against her beaded nipples. Her gaze slid away. "Are you crazy? I'm in my nightgown."

Justin took a step closer, leaning down to whisper just above her lips. "I'll wait while you change."

She sucked her bottom lip between her teeth. "You have to turn around while I get dressed."

"Baby, I've already seen everything you've got."

Her nose wrinkled. "Can't you be a gentleman for five minutes?"

"No one ever taught me manners. Expect me to learn right now?"

Dani huffed away, stepping inside her closet and closing the door behind her.

He hadn't expected that, but he grinned. He'd let her think

she'd won this round.

By the time she'd changed and they'd climbed down the ladder, only ten minutes had passed. Justin led her to where he'd tied his horse off behind the barn and helped her into the saddle before climbing on behind her. "Scootch up," he said, nudging her bottom.

"We're not going far, hear me?" she said, but she scooted toward the saddle horn.

The hard-on pressing against the leather saddle had him silently agreeing. Justin reached around her, ignoring her stiffening spine, slipped the reins he'd looped around the horn and clucked softly to get his horse moving.

While Dani remained rigid, he relaxed. Sitting this close, inhaling her sweet, musky scent was heaven enough. For now.

He had a pretty good idea how Dani felt about him. They shared the same intense, animal attraction. But she'd always tried to resist it, aware of his reputation and wanting to remain loyal to Rowe.

Today's revelation had to be making her nervous as she reassessed her feelings. If he could find a way to tap into her attraction for him, use her love for Rowe, maybe they could all be happy.

"Do you have to breathe down my neck?" she whispered, sounding grumpy.

"I can't move back any farther and not fall off this horse. Tell the truth. I make you nervous."

"I'm not nervous. But I don't know why you thought this might be a good idea. We don't have anything to discuss."

"Rowe's worried about you."

"He could have picked up the phone."

"I didn't want him to. I thought maybe we should clear the air between us first."

"How will that help? You're the problem."

"Yes, I am," he said cheerfully, knowing it would put a kink in her tail.

Moonlight filtered through the live oaks framing the trail he chose. When they were far enough away from the house their voices wouldn't be heard, he turned toward a rise that emptied into a dark hollow.

They both dismounted and he unsaddled his horse, stripping the saddle and the blanket from his gelding's back.

Dani eyed him suspiciously.

Justin shrugged, widening his eyes innocently. "We may be talking for a while. Might as well get comfortable."

Her eyes narrowed to suspicious slits. "So long as you stick to your side."

He spread the blanket beneath a tree and took a seat, leaning back against the trunk and lifting one knee.

Dani sat cross-legged in front of him, staring at his boots. "All right, you have me here. What do you wanna talk about?"

Justin nodded then took a deep breath. "What you saw today..."

Dani shook her head. "It's none of my business. You needn't worry about me saying anything. I'd never want Rowe to be embarrassed or worse. I know how people are around here."

The fact she didn't give a damn what people might think about him stung. "You're not shocked?"

"Just a little disappointed. I'd thought Rowe and I..." She shrugged and raised her head. "Guess you know."

"Don't be so hard on him, Dani. I don't think he intended for things to go this far. He was just curious...at first. Like you."

Dani's sharp intake of breath said she hadn't expected the conversation to drift back to their one encounter. "That was a long time ago."

Justin paused, letting her remember. "And yet, you never told Rowe about it," he said slowly. "Not something a woman who expects a ring should ever do."

Her lips tightened. "So I'm not perfect. He never gave me a blow by blow of every girl he ever dated. Besides, we hadn't made any promises."

"Still haven't." Justin drew a deep breath and let his gaze trail over Dani's hair. It shone as bright at the moon above them. "Maybe Rowe's just sowing some wild oats. Think you can forgive him? Could you put this behind you?"

Dani's haunted gaze lifted to his. "I could. But I don't think Rowe can let it go. I saw his face, when you...were making him do those things. He wanted it bad, even while he was ashamed. How the hell can I compete with that kind of need?"

"Do you really want to?"

She gave a soft, feminine snort. "I always had this vision of myself, my future. On Rowe's ranch, raising kids with him. It's all I ever wanted."

"Can't be completely true. You stayed gone a long time."

"I wanted to make myself the best possible partner. Run the business end of the ranch."

Justin nodded although he remained dubious. "What about the married part? Him and you. Is that all you ever wanted? Can he give you everything you need?"

A bitter grimace stretched her mouth. "This the part where you tell me you know I hesitated because he couldn't fulfill all my needs?"

"I wouldn't say that to you." When her eyes narrowed, he smiled.

Dani tilted her head as she stared at him. "What's in this for you? Why do you care if I'm not happy married to Rowe? You want to be my little bit on the side if I keep quiet about you two?"

"Not what I was going to say, but interesting you went there."

Dani's mouth crimped into a sneer. "You're impossible. Don't know why I thought we might actually have a conversation without you ending up mocking me again."

"But we are talkin'. Maybe it's not all that civil. But I haven't touched you." Justin gave her a sly smile. "Is that why you're gettin' all worked up?"

"I'm not all worked up!"

Justin's body hardened the hotter Dani grew. That he could get under her skin so quickly had to mean something. "No? Are you angry I didn't comment on the fact you aren't wearin' a bra?"

Dani's shoulders hunched. "Maybe I just didn't want to take the time."

"I think you're still hot and bothered. You came because you hoped something would happen. That I'd take the choice of exactly what might happen right out of your hands. You're not so different from Rowe, you know. You both like to pretend you're better than this."

Her eyes glittered in the darkness. "You're so full of yourself. Do you get off on being the one in charge?"

Her defiance pleased him. And he almost softened toward her, but he knew instinctively this wasn't the time to let her know she could trust him. Dani was stubborn. Liked to think she wanted to be in charge. "Tell the truth. The only reason you're angry right now is because I haven't made a move on you."

Dani's breath blew out, but she didn't respond with a caustic comeback.

Justin lifted an eyebrow then eased away from the tree, coming to his knees in front of her. "Did I guess right?"

Her head bowed. "I hate you."

Her softly muttered statement didn't wound because he knew she lied. Eyeing her bent head, tenderness filled him. He took a breath, and forced steel into his voice. "No, you don't hate me or you'd be backing up fast." His hands closed around her upper arms and he pulled her to her knees. With his mouth hovering just above hers, he whispered, "Last chance, Dani-girl."

Chapter Three

Dani still didn't move, didn't fight his hold. Her green eyes remained wide open—whether from fear or excitement, he didn't really care. He could make either work.

She waited for him to make that first move.

Justin laid her on the blanket and knelt over her. "Open your legs," he said gruffly.

Hesitantly, she did so, spreading herself while a deep, delicious sigh sifted through her lips.

Justin stretched his body on top of hers, anchoring her to the ground. His cock rode the top of her feminine mound.

Her eyes glittered in the moonlight. Her tongue stroked her upper lip then disappeared.

His body, already hot and hard, tensed, and he fought the urge to ravage her. He wanted to savor the moment. So much had changed in the six years since he'd last taken her. She'd been a slender girl, now all those lush, womanly curves lay beneath him, ready for him to explore.

He settled onto her and bracketed her face with his hands. He rubbed a thumb lazily over her moist mouth and glided his lips along her cheek before drawing back. "I'm sorry you had to find out the way you did. About me and Rowe. But I'm not sorry at all that you know."

Dani drew in a short, shivering breath. But her hands glided along his sides. "It's wrong. You. Him. Me."

"Why?" he asked, pressing his mouth against her then

pulling away again. "Because this isn't what you saw for your future?" He nuzzled her cheek, her ear, felt her tremble and smiled before lifting his head again to watch her expression.

"Something like that. I don't know where this can all lead except to hell."

He scraped his thumb across her plump lower lip. "Do we have to be going anywhere?"

Her tongue darted out, wetting her upper lip again then gliding over the tip of his thumb. "Our families…"

Justin watched her hot little tongue, fighting the image of it stroking his cock. "Your brother. Rowe's on his own now. Just like me. Who's gonna care?"

"You say this doesn't have to go anywhere, but is that what you really want? Because I don't know if I can settle." Dani's voice was breathy, but her gaze didn't waver.

Justin nearly growled. She'd all but admitted she wanted a long-term affair. "I'd like you to consider the possibility of having more than one man in your life."

"Are you saying you want the three of us…?"

Justin flexed his buttocks and gently pressed his cock against her. "I think we'd all do well together. We might not all have the same upbringing, but we do love this life. Working a ranch together, sharing the burdens—"

Dani frowned. "Sharing the same bed…that's what you're really thinking about."

Justin grinned. "Can't say that thought hasn't crossed my mind." Again, Justin ground his cock against the juncture of her open thighs. "Don't try to tell me you haven't been thinkin' about it too ever since you saw Rowe go down on me. I saw your face. You were creaming just watching us."

Her body quivered beneath his, but she didn't deny it.

"Now, shut up. I want that mouth of yours doing something other than telling me all the reasons this can't work."

Dani's eyelids drooped. Her lips parted.

Justin recognized the invitation and swooped down to kiss her.

His tongue stroked inside her wet, warm mouth and he groaned. "Wearin' any underwear?" he whispered when he broke the kiss.

She shook her head.

"*Goddamn.* Already you please me." He kissed her again, then rose from her, straddling her hips and raking up her shirt, pausing to take it over her head. Then he bent again, and his mouth glided over hers, sucking on her bottom lip and releasing it. *Fuck*, she tasted sweet.

He glided downward, pressing kisses against her shoulder blades and the tops of her breasts. When his lips closed around a tightly beaded nipple, her fingers dug into his scalp, holding him there. He scooped the nipple into his mouth, tongued the hardened tip and suckled hard until her body moved restlessly beneath him.

Justin remembered the taste of her, remembered how sweetly she'd surrendered the last time he'd been intimate with her.

Even then he'd known she was special. He'd watched her with Rowe, caught fleeting glimpses of her in town. But the few years' difference in their ages had kept him from acting on his attraction because he'd known she was too young, and her brother would kill him. Too, he'd needed to keep his job, and while Mr. Ayers liked him, Justin seriously doubted the old man would have stood up for him if he messed with his neighbor's daughter.

So he'd bided his time, letting her fill his dreams while he'd plowed through women like he was planting a crop. She'd been the girl he'd set on the pedestal, unattainable, until one day not long after she'd graduated high school, he'd found her alone.

She'd been sitting beside the creek that fed the many ponds on both properties, waving her hat in front of her face to cool her skin, watching him as he approached on his horse.

"You're a long way from home," he'd said, wondering why that was, and why she looked like she'd been running.

Her face had glistened with sweat, her shirt had stuck to her slender frame. Her nipples poked against the fabric of her thin bra and he hadn't been able to look away because the rigid points sat on the upper swell of breasts. He knew if he stripped her naked, he'd only have to lean down to take a sexy sip.

Her expression didn't change, remained closed, but her eyes trailed down his body then back up.

He'd hardened in an instant. "Need water?" he'd said, his voice rasping.

One pale eyebrow lifted and his cheeks burned. She was sitting beside a creek after all.

"Clean water." He untied the canteen from his saddle and leaned down to hand it to her.

She'd taken it and lifted it to her lips, taking a long draw that overspilled her mouth and ran in rivulets down her throat.

"You worked up a thirst. Mind tellin' me why you're so far from home without a horse? Did you have a fall?"

She shook her head, but her eyes filled.

Justin had sighed and slipped off the saddle to kneel beside her. "What's wrong, Dani?"

Her gaze had climbed up his chest and lingered on his lips.

His mouth went dry as her interest became apparent. The question of why she was here and all alone faded from his mind as he bent and pressed his mouth to hers. He'd waited too damn long, stayed awake too many nights thinking of her to ignore the invitation.

Her soft, lush mouth yielded, and he plundered it, and when he drew back they were both gasping from breath. His gaze dropped to her breasts.

Surprisingly, she hadn't stopped him when he'd given into the urge and nuzzled her breasts through her clothing. She'd sat wide-eyed, her mouth gulping, but she didn't resist when he'd opened her blouse and made a feast of her small globes. Her pink nipples blossomed under the lash of his tongue.

She didn't do more than moan when he'd stripped her pants from her long legs and settled between them. The sight of her pale blonde ruff and the deep pink, inner lips framing her entrance, took his breath away.

Complete silence had surrounded them, not a word passing between them while he'd taken her. She hadn't offered a single word of complaint when he'd turned her and hammered into her tight little cunt from behind.

And when they'd both come, he hadn't been able to break the magical silence because he hadn't wanted to spoil the moment.

They'd ridden together on his horse to a spot nearer her home and he'd watched as she walked away. Later, he'd found out from Rowe that it had been the anniversary of her parents' deaths. But he'd never regretted taking advantage of her sorrow.

And to this day, he hadn't understood why she'd let him have her, why she'd remained mute throughout. Dani wasn't the quiet type, didn't like to give up an ounce of pride without an argument to get her good and hot.

He should know. He'd watched her and Rowe often enough. She'd goaded his friend every time into giving her what she craved.

Only now, as then, she didn't say a word to him, simply melted against him, letting him place her hands above her head.

A gentle push against the blanket was all it took to tell her not to move them. He stripped her efficiently, without a single caress to entice her into surrender.

Like a ragdoll, she lifted her hips when he tugged at her pants and let him slide them down. When he pressed against her inner thighs she opened. When he cupped her bottom, she rocked her hips upward, only as far as he wanted. When his hands slipped from underneath her bottom, she stayed in place, offering her sex for his eager mouth.

A perfect little supplicant. And she'd never been that way for Rowe.

Fierce, hot elation swept through him, and he tugged her folds into his mouth and sucked, slipping his tongue between them and stroking into her entrance, just to acquaint himself with her spicy taste.

Then he sat back on his haunches and drew his shirt over his head, stood and toed off his boots, shoved his pants down his legs and kicked them away. When he came down on his knees, she didn't move...not to get away...not to embrace him.

That gave him pause. Almost made him angry. She might surrender her body, but he wouldn't be satisfied until she gave him her uncensored response.

"Roll onto your belly," he said, keeping his tone even.

Dani bit her bottom lip but rolled, lying there, her slender back tense.

He bent and kissed each cheek of her ass, giving them a bold caress of his hands, rolling them, parting them.

Her breath hissed between her lips, and a quiver worked its way down her spine. She didn't resist, but she also didn't urge him to move faster.

"I want you on your knees."

"God," she finally whispered, pushing up on her arms, her bottom lifting toward him.

Justin bent and licked her from behind, stroking his tongue over her clit, sliding into her entrance, then up, following the tender region behind her folds and trailing upward until his tongue grazed her little asshole.

Her body jerked away.

He pinched her bottom in warning. "You don't get a say in what I do."

"I've never..." she started to say in a little voice.

"Rowe never take you in the ass?"

Her head shook, and so did her whole body.

"If that's what I want, will you stop me?"

She gasped. Then, she whispered, "M-make me."

Justin closed his eyes. He hadn't known it any more than he had when Rowe's unexpected surrender had come, that this was what he wanted of her. Capitulation. No questions, only a show of resistance.

God, it was going to be sweet training her to suit his needs. *Their needs.*

Dani couldn't believe what she'd just said. Or how she'd said it—in a small, timorous voice, like his response mattered more than anything, even her pride. What was it about him that made her so completely crazy for him to take control?

For as long as he'd worked at the ranch next door, she'd been aware of him, and knew he was aware of her. When she'd ride along the fence toward the shack, she'd see him outlined against a far hill, sitting atop his horse. Alone and lonely. She'd known that. But he'd always frightened her because she'd known deep inside that he'd demand complete control, and she hadn't been ready to surrender.

She needed to be pushed beyond endurance, beyond any sense of self-preservation before she could allow him near her.

Just like the first time, when she'd been running from her problems and needed time away from Cutter and the home that was still filled with memories too painful for her to face. She'd wanted him to take her. Make her forget. He could do it with just the hard edge of his voice.

Sure, she'd always loved goading Rowe into being forceful, into spanking her. But it had been a game they both played for their mutual pleasure. With Justin, she needed him to force her to accept him, needed him to command her body.

Was this how he'd gotten to Rowe?

A palm cupped her sex, fingers strumming over her folds. Moisture seeped against his palm. A low, sexy chuckle sounded behind her. His hand swirled over her then dropped. Before she had a chance to moan in complaint, Justin slapped her pussy.

Shock held her immobile for a long moment, then her whole body convulsed. Her back sank, and her bottom rose higher.

Again. She wanted him to do it again.

The next slap was harder, sharper. It warmed her sex, sent a jolt of heat arcing through her, trembling up her channel to her womb. Her bottom wriggled, her thighs clenched, she rocked against his gliding hand.

"Like that?" he asked softly.

"Mmmm..."

He spanked her pussy—rapid little swats that got noisier as her body released fluids to drench his palm and trickle down her inner thighs.

When he smeared his wet hands over the globes of her ass, she didn't shy away from the nastiness. She damn near purred. But it was only a short respite.

His hands landed on her backside, warming every inch of her bottom while her pussy swelled and her inner muscles rippled up and down her channel around tight, cramping clenches.

"Jesus," he said, laying his cheek against her ass. "You're so goddamn wet."

So fuck me anyway, she wanted to moan, but he'd just make her wait longer.

"Want me inside you?" he whispered, his tone harsh, his breaths jagged.

She didn't answer, just shook as her arms began to tremble.

His mouth nibbled at her bottom. "Don't know if I want your ass or your cunt."

God, he did not just say that word. The dick!

"Don't like cunt?"

"I said that out loud?" she groaned.

"Sure did." He chuckled. "Cunt," he rasped, his breath blowing over her moist pussy. "It's brutal, isn't it? Nothing pretty about the word, nothing cuddly...like pussy. But men like it. Like how nasty it sounds. Like to say it out loud."

"Don't give a shit what you call it," she groused.

Fingers traced the sensitive edges of her thin inner lips. "Not now, you don't. You just want me to sink inside it. Don't you?"

She nodded, but he couldn't see. She pressed her lips into a thin line.

"I don't think I like the quiet you anymore. I've watched you with him, you know. Watched you prick at him, tease him, fight him when you wanted him to get a little rough."

A finger teased inside her entrance. Too narrow to fill her, too shallow to stroke over her magic spot. God, would he ever just get busy? "I knew he'd never hurt me," she said softly.

"Not so sure about me?"

"I hardly know you."

"Didn't really know Rowe at all, did you?" He licked her pussy, lapping at her arousal. "If you want more from me, want me fucking you hard...you have to give me a little trust too. Can't play coward now."

"I don't want to fight you. I'll give you what you want."

"What if I need a little resistance from you?"

Her pussy clasped, more sweet juice greeted his tongue. "Can't."

He sucked her folds and let them go. "Are you afraid of me?"

A soft sob shook her slender frame.

Justin grew still behind her and eased his grip on her ass. But he couldn't resist skimming his palms over her soft skin. "I'm not much bigger or stronger than Rowe."

Dani lifted her ass, pressing against his hands. "Rowe's my best friend. We were each other's firsts. I know he'd never hurt me. I don't know you. And from what you've let me see of you, I know I don't like you very much."

"And yet, you're here with me now."

Her breath gusted in a huff. "Can't help myself. Can't resist."

Something inside Justin twisted. He leaned away and took his hands off her hips.

Dani glanced over her shoulder then knelt, her hands covering her breasts. "Why'd you stop?"

"You can't resist. Means you wish you could. Am I not good enough for you, Dani?"

Dani's mouth opened then closed. Her brow lowered.

"You're just not the same as Rowe."

"I'm a man."

"But I wasn't raised next door to you. I haven't known you all my life."

"That wasn't exactly possible, now was it?"

Dani wrapped her arms around her breasts. Her large eyes glittered. "What do you want from me?" she asked, her tone ragged.

Justin didn't want to beg. Didn't want to let her see how vulnerable he really was. He ground his jaws together. "I want your trust. And for you to see me as a man with every right to be in your life."

Her brows rose. "You wanna date me?"

"Am I reaching too far?" he asked quietly, holding himself still.

She shook her head, a frown building a furrow between her brows. "My brother..."

He let one side of his mouth curl. "Yeah, he'd have a problem with me, wouldn't he?"

"He doesn't know you. He'd expect...well, someone different for me."

"He'd expect someone like Rowe. Someone with prospects."

Dani shook her head again, but then her shoulders slumped. "He'd expect someone who would want to take care of me."

"You think I don't want to do that?" he asked, keeping his voice dead even while anger formed a hard knot in his belly.

Dani's glance fell away for a moment. When she raised her head again, her eyes were wide and wet. "Why should I think any differently, Justin? The only time you've ever come close to me was to get into my pants. Why should I think I'm any different from any other woman you've fucked and left?"

Justin drew a deep breath. How could he change her mind now about his intentions? His reputation was a huge obstacle. Their shared past was another. He'd used her when she'd needed tenderness. And his relationship with Rowe was the two-hundred-pound gorilla in the room they still hadn't addressed.

Justin forced emotion away, reminding himself that she didn't want that from him.

Dani Standifer was only curious, slumming with the bad boy. In the end, she'd turn away from him. So why shouldn't he take what he could while she was still willing and eager for him to use her?

Justin's expression shuttered, growing remote. And Dani had the sinking feeling she'd hurt him. "I was just being honest. Do you want...something more...?"

His mouth curved into a bitter smile. "Come closer. I want you to straddle me."

Dani eyed him, wondering what he was thinking now. Gone was the lazy charm he'd used that had curved his lips and kept his sharply masculine features from slanting into the scary mask he wore now. "Maybe I should go back," she said softly.

"I'm not finished with you."

She wanted to say that maybe she was done with him. But it wouldn't have been true. She still needed something from him. She needed to feel desired. Needed his brand of sensuality—dirty, relentless, harsh. She needed to feel the stretch of his cock, the heat of his hands and mouth. Maybe she wanted to use his body, but that's all he wanted from her anyway, wasn't it?

She crawled across the blanket toward him, then awkwardly placed her knees on either side of his hips and settled her hands on his shoulders.

His gaze dropped to her breasts, and her nipples tightened. Her uneasy breaths caused her chest to quiver.

"Slide that juicy cunt over my dick," he said softly.

She gasped. His steady glare said he wanted to shock her. Maybe he half-expected her to try to escape him. His hands closed hard around her hips.

She lifted her chin. "Do you have a condom?" she asked,

proud her voice hadn't quivered.

"In the pocket of my jeans. You'll have to reach for it if you want it that bad."

She firmed her lips and her glare, but reached beside them to his crumpled jeans.

"Front pocket."

His cock already nudged between her folds. God she was tempted to slide right down this very moment. But she rooted into the pocket and pulled out the small cellophane-wrapped square, holding it between them.

He plucked it from her fingers, tore it open with his teeth, and cloaked himself expertly. When he was done, he arched one dark brow.

She gritted her teeth, really hating that expression he donned every time he expected her to bolt. Instead, she centered her sex over the tip of him and drove downward.

He didn't help her, didn't move, just sat on his haunches while she tried to still the trembling inside her and forced herself down his shaft. When she was seated, her pussy clenched tightly around him, their faces were even.

She read anger in his expression.

She wondered what she betrayed. Regret? Because she was feeling it now. She wanted to take back what she'd said, wanted him to caress her body like he gave a damn about her.

Dani took a quivering breath. "I'm sorry."

"For what, Dani?" he said, sounding a little tired.

"I don't know...precisely."

He snorted. "What do you need from me? *Be precise.*"

With their bodies connected, she felt a little less inhibited by her own pride and tried to reach out, tried to breach the emotional distance separating them. "I want...for you to care."

"But this is just a fuck, isn't it? Revenge, maybe, because I shot your dreams all to hell." His words were harsh, but his hands were cupping her ass gently.

"You didn't dash my dreams. You couldn't. They were mine and based on...nothing. I didn't know."

130

A muscle alongside his jaw flexed and he dragged in a deep breath. "What do you want from me, Dani?" he repeated, his gaze lifting above her head.

"I'm not sure," she said, leaning closer and nuzzling his neck.

"Don't lie."

"I want you to touch me. I want you to hold me."

His hands roamed up her back, lightly. Teasingly. "Like this?"

She shook her head and gave him a sheepish glance. She bit her lip. "Leave bruises."

He grunted. "Want me to mark you? You won't be able to forget me in the morning."

Dani let him see the longing in her face. "Justin, I never forgot you."

"And yet, you never sought me out again," he whispered. "Couldn't meet my gaze whenever we passed on the street."

"I'm sorry." She set her hands on his shoulders and smoothed them up his sturdy neck, locking her gaze with his. "You scared the shit of me. I was really young. I didn't know I wanted those things."

"What things?"

"Damn you, you know. I let you do whatever you wanted, would have loved for you to take so much more."

"So you turned to Rowe. Made him give you what you needed."

She nodded, and it must have been the answer he'd wanted because he gripped her harder and lifted her, driving her down on his shaft. Dani's eyelids drifted closed.

"Don't," he said roughly. "You have to look at me while I fuck you. I don't want you pretending I'm anyone else."

Her mouth opened, her jaw sagging as his strokes heated her inner walls. "How could I?"

"Dani," he breathed and his head fell against her shoulder.

Dani wrapped her arms around his shoulders and placed her cheek against his. "I never forgot. Always tried to recapture the feeling...but it was never the same."

"Don't care why. Not now. *Jesus*, hold tight." Justin leaned forward, cupping her bottom to keep her pussy clutching his cock, and got his knees under himself to take her down to the blanket. Balls-deep inside her, he pushed into her, rooting deeply, his hips lifting, pulling his cock away, then slamming deeper still.

She wrapped her legs around his waist and sobbed into his ear. "Justin, more. God, please, *please*, don't stop."

His arms shot under her knees and he pressed her legs upward. His cock dug impossibly deeper, forcing out her breaths in short feminine grunts. He unleashed a storm inside her, thrusting endlessly, his strong, muscled body dominating her in the most fundamental way.

Dani couldn't breathe except to drag in his breath, his scent. She couldn't move except to counter his strokes, lifting her bottom to slam her pussy against his groin. She couldn't think about anything except the way he filled her, rushed into her, cramming so deep, filling her so completely, she never wanted it to end.

But at last, his frenzied movement built the sensual tension that curled around her womb...tightening...tightening— until he rocketed her into an orgasm that left her shaken, shivering and gasping for breath.

His strokes slowed even though his cock lost rigidity as though he too didn't want the experience to end. When he halted, she slowly opened her eyes.

His gaze bored into her, glittering with triumph.

Dani felt a chill pass through her. "I can't breathe," she whispered, pushing against his shoulders.

He rolled away and covered his eyes with his forearm while he dragged in deep breaths.

Dani sat up, wrapping an arm around her breasts and pressing her thighs together to still the tremors that faded slowly away. God, she'd given him everything he'd wanted. More than she'd intended. And now, he meant to mock her?

"I need to go home," she said, keeping her voice even by sheer willpower.

His chest lifted and he lowered his arm. "Right. Get dressed."

He rocked to a sit and reached for his shirt, dragging it over his head. Then he stood, his cock glistening in the moonlight, and quickly stripped off the condom and dragged on his jeans. He was dressed before she'd moved and standing with his hands on his hips.

Dani moved like an automaton. She managed the pants, but her hands began to shake so badly, she couldn't get the shirt over her sweat-sticky skin.

He sighed and turned her away. His hands gripped the lower hem and pulled the shirt efficiently down.

Then he whistled softly and his horse ambled toward them. Before she could gather her thoughts and her shattered pride, he had the horse saddled and was helping her up. They didn't speak all the way back to the house. Dani didn't know how she made it up the ladder, must have been the hands steadying her legs and ass all the way up, but when she'd entered her bedroom, she closed her doors and turned the lock, drawing the curtains closed behind her.

A light clicked on behind her and she stiffened. *Sweet Jesus, not now.* All she wanted to do was crawl into bed, pull the covers over her head and weep.

"I heard a noise and got worried," Cutter rasped behind her. "Imagine my surprise when I saw you disappearing over the balcony."

Dani closed her eyes briefly then turned to glance over her shoulder and meet her brother's enraged glare.

"Cutter..."

He rose from the armchair next to her bed and strode over to her. Before she could back away, he lifted his hand and turned her face into the light. "Didn't even bother to kiss you goodnight? Don't know whether I should chase him down and beat the shit out of him or not. Who were you with, Dani?"

"Rowe—"

"Not Rowe. I called him. He hedged, so I guess he knew damn well who you were with. Which leaves me wondering…" His gaze bored into hers. "Couldn't have been Cruz. You have better sense."

She flinched, giving him his answer.

Air hissed between clenched teeth. "You haven't been back even a day. Or did you stop by to set up your little rendezvous before you came here?"

"It wasn't like that."

His jaw ground, then he shook his head. "Guess you're old enough to make your own decisions, but if Cruz thinks he's gonna get a piece of this spread, he's in for disappointment. Mom and Dad had the good sense to leave this place in my care."

"He's not after this ranch."

"You know that for a fact?" He raked a hand through his brown hair. "What's he want then? You? Think he's been waiting around for you to come home?"

"I'm not sixteen anymore. I don't need you to protect me or vet my dates. Justin isn't anyone special to me."

"Well, that makes me feel so much better," he snarled.

She stared at him through a wall of shimmering tears. "Dammit. Don't you dare make me feel like a whore. You aren't exactly a monk."

"I don't sneak around. Any man who is a man will come to our door."

"Like you'd let him date me?"

"You said it. You're not a child." Cutter's gaze condemned her one last time then slid away. "I'm tired. I'll say goodnight. I hope I don't have to worry about anyone else knocking at your window tonight."

Dani let out a deep breath and sat hard on the edge of her bed. Her relationship with Cutter had always been a little one-sided, his way or the highway, but he was right.

She couldn't sneak around. Not and keep her self-respect.

Not that Justin hadn't stripped it all away from her already. He'd used her tonight, proven he could get to her with very little effort.

Damn him. And damn Rowe for putting her in this position.

The things they both made her want were all wrong. However, she couldn't get the image out of her mind of Rowe closing his eyes and sinking down Justin's cock while Justin's hot glare nailed her. She'd quivered then grown wet.

Hot, nasty lust still held her in its grip and she thought she might be like a crack addict, haunted by visions of what her life could be if she could just shake the gnawing need.

But Justin hadn't fully appeased her appetite tonight, hadn't slaked her thirst for his brand of loving. He'd given her teasing glimpses of the man he could be before slamming the door shut. The haunted intensity of his gaze when he'd knelt in front of her couldn't have been just another weapon in his seductive arsenal. If there was even a slim chance she could chip away his armor and prove a caring man really did exist, she had to give it a shot.

Dani didn't know how she knew it, but she knew that she and Rowe would never be completely happy, completely free, if Justin wasn't there with them.

Chapter Four

Rowe found Justin in the barn the next morning, saddling his mount. Another ranch hand was mucking out stalls, but Rowe gave him a jerk of his head, telling him silently to get the hell out. "Justin, we have to talk."

Justin glanced over his shoulder, his face settling into a frown. "What's wrong?"

The chilliness in Justin's voice didn't put him off a bit. Rowe wasn't in the mood to pussyfoot around. "What the hell happened last night?"

Justin aimed a cool glare his way. "Gonna ride my ass for seeing Dani? Told you I'd handle her."

"I got a call from Cutter, looking for her last night. After I stuttered my way through a lie, I took a look around. You weren't here. I would have appreciated knowing I had to cover for your ass."

Justin's dark eyes glittered with amusement. "You don't. And I didn't know I had to ask your permission for a damn thing. Dani's a big girl. She can take care of herself."

Where Justin was concerned, Dani was a lamb being led to the slaughter. And Rowe should know. Even now, as irked as he was, Rowe hated Justin's cool tone. Hated himself for feeling this needy when he wasn't sure where he stood with Justin. "Dani loves Cutter," he said, his tone softer. "He's always looked out for her. Stepped up when their parents were killed. She might not like him bossing her around but she doesn't want to hurt him."

Justin smoothed his hand over the bay's side then reached for the cinch. "Is she willing to stay his little sister forever?"

"All I'm saying is, if we want this thing to work with her, we have to have some respect."

Justin's flinty gaze showed no sign he understood what Rowe was really asking. "You think I don't have respect?"

Anger tensed his muscles, but Rowe saw a shadow cross Justin's face. Justin didn't know how to give respect, because damn few people had ever given it to him willingly. But Justin's pride was a prickly thing. He reacted better to sarcasm than empathy.

Rowe snorted. "I'm pretty sure you don't have any for her or me. Didn't bother me too much before, but I knew what I was getting into. I've had time to think it through. But we kinda blindsided her yesterday."

Justin's lips curled into his trademark smirk. "Buddy, the girl likes to be overwhelmed."

Rowe stepped closer and braced his legs apart, ready to fight if that's what it took for Justin to stop acting like an asshole. "Maybe when it comes to sex, but there's more to her, more to most people, than pleasure."

Justin glared, and then turned back to the horse. He pulled the strap hard beneath his horse's belly and buckled it.

Rowe sighed. He hadn't gotten through.

"What do you want me to do?" Justin asked quietly.

Rowe closed his eyes for a second, relief washing over him. "Cutter's probably put two and two together and figured out you were with her last night. He's not gonna be happy."

Justin snorted again. "What's he gonna do, ground her?"

"Cutter's not a complete control freak, but he's protective. He's had to be parent and brother to Dani. And it's hard for him to see her as anything but his kid sister. It's why Dani and I used to meet on the sly. She didn't want to disappoint him, and frankly, he used to scare me."

Justin's lips twitched. "Hard to picture that, looking at you now."

Rowe shrugged. "Everyone grows up. And I never gave Cutter a reason to want to call me out. Besides, I don't think he would have minded it being me all that much."

"You have to plenty to offer," Justin said, his voice dead even.

"You think Dani's all about what a man can give her financially?"

"Why shouldn't she be? A woman has a right to expect a comfortable life."

"You can support a wife and family. I know what I pay you."

Justin flashed a quick smile, and then rubbed the back of his neck. "With the two of us, she'd never want for a damn thing, but do you really think she'll go for it?"

"We won't know unless we try. But Cutter's a problem. Dani won't be happy if he can't accept this. He's all the family's she's got left."

"So what do you want me to do?"

"You need to make it right. Go to her place, her front door, and ask her out. On a date. Let's ease Cutter into this thing."

Justin gave a soft, amused huff. "A date? Dinner and movie?"

"Dinner for starts. What happens after that is between consenting adults. But let's give it a rest for a couple of days. Let everyone cool down."

"Friday night, then." Justin's smile was tight-lipped. "Want to make it a threesome?"

Rowe grinned. "You get her off her ranch. I'll join you later. No use getting Cutter hotter than he already is. She might be all grown up, but she's still his kid sister. If he gets a whiff of what we wanna do with her, he'll skin us alive."

Justin gave him a steady stare. "You're okay with this? You got over your reservations pretty damn quick."

"I saw Dani's face yesterday too. She wanted in. She just doesn't know how to surrender."

Justin's expression lost its usual hard-edged certainty.

"Dani's gonna want more than a wild fuck. A helluva lot more. She expects a ring, a fancy wedding. Kids. Can't have two grooms. Once we start her down the path, which one of us is gonna step aside?"

Rowe locked gazes with Justin and wished he could step closer and put his arms around the other man. He'd known him long enough, knew enough about his past to understand his insecurities. Justin was a strong man, sometimes damn hardheaded, but he needed to be loved.

However, public displays would never be something they could share. There were too many people around, and as long as they lived in Two Mule, their relationship had to stay on the down low. "Let's take it one step at a time. You've already got me convinced we can share. Maybe we'll find a solution that won't leave one of us out in the cold."

"Afraid I'll change my mind? That I won't choose you?"

Rowe drew a deep, slow breath and dared to state the bald truth, however much it might get Justin's back up. "I'm not stupid, Justin. You like what we have. You get off on the power you wield over me. But you need me more than you know."

A snarl curled Justin's lips. "It's just sex. Damn good sex, but don't think it's anything more than that."

"And who else have you fucked since we started this thing, besides Dani?"

Justin's face hardened. "Maybe I've just been a little busy. You're pretty demanding."

Rowe couldn't help it, one corner of his mouth tilted up. "I'm not the one issuing the orders, bro."

Annoyance flushed Justin's cheeks, but Rowe strode away whistling.

His phone vibrated against his hip and he unclipped it from his belt. "Dani. I was just thinking about you, darlin'."

"We've gotta talk," she said, her voice small and miserable.

"About what happened last night?"

"You know?"

He snorted. "Who doesn't?"

"I sincerely hope you're just being cute."

"The only people who know are the important ones. Promise. Now, what's bothering you?"

"Damn. It's hard, talking to you about another man."

"Almost as hard for me," he said smiling. "Tell me, did big brother bust you?"

"Cutter was waiting for me when I got back. Like I was a teenager who'd snuck out to toilet paper a house. He was furious."

"Must have been worried about you."

"He figured out real quick it was Justin who snuck up to my bedroom window and lured me away. You'd have thought I'd consorted with the devil himself the way he acted."

"He's always had a thing for Justin," Rowe murmured, knowing full well what drove the animosity between the two men.

"I don't get it. I mean, yeah, I know Justin doesn't have the best reputation when it comes to women, but it seems more personal."

"It is, sweetheart. But Justin or Cutter's gonna have to tell you about that."

A soft, feminine snort sounded in her ear. "Like either one of them are big talkers." She sighed. "I still can't believe I let him talk me into it."

"Can't blame it all on him. You could have said no."

"As if! Tell me you can resist him when he uses that sexy growl. And he got me mad first."

Rowe chuckled. "Mad enough to forget you don't like him?"

"Mad enough to do whatever the hell he wanted."

Rowe blew out a deep breath. His body tightened. "Jesus, wish I'd been there to watch," he whispered.

A long silence followed. "You could really do that?" she said softly. "You could stand back and let him have me...like that?"

Dani didn't sound shocked or disappointed. Her soft voice had grown husky. Rowe lowered his own voice and growled. "Might join in too, if you'd like."

Dani gave a short, choked laugh. "God, I can't stop thinking about it. About us, all of us. It's wrong in so many ways."

"According to whom? Whose opinion really matters?"

"Cutter's matters."

"I think Cutter only wants you happy. If you're circumspect, and don't flaunt it to raise eyebrows, I don't think he'd care if you kept a harem. He just wants you safe and loved."

"He thinks Justin doesn't respect me."

"Justin has some things to learn about us. He thinks he knows us inside out. And while he knows how to get to us sexually, he hasn't learned to trust us."

"Trust." She huffed. "He all but demanded it of me."

"He has to learn to give it before he can expect it back."

"And how do we teach someone as stubborn as him?"

"Maybe we should push him outside. Make him watch. We can show him a thing or two about what two people who love each other can do for each other."

"You still love me?"

Rowe smiled at the thickness of her voice, envisioning her soft green eyes moistening. "Always have, Dani. We're the same people. We have the same dreams. I think bringing Justin into the fold will be good for both of us."

Dani groaned into his ear. "I have to help out with the books and payroll today. Now you've completely blown my mind."

"Leave it all to me. Whatever happens on Friday, just go with it."

Rowe closed the phone and grinned. Feeling lighter, like all the pieces of his life were finally coming together, he strode toward the house and his office. He'd always known his future would include Dani, that they'd marry one day, but he'd still felt like his heart had room for more.

Justin knew Rowe was hooked, but he probably didn't have a clue how deep his feelings really went. Justin was a hard case. He didn't trust anyone but himself. Didn't rely on anyone to give him happiness.

And other than his little sister, he didn't love a single soul.

Every time Justin and he were together, the glimpses of tenderness only came when Justin was spent, too exhausted to fight the ties binding him closer and closer to Rowe.

Justin was a sensual guy, a hedonist when it came to finding pleasure, which was the only reason he'd given into the urge to take Rowe as a lover. But he was a hetero man at heart. Love would have to be strong to overcome his proclivities in the long run.

Rowe wasn't as sure about his own natural bent.

Dani was his friend, his playmate. If it didn't sound completely gross, he might have labeled his affection...brotherly. But that didn't mean he didn't desire her, didn't get off on sinking into her hot little body, didn't crave the clasp of her mouth and hands wrapping around his cock.

When wicked humor glinted in her eyes, issuing a feminine challenge, every muscle of his body hardened...and he was there. And he knew she felt the same way about him.

And yet, he'd seen the way she'd stared at Justin. Kinda like he wished he could. All that heat and yearning burning in her eyes told Rowe everything he needed to know.

Dani could be happy with the both of them. She'd share her body, share her life and a home. But he had to tread carefully. Justin was stubborn enough to hold himself apart from them, try to keep them dancing to his tune. The bastard thought he had to be in control.

It was going to be tough figuring out how to get the ornery cowboy to surrender to love.

Dani signed the last payroll check and closed the checkbook. Everything was ready for Friday's payday.

The past couple of days hadn't been bad between her and Cutter—exactly. Since he was up with the roosters and she hadn't quite gotten used to the early mornings, they only shared the dinner meal together. Most of the day, he came and went, ducking his head into the office to see if she needed anything, which she didn't. She'd spent her summers taking care of the admin side of the ranch since high school.

And she didn't mind doing it now, even though nothing had been settled between them. Cutter ground his jaw every time she tried to talk to him about that night, so she'd let it go.

Likely the problem would fester into a sore the size of Texas before Cutter relented. He was the most stubborn man she'd ever known. Even more so than their father. And that was saying a lot.

She'd loved them both despite the flaw.

Dani pushed the chair away from the desk and stood, stretching her arms over her head and rolling her shoulders to ease the ache. She'd spent too many hours tallying columns of numbers in the ledgers. Cutter refused to automate.

Sunshine gleamed from the window and she glanced outside, sighing as she watched a ranch hand pounding nails into the wooden fence surrounding the corral. Everyone else was out riding herd, moving them to fresher pasture or following the fence line to check for breaks.

She'd have liked to join them, but then again, she didn't really want to talk to anyone right now. As edgy and grumpy as she was, she'd snap. Sleep hadn't come easy the previous night. The memory of Rowe and Justin played back, over and over, only she'd rewritten the scene in her mind.

In her dream, both men were naked. Rowe was still on his knees and suctioning hard enough to make Justin's toes curl into the plank floor. When Justin challenged her with his hard gaze, she didn't bolt. Instead, she'd imagined herself walking nude toward both of them then sinking to the floor beside Rowe. Together they'd pleasured Justin until his whole body quivered and shook. When he came, she and Rowe took turns lapping the sticky white stripes from each other's faces.

The image was burned in her mind. Kept her body tense, her sex and breasts aching. She was half afraid that anyone

143

looking at her now would know exactly what she was thinking because she couldn't stop sweating.

Frustrated, she decided to get out of the house and ride. Maybe the wind rushing through her hair would cool her down.

But even her horse seemed to know what she wanted, because without so much as a single nudge or pull of the reins, the mare headed straight for the cabin.

Someone else had read her mind. Dani flashed Rowe a grin and slid off her horse.

Rowe sat on the porch, his lean face breaking into a smile.

"Waiting for Justin?" she drawled.

"Nope, I was waiting for you."

Dani tilted her head in a silent question. "You have a spy at the house?"

"Nah, just knew you'd never hold out until Friday."

She wrinkled her nose. "I hate being predictable. But I'm glad you're here."

"Want to talk?"

"Can we talk and get busy at the same time?"

His soft chuckle was all she needed to hear. He stood and gripped her hand, tugging her up the steps and through the door.

They undressed each other, kissing every inch of skin they laid bare until they were naked and lying on fresh sheets in the bed that still sat in the center of the floor. Rowe cloaked himself in latex, and then they faced each other, heads supported on one hand, while their free hands roamed.

Rowe pinched a tightly beaded nipple. "You know, it's not because I don't love you."

Dani knew exactly what he was talking about, and was relieved they still seemed so in tune. "I know." Her fingertips scraped down his belly, heading toward his cock, which jerked as though excited about the attention coming its way.

"It's always been good between us."

Dani wrapped her hand around his shaft, enjoying his steely hardness and the heat radiating through the condom.

"But not fantastic, right?" She darted a glance his way, intending only a peek, but his soft, regretful smile held her.

"I didn't know I wanted more. Not until it happened."

Dani kept her expression set. If she got too emotional now, he'd feel like hell. "I would have tried."

"I know that." His hand cupped her breast and squeezed, then he tucked his fingers between her legs and traced the edges of her folds.

"Justin...he gives you everything you need?" she asked, afraid of the answer, and hoping she wouldn't betray her sadness by tearing up now. Rowe needed to tell her this. Needed her understanding.

Rowe rolled over her and settled his cock between her legs. The tip pushed against her pussy then slid rapidly inside, not stopping until every inch of him filled her. "He doesn't give me everything I need. He can't. He isn't you."

The tears she'd wanted to hide leaked down the side of her face. "I was afraid you were done with me. I think that's why I was so shocked yesterday."

Rowe kissed her. Settling his weight on his elbows, he combed his fingers through her hair. "I will always love you."

Dani stared into his pale blue eyes. "But...?"

"You give me warmth and laughter. Justin..."

"Overwhelms you?" she whispered.

"Yeah, he completely blows away every inhibition I ever had. He's like a goddamn drug." He sighed. "I'm sorry if I've hurt you."

Dani swallowed the tears down her throat, hating the regret in his gaze and feeling guilty because he thought he'd betrayed her. "I have something I should have told you a long time ago."

Rowe pressed a finger against her lips. "You've been with him too. I picked up on that. It's okay. I'm kinda relieved actually. It means we both have the same taste."

A gust of laughter caught her by surprise. "It was only the one time. Right after high school. And I hated myself for being weak."

145

His wry grin said he knew exactly how she'd felt. "Even if I hadn't become his lover, I would have forgiven you. We have too much history, and we were so damn young. It's a wonder we've come this far."

"I'm sorry I never told you. Maybe it was meant to be this way." She blushed, feeling foolish saying that, but Rowe's crooked smile said he felt the exact same way.

But in true Rowe fashion, his expression slipped from tender to wicked in a heartbeat. He lifted a brow, Justin-like, and growled, "Want to make me spank you first?"

Dani laughed. "I think I just wanted a hug, and this is the sexiest kind imaginable."

"'Nough talk then." Rowe's sweet breath entered her mouth a moment before he kissed her hard. His tongue stroked deep, sweeping along the edges of her teeth, and then dueled with hers.

Dani raised her legs and hooked them behind his back, tilting her pussy to take him deeper and squeezing her inner muscles around his shaft.

As he began to thrust, the slow, steady throb of her heart picked up the pace; her breaths quickened. The slick, wet sounds they made as they came together were just nasty enough to thrill her, and the familiar musky scent and feel of the man working above her smoothed away the edges from her earlier unrest.

Sex with Rowe had always been comfortable and comforting. He worked hard to please her. Convinced he still loved her and that she still had a place in his life, she gave herself over to his loving, gliding her hands over his chest then clutching the tops of his shoulders when his thrusts quickened.

The climb ended quicker than she'd thought it would. Tiny, pleasurable convulsions began to pulse all along her channel. She arched her back and slammed her hips upward, meeting his strokes, gasping as the sudden wash of her orgasm took her breath and swept her away.

When she came down, Rowe wore a one-sided smile. "I think I got it."

"You did. Just what I needed," she groaned and tightened her legs and arms around him to hold him closer.

Rowe kissed her forehead and waited while she unwound herself from around him. He padded to the small sink and poured water from a bottle onto a clean cloth. On his way back, he glanced at the window and hesitated.

"What is it?"

Rowe shook his head. "Thought I saw something."

When they'd both cleaned up and dressed, he helped her onto her horse. "Ready for tomorrow?"

She slid her boots into the stirrups. "Just what's supposed to happen?"

He winked and gently slapped her horse. "Wear something sexy."

Dani made a face at him and tugged the reins to turn the horse. When she pulled away from the trees, she glanced to the far hilltop.

A lone cowboy sat atop his horse. Even from the distance, she knew it was Justin. She started to lift her hand to wave, but something about the way he held himself—his posture straight, his aura so vigilant—stopped her.

She didn't know if he was angry or jealous, or if he cared at all. But she did like the fact he didn't move, following her with the turn of his head as she headed back to her brother's ranch.

Chapter Five

Dani's body hummed. Rowe had told her to cool her heels until Friday. Even if he hadn't set the date, she'd have known something was going to happen tonight. The stillness of the air outside, the sharp edge of summer heat, the energy buzzing inside her own body kept her anxious and excited. If only her brother wouldn't put a damper on her emotions. Not now.

Cutter sat across the table from her, toying with the food on his plate. His glance had raked her once before he took his seat, but he hadn't commented on the fact she'd showered and changed. But his gaze lingered on the thin straps of her silky green top.

She hated the tension between them. Hated that he was disappointed in her. But she wasn't fifteen anymore. Setting down her fork, she took a deep breath. "We should talk."

Cutter gave a sharp shake of his head and kept his gaze glued to his plate.

Tears filled her eyes, and then she grew angry. She'd only feel guilt over what happened if she let him lay it on her. "You've gotta know I'm not a virgin."

His face screwed up in disgust. "*Jesus*, Dani. I don't want to talk about this."

"You don't want to talk about anything," she said, feeling miserable. "And I can't stay here with you, feeling like this."

Cutter's expression became impossibly darker. "What are you saying? You wanna go? Wanna shack up with Cruz? Think he'd even have you? You might cramp his style."

Dani tossed her napkin on the table. "Would you stop it?" What he said was true, and she knew it. But it still wasn't any of his damn business.

Cutter's lips curved into a bitter smile. "When I thought it might be Rowe—that was bad enough. You two were always thick as thieves, and don't think for a moment that I don't know you've been getting it on for years with him."

Dani lifted an eyebrow. "What's wrong with Rowe?"

"He strung you along. Never stepped up to make an honest woman of you."

Dani snorted. "What the hell? Do you think this is the Old West? I don't need anyone making me *honest*! Did you ever think that maybe I was the one dragging my feet?"

Cutter's expression, a mixture of anger and confusion, frustrated her. He didn't know a thing about what was inside her. She blinked to dry the tears quickly filling her eyes.

Cutter shoved his half-finished plate forward. "Why would you drag your feet? You sleep around with him. You're obviously compatible. Why not marry the man?"

Heat flooded Dani's cheeks. "*I fuck him*, Cutter. Can't you call it what it is?"

"Don't push me," he said, raising his voice. "You want me to go ballistic on his ass? You're my little sister. My responsibility."

"I'm twenty-freaking-five. All grown up. I don't need you babysitting me. And I don't need you choosing my boyfriends."

"Gonna have more than one? Does Rowe even know you're seeing Justin?"

Dani crossed her arms over her chest and narrowed her eyes. "As a matter of fact he does. And yeah, maybe I like having more than one."

His mouth opened then his eyelids fell halfway. He clamped his jaws shut.

"Yeah, think about it," she said softly, rising.

The doorbell rang, and Cutter shot out of his chair.

Dani hurried to the door, her brother right behind her. When she swung it open, her stomach dropped. If it had been Rowe this would have been so much simpler.

Justin stood on the stoop, his hat crushed in one hand, his dark, hooded gaze landing on her, giving her a once-over that left her trembling before his gaze lifted beyond her shoulder. "Cutter." He gave her brother a nod.

Dani risked a glance over her shoulder at her brother, who was equal in height and breadth to Justin, and wondered if a fight was about to break out. Both men bristled with animosity.

And what was up with that? Sure, Cutter had his reasons, but what was with Justin? "You here for a reason?" she asked breathlessly, clinging to the doorknob behind her.

"Came to see if you'd like to grab a bite to eat," Justin said, his voice a low rumble.

"She already ate," Cutter bit out.

Justin cleared his throat, his glare softening when it landed on her again. "How about we head to Lafferty's? Maybe you'd like to dance."

He wasn't really asking; he'd inserted the "maybe" for Cutter's sake. Dani felt herself easing away from the door under the influence of his rough persuasion.

"Cruz, you and I need to have a little talk," her brother said, his expression looking as though he'd swallowed something bitter.

"Cutter—" Dani broke in.

"He's right, Dani," Justin said, closing his hands around her shoulders and gently pushing her aside. "Your brother's got a problem with me. Shouldn't take more than a minute. Get your purse."

Dani's nervous glance went to Cutter. He'd stiffened when Justin issued his order. God, what would he think?

"I won't be a minute," she said, aiming a warning at Cutter.

Cutter held out his arm, indicating Justin should precede him.

The corners of Justin's mouth curled, but his eyes

remained narrowed. Dani stared as the two men headed to the downstairs office. Once the door clicked closed behind them, she raced for the staircase. Soon as she grabbed her purse, she'd be hammering on the door.

Justin walked into the office and heard the door close behind him. The hair on the back of his neck lifted, but only in the way a male scenting another might. He had no illusions Cutter would kill him where he stood if he thought he could get away with it.

"She doesn't know we've had our run-ins," Justin said quietly in case Dani had her ear pressed to the door.

Cutter fisted his hands on his hips. "Maybe we should tell her. Might give her insight into your character."

Justin kept his posture casual, not responding to the unspoken threat rippling through Cutter's rigid frame. "She knows I haven't been a choirboy."

"Probably what attracts her too, dammit."

Justin gave him a quick, tight-lipped grin. "Maybe."

"Does she have any idea what a man-whore you really are?"

"Like I said. Dani has no illusions about me."

"You seein' anyone else?"

Justin wondered whether Cutter knew, but Cutter's shuttered expression spoke of personal interest. "I haven't seen Katie in over a year—if that's what's bothering you."

Cutter's jaw hardened to granite. "Not what I was asking, but since you mentioned it, did you have to set your sights on her too?"

Justin's gaze slid away. He wouldn't admit it in a million years, but Cutter's condemnation made him feel...ashamed. He shrugged to get rid of the momentary twinge of remorse. "I didn't do it to spite you. Back then, any woman I hadn't slept with was a challenge. Katie gave me more of a run than I expected. She didn't go down easy."

Cutter's lips lifted in a snarl. "Whatever you're doing sniffing around my sister, it's not gonna get you any part of my spread."

Justin felt the stab clear to his gut. Cutter might let her roam a bit, but he'd never give his approval. That might matter to Dani. "I don't need your land. Don't need what she brings other than her pretty little self."

Cutter stepped closer, his gaze boring into Justin's with deadly intent. "This isn't over. She's gonna come through that door in a minute, so I'll make this quick. You're trash, Cruz. Not because of what you came from, but because of how you use people. My sister deserves a whole lot better than you. You hurt her, I'll kill you."

Justin met his glare with one of his own. He believed him.

A sharp knock sounded on the door, but neither man looked back as it shoved open. Footsteps clicked on the floor. Dani's hand smoothed over Justin's sleeve. "Ready?" she asked, sounding breathless.

Justin turned to glance down at her. She'd glossed her lips with pink. He wondered what big brother would do if he bent and wiped it off with his mouth. "We done?" he asked Cutter without lifting his glance from Dani's anxious face.

"Dani," Cutter bit out, "I wish you'd think about this."

"It's just a date," she said, lifting her chin. A deeper pink than tinted her lips washed over her cheeks, but she didn't hesitate. "Don't wait up for me."

Justin felt like growling his approval. The woman made him feel that way. Primal, possessive. Already his cock filled, pressing against the front of his jeans.

He turned, crooking his arm for her to settle her small hand along his forearm. "Those shoes comfortable?" he asked, glancing down at the high-heeled sandals peeking under the hem of her crisp blue jeans.

"Don't you worry about my feet," she tossed back. "I think you're a better dancer than to stomp all over my toes."

Justin glanced over his shoulder one last time at Cutter, whose expression had turned bleak. He felt a moment's pity for the man, but quickly squelched it. Sure, he knew how it felt to worry about some scumbag taking advantage of his little sister, but Dani knew what she was getting into. If she thought she could handle everything he'd bring—so be it.

Inside the truck, Dani fidgeted on the bench seat of his pickup. "So did Cutter lay into you about the other night?"

"He never mentioned it."

"I'm sorry if he gave you a rough time."

"He's your brother. It's his job to worry about you."

Dani drew in a deep breath and nodded. "You look great by the way."

Justin glanced down at his clean jeans and crisply ironed blue shirt. "Thanks." Then he realized what she really wanted to know was that he appreciated the effort she'd gone to over her own appearance. "You look pretty tonight," he murmured.

Her head swiveled his way. Her green eyes flashed. "And I didn't every other time we saw each other?"

Justin wondered where the hell his ease with women had gone. Right out the window apparently. Or maybe they were both wound a little tight after the fuss her brother had made. "You're beautiful—makeup or no. Pretty blouse or naked," he said, smiling because he knew exactly how she'd react to that little comment. *Let the game begin.*

"You're an ass," she said, crossing her arms over her chest and settling back in her seat with a scowl.

"Just bein' honest. You have pretty skin—milky white where the sun never gets, pretty pink nipples, pretty pink—"

"Justin!"

He chuckled. "I love it when you get fired up."

"Why would you want me angry with you?"

"Because you forget about being scared and embarrassed when you're blowin' hot."

"You know, I'm not exactly scared of you." Dani pulled her lower lip between her teeth then released it. "I thought all week about what we talked about. I think I'm scared because you make me feel out of control."

"But you love me taking control," he said, his voice sliding into a low purr.

"Doesn't mean it doesn't scare me. Guess I worry about what will happen afterward...with us."

Justin silently cursed his own past. "Think I'll be in a hurry to move on?"

She shrugged. "Cutter's right. You do have a certain reputation. Love 'em and leave 'em."

"I never loved any of 'em," he said quickly.

"That makes me feel so much better. Damn, I sound just like Cutter now," she said under her breath.

"Dani," he said softly. "Just 'cause I never have, doesn't mean I don't want to learn how."

Her head turned slowly toward him, and he met her gaze for a charged moment before staring through the windshield.

Dani unclipped her belt and scooted closer.

Justin's chest swelled around a deep, relieved breath. "I think I'm sitting on the other belt," he said, lifting up in the seat while she rooted.

"Got it." She sounded breathless. When she was safe again, he stretched his arm behind her and she leaned her head on his shoulder. Justin liked the way it felt, her snuggled close, her body heating his side, her sweet floral scent wafting over him.

When he pulled up in front of Lafferty's, he cut off the engine. The perennial Christmas lights tracing the line of the roof and the door of the little bar sparkled. Music blared through the windows.

"Let me get your door."

Dani smiled and waited while he circled the front of his truck. He opened her door but didn't step back. "Don't think I can wait for a kiss."

"I was wondering when you would get around to it." Dani scooted toward the edge of the seat, opened her legs to cradle his hips, and he leaned in.

Justin tilted back his cowboy hat, bent to press his lips against hers and was lost.

Her lips opened beneath his, her sweet breath seeping into

his mouth. Her tongue touched the tip of his then retreated, inviting him to follow. He slanted his mouth over hers, rubbing lips together, stroking his tongue over hers, spearing rhythmically while he rocked his hips against the juncture of her thighs.

Dani wound herself around him like she did when they screwed, arms and legs hugging him close.

He rutted between her legs, making them both groan. When they came up for air, her mouth was blurred, and he suspected he wore as much of the pale pink lip gloss as she did.

Her pleased little smirk told him it was true. And because he enjoyed the sparkle of humor in her eyes, he didn't bother wiping it away. He stepped back with her still wound around him.

She slowly dropped her legs and sagged against his chest. "Sure we have to go inside?"

Justin nuzzled her fragrant blonde hair. "I've been looking forward to dancing with you all day."

"You asked me to dinner first."

"Exactly."

She leaned away and wrinkled her nose. "That didn't make a bit of sense."

Justin grinned and readjusted his hat. He reached behind her for her purse, placed it in her hands, and then crooked his elbow again.

Every glance swung their way when they pushed through the doors, and he knew what everyone was thinking.

Justin had himself a fresh conquest. This time he didn't enjoy the little charge of triumph. He didn't like the men eyeing Dani and wondering if they'd have a shot at her when he dropped her. He'd be damned if he let a single one of them near enough to ask for a dance to put the idea into her head.

This snarling possessiveness was new for him, and he knew he had to pull back a bit or Dani would wonder what the hell had gotten into him. Then he spotted Rowe sitting alone at a table in the back and he sighed. Damn, he knew what the name of this game was, but he didn't want to share her quite so soon. However, he couldn't alter the plan now.

He bent toward Dani. "Rowe's here, sweetheart."

Something flashed in her eyes. Was it a moment of disappointment? Then color flooded her cheeks. Excitement shortened her breaths.

And just as quickly, Justin forgot the twinge of jealousy because he couldn't wait to see how the night unfolded. He might have a reputation for his wild sexual exploits, but he'd never shared a woman with another man. He'd always been too damn selfish. Tonight was different. These two people drew him. Individually, he'd desired them both.

But would he be left to feel like a third wheel as they loved each other, or would they welcome him between them? He was eager to find out. Hopeful like he'd never been before that, for once, he wouldn't be left on the outside looking in at an elusive happiness.

Rowe watched Dani and Justin weave their way through the tables to join him. He didn't miss Justin's momentary grimace when he spotted him. *Too bad.*

Rowe had big plans for tonight. And there was no time like now to start the wheels in motion. Justin wouldn't be the one in charge and he wasn't likely to embrace the change. Rowe admitted a twinge of disappointment that he wouldn't be on the receiving end of Justin's attentions, but this new start was too important.

To further complicate matters he had to enlist Dani's help. And she might hesitate because she was enamored of the idea of sensual enslavement.

He understood the feeling. Craved it himself. But Justin couldn't be allowed to think that he controlled them beyond the bedroom.

Rowe laid his hat on the table and stood when they drew near to hold out a chair for Dani. She slid silently into it, giving him a small, tight smile, her eyes glittering in the pale light shining from behind the gleaming, wooden bar.

Justin hovered for a second, but Rowe held the back of her chair for another unnecessary moment, offering the other man a silent challenge.

Justin's head tilted, his eyelids fell halfway. Then he grunted and took the chair opposite Dani's, sliding it toward her so that he could sit close.

Rowe suppressed a smile as the music changed. A waltz. His hand cupped Dani's shoulder, drawing her gaze upward.

He lifted his chin, and her smile broadened. She rose immediately, sparing Justin a quick wink, then taking Rowe's hand. "People are gonna talk," she said under her breath.

Rowe leaned close, knowing the picture they presented, bent toward each other as they escaped Justin's frowning presence. "That scare you?"

"Not a bit," she whispered. "But Justin's not gonna be happy. I just abandoned him."

"Want to see how much it takes to break him?"

"Break him?" Her head tilted back and she eyed him with suspicion.

Rowe's hand slid along her lower back, turning her toward him, and he brought her slender body flush with his. Her breasts softened against his chest. Her hands clutched his upper arms before sliding slowly over the tops of his shoulders.

"Justin's a bit bossy," he drawled, shuffling his feet in a semblance of dance and pulling her along. "Do you want him to think you're a doormat?"

"You think he doesn't respect me because he can get to me so easily?"

"What do you think?"

A frown bisected her smooth forehead. "I haven't really had time to think...about what his expectations are. About what mine should be. This is all new to me."

"Begin the way you mean to proceed," he replied in a glib tone.

Dani shook back her pale hair and lifted her chin. "But what if I like how he is...what he does."

The wicked sparkle in her eyes told him she was thinking about all the possibilities. "Baby, you're not giving that up," he said, lowering his voice. "You're defining yourself. Impressing on him that he's not the only one whose needs should be addressed."

Dani's gaze slid toward the cowboy at the lonely table. "He's not selfish. Not in his heart. He works too hard at pleasing a lover."

"You don't think ego might have something to do with that?" he drawled.

She turned a pensive glance his way. "You've been with him longer than I have. Is that what you think?"

Rowe sighed and turned her on the floor, glancing at the table where Justin had tilted back his chair and was staring at them from beneath the brim of his hat. "I don't know for sure. Justin doesn't share what he's thinking or feeling. I don't think he knows how to love. But we do. Don't we, Dani?"

Her expression softened. She placed her head against his chest and snuggled closer. "We do know how. We've been lovin' each other since we first exchanged notes in middle school."

"Let's show him how it works." Rowe's lips slid down the side of her face.

A soft, sexy chuckle gusted against his neck. "You tryin' to make us the talk of the town?"

"It won't do you any harm—two handsome cowboys makin' moves on you."

"Think a lot of yourself, don't you?" She shivered when his tongue glided along the curve of her ear.

"Don't you think I'm handsome?"

Dani laughed and pulled back her head. "Think he'll just sit back and watch you flirt with his date? He has a big bad reputation to uphold."

"Relax, he's not gonna start a fight in front of everyone."

Dani's gaze darted back to the table. "I don't know about that. He's giving us that dirty squint of his."

Rowe's mouth curved. "Let him. We can't worry about the

fact he might be angry."

"Why not? I don't want to hurt him."

"Dani, this isn't just about tonight. We want him to be ours, don't we?"

Rowe's hand pressed against her lower back as he guided her around the floor. Dani had a hard time keeping her mind on the conversation because she'd gotten a look at the bar—every gaze followed them as they danced then darted back to check Justin's reaction.

For his part, Justin nonchalantly rocked his chair on its back legs, sipping a beer. Acting as though there wasn't anything unusual about his date cozying up close to another man.

But Dani saw the banked heat in his narrowed eyes. He wasn't happy at all. "Do you really think he can share? That he'd want more than just a night with us? He's never kept a girlfriend for long."

"Maybe he's ready for a change. But if we want this to work, we can't let him have everything his way. He can't lead us around with a bit in our teeth while he cracks a damn whip."

Dani wrinkled her nose. "What if that's what I like about being with him...him taking charge?"

"Baby, before he can master us he has to love us. Both of us."

And because that's exactly what she hoped, she gave in, snuggling closer still, drawing on Rowe's strength and warmth. "You think he really can?"

"I think Justin's ready for it, dyin' for it. Up until we started...meeting, he ran through women like he was still the high school quarterback, but he wasn't happy."

"You think he can be happy with us?"

"I happen to think we have a lot to offer."

Dani ducked her head. "Cutter thinks he's after a piece of the ranch."

Rowe snorted. "That thought has probably crossed Justin's

mind, but do you really think he's greedy?"

"I don't know." Maybe she looked at him through rose-colored glasses, reflecting her own hopes and dreams on him.

"Dani, he drives the same dinged-up truck he bought after he started working at the ranch. He's not a flashy dresser, doesn't spend money he doesn't have. If he covets what we have, I think he wants what it represents. Stability, roots. That's not such a bad thing to want, is it?"

"How's that gonna happen for him…with us? Cutter's already said he'll protect the ranch against him. And *you* certainly can't marry him."

Rowe snuck his thigh between hers and dipped his hips, forcing her to ride him. "If this works, we won't need a damn thing from Cutter. I have enough to support us all."

Dani closed her thighs around his and shivered. "You do like playing with fire. I still don't get how you think this will amount to anything but a good time. For a while anyway. How in hell will we make it last?"

"If this is something we want bad enough, we'll find a way. But for right now, we need to teach Justin a lesson or two."

Rowe rubbed his leg against her pussy, which was still sensitive after Justin had teased her in the parking lot. She bit back a groan and took a deep breath, hoping to clear her head. "He's so damn sure of himself," she said, lifting her gaze to Rowe's. "Maybe he's unteachable."

A crooked smile betrayed the fact he knew exactly what she was feeling. "That pride of his is a mask. I promise you that."

"How do you propose we do the teaching when he'll want to be the one arranging us for his pleasure?"

"Well, he's damn sure not likely to let us tie him up. We'll have to slip it in when he's least expecting. Leave him wondering when he lost control."

Losing control—that's what she'd like to do right now, but there were too many interested gazes following their every move. "I like the sound of that," she whispered.

"Thought you might." Rowe bent closer. "Don't look now."

Dani grinned. "He didn't hold out long, did he?"

"You look amazing tonight. Did you think either one of us wouldn't be following you like a couple of hound dogs, tongues hangin' out?"

She giggled against his chest. "You like the blouse?"

"What there is of it."

"Cutter nearly choked when he saw me."

"Bet he wished he could have choked the life out of Justin."

"Was it your idea for him to ask me out? Somehow, I can't imagine him thinking of arriving hat in hand to woo a girl."

"Uh-huh."

"I'm cutting in." Justin's deep voice sounded strained. Tight, like he was a hair away from making a fuss. "I came in with her, buddy. Looks damn strange."

Rowe lifted Dani's hand and twirled her under his arm, letting her reel out toward Justin then snapping her back against his chest.

Justin shook his head.

Dani laughed.

Rowe underestimated Justin's lack of embarrassment. Justin reached out and clutched Dani's hips then moved in, snuggling her ass against his groin, sinking his face into the corner of her neck.

Dani's breath caught, and she groaned against Rowe's chest. Then she turned her head to see his expression.

Justin's eyes narrowed; his smirk was firmly in place. "Don't play games you aren't willing to finish."

Chapter Six

Rowe felt heat creep across his cheeks. All eyes clung in fascination to the trio swaying together on the dance floor. Rowe lifted his chin in defiance, and slid his hand around Dani's waist to pull her closer.

"Guys?" she said softly.

"Yeah, sweetheart," Rowe muttered.

"You're killin' me. And Cutter will have a cow when he gets wind of this."

Justin brushed his lips against her cheek and bent toward her ear. "You care as much about what Cutter thinks as where this is leadin'?"

She moaned and snuggled closer to Rowe. "You and your bright ideas," she muttered.

With her soft body pressed so close he could feel her heart beat against his chest, Rowe stopped caring about the little competition he and Justin waged. "Would you be embarrassed if we left right now?"

Dani's soft laughter vibrated against his chest. "I think I'll be more embarrassed if we wait much longer to get out of here. You're both pokin' at me."

Justin's mouth stretched into a wide grin, and Rowe couldn't help responding—just two guys reacting to a little feminine distress.

Rowe cleared his throat. "Since he came with you, I'll be the first out of the door. But keep me waiting long, and I swear I won't care who sees me drag the two of you out of here."

Justin locked gazes with him. "Your bed or mine?"

"Mine's bigger," he said waggling his eyebrows.

Justin grunted and pulled Dani closer.

Rowe let her go and stepped back. Conscious of all the gazes trained their way, he lifted his hand to tip his nonexistent hat to Justin and left them.

As he walked through the saloon, he met the gazes of several of the interested patrons and aimed glares their way. Their lips twitched, but they turned back to their beers.

Satisfied that no one would think anything other than a sly rivalry between suitors had occurred, he pushed through the double doors and strode down the steps toward his truck. No use letting the whole town in on what was happening among the trio. Soon enough, they'd get wind of the fact that Dani couldn't make up her mind between the two of them.

How he and Justin handled the truth over the coming months would set the tone for how everyone treated them. He didn't want Dani to become uncomfortable in public. If he and Justin had to settle matters in true Texan fashion with anyone who looked sideways at them—behind a barn and with fists—so be it. But Dani would never know.

If things turned out the way he hoped they would, he'd never let Dani or Justin regret their decision. And he had the money and the family name to back him.

The meager light from the dash didn't pierce the intimate silence that settled inside the cab of Justin's truck. Dani snuggled close to Justin all the way to Rowe's ranch. His hand smoothed along her side, sliding under her arm to cup her breast and squeeze. She lifted her arm to give him access. Then his hand glided down, right between her legs, and she eased her thighs apart.

"Should have worn a damn skirt," he grumbled.

She laughed and unbuckled her belt, opened her pants and

eased back, giving him room to sneak his hand inside.

His fingers slid into the melting excitement that oozed from deep inside her. Callused fingertips glided over her hard little clit and right inside her pussy, but not deep enough to ease the ache.

"Justin...Justin..." she moaned, rolling her head on his shoulder as he swirled.

She dropped a hand between his legs and cupped the hard bulge of his cock.

A soft curse lifted her hair, and the truck veered off the road.

Dani smiled and opened her eyes as the truck's tires ground in gravel.

"Get out," he said, roughly.

Rowe's warning about Justin not appreciating an easy conquest flitted through her mind, but her body overruled her common sense.

Ever since the two men had pinned her between them, dueling cocks grinding into her soft belly and ass, she'd shivered with excitement, tension building tightly inside her core. That tension had only continued to build to the point that, now, she thought she'd explode the second Justin pushed his cock inside her.

She scooted across the seat, opened the door, and slid to the ground.

Justin's door crashed, and he stomped around the truck. His jaw was taut, his eyes glittering with sexy menace in the moonlight.

Dani quivered at the tension radiating from his bunched shoulders. He opened her door wider and grabbed her hips to lift her to the edge of her seat. Her sandals fell away; her pants were peeled down her legs. His zipper scraped, he donned a condom, and then he was there—stepping up on the running board and pushing his cock inside her.

His groan was only slightly less desperate than her own. He pulsed his hips, grinding into her. A thumb flicked her clit, but

Dani needed more. She lifted her legs and slid her calves over the tops of his shoulders.

Justin grunted his approval and slammed deeper.

"Hardly seems fair..." she groaned.

"What?" he asked, sounding irritated.

"We're keeping Rowe waiting." Not that she really cared with Justin's cock plunging fast and deep, but she did like to talk.

"He'll figure it out. It's his own damn fault anyway."

"How's that? He wasn't the one with his hand down my pants."

"He pulled you onto the dance floor and shoved his dick against you while everyone was watching."

Dani grinned. "Only person who gave a damn was you."

"Your point?" Justin halted his movements and pulled out most of the way. His hand slid around the base of his cock and he squeezed, closing his eyes and dragging in deep breaths.

Dani wished he hadn't stopped, but she did enjoy the sight of him, tight-faced and trembling, as he fought for control.

At last, he drew one long, shuddering breath and opened his eyes.

Dani locked gazes with him and reached down to slide her hands beneath her shirt and push it up to expose her breasts. Then she tugged her nipples, panting as her whole body quaked at the heat tightening his face.

Justin leaned back and plucked her clit with his thumb and forefinger.

Her pussy clenched around him, and tension curled deep inside her body. "You have an effective way of ending a conversation," she gasped.

"Not in the mood to talk."

"I've noticed that about you. More an action kind of guy, huh?"

"Can't talk...my dick's ready to blow." He leaned over her again, his hands landing on the seat on either side of her waist.

"Don't you think you ought to hurry it up a bit? Someone

might see." Not that she really gave a damn, she was that close.

"Don't see any cars. You want me to hurry?" His hips circled, and he slowly screwed his cock inside her.

Dani felt like her skin was on fire. "God, *Jesus*..."

"Got a whole damn host of saints here, baby. Come for me."

Dani braced her feet against the dash and door, widened her splayed thighs, and tilted her hips.

"That's it." Air hissed between clenched teeth. "Let me all the way inside."

"Justin...?" Dani lifted her head and stared at him. His lower body was hidden in shadow, but the side of his face where moonlight struck shone on sharpened cheeks.

His mouth opened, and his teeth gleamed between tight lips. "Come for me, baby."

Another quick stroke and another slight swirling twist of his hips, and she came apart.

"That's it, that's it," he crooned, thrusting in rapid bursts until the earth stopped tilting and she could breathe again. He pulled free and rolled the condom off his cock. Then he pulled her hand, bringing her up.

Dani reached for his cock, sliding her hand around his hot shaft, and stepped down from the truck on shaking legs. Then kneeling in the dirt beside him, she took him into her mouth.

His fingers dug into her scalp, then relaxed, threading through her hair and stroking her softly as she sank forward then drew back, over and over. She stroked her tongue along his length, learning his scent, his taste, loving the satiny texture of his skin, the tight, hard steel beneath.

He dragged one hand from her hair and gripped his shaft at the base, and stroked himself, his fingers meeting her lips each time she engulfed him.

Dani gripped his hips, bracing herself and quickening her motions, craving more, suctioning hard to get him to hurry and give her what she wanted.

Her cowboy groaned and began to crank his hips, pistoning steadily, driving past her tongue, tapping the back of her throat, his motions tight and controlled.

No way was he going to take charge when her mouth was doing all the work. Dani slipped a hand beneath his cock and cupped his velvety sac, gently tugging his balls.

A soft laugh gusted above her. His balls contracted, drawing closer to his groin, but she continued to massage them, strengthening the suctioning of her lips until his body shuddered and his thrusts lost rhythm.

Without a single grunted warning, salty gushes of come spilled into her mouth, coating her tongue.

Her tongue glided in it, painting his cock inside her mouth as she sipped it down, making more noise than he allowed himself, eager to please, eager to prove she was ready for him, wanted him. All of him.

Justin's hands cupped her cheeks, his thumbs pushing on her bottom lip until she came off him. Then he pulled her up, bending to meet her with a kiss that smoothed the come on her lips, sharing the taste, and sliding into her mouth until her body quivered and she thought she might never want to leave this spot beside the road.

But an engine growled in the distance, and Justin's head lifted. His eyes narrowed at the approaching lights. His expression shuttered. He dropped his hands and stuffed his shirt into his pants. "Better get dressed."

He'd done it again. Turned off like a light switch once he'd had what he wanted of her. Dani bent and whipped her pants off the ground and climbed back into the cab to pull them on.

Justin strode casually around the truck and climbed back in. Without looking her way, he started the truck and pulled back onto the road. "Get buckled up."

No more tender "baby", she guessed. The stern voice was back.

But was it really because he'd gotten everything he wanted, or because he needed to take back control?

Dani thought that maybe Rowe was onto something. She finished shimmying into her tight jeans and scooted close to

Justin again, buckling up and leaning her head on his shoulder.

His arm lowered. His hand clasped her upper arm and squeezed.

She sighed and closed her eyes. It was enough for now.

Justin let himself and Dani into Rowe's darkened foyer and, with a hand at her back, guided her through the living room and down the hallway toward the bedroom at the end of the long corridor.

Rowe's house wasn't as large as Dani's. Just a plain old-fashioned ranch house, single-storied, a white clapboard exterior with a porch stretching along the front. The interior wasn't fancy, but the furnishings were sturdy, well made. A far cry from the cheap cinder block and plain pine furniture he'd grown up with. This time, his gaze didn't roam the rooms, cataloging the differences.

Light fanned into the hallway from the crack of an open door. Dani's steps slowed.

"You know what's gonna happen tonight..." he whispered, wondering if she was getting cold feet.

"Think I'm gonna back down?"

Justin drew a deep breath, warning himself to slow down. "Anytime you get nervous or scared..."

One pale brow arched. "You'll stop?

A smile lifted one side of his mouth. "I'll slow down. Don't know if I'll be able to stop." Justin pushed open the door. The sight that greeted him had him grinning.

Rowe lay against the pillows, completely naked. The set of his chin and his lowered eyebrows said he knew exactly what had kept the pair. By the rigid state of his cock, Rowe had tried to relieve a little tension on his own. "'Bout damn time," he grumbled.

Justin pushed the small of Dani's back, urging her forward. Her cheeks were a bright red, but she gave Rowe a small, sheepish grin, then shrugged.

"What was it?" Rowe said, his gaze skimming Dani's mussed appearance. "Justin had to start the party without me?"

"Fuck you," Justin said, aiming a glare the other man's way. "Dani, get your clothes off."

Dani's head swiveled his way, a frown furrowing her forehead.

Justin gave her a single arched brow, echoing her own tart response seconds ago.

Her attention went from him to Rowe and something passed between the other two. Like a coded glance. Their gazes locked and lips pressed into straight lines.

Justin didn't like being left out of the "conversation" one damn bit.

He toed off his boots while he unbuckled his belt and slid it free, wrapping it around his fist while he glared at Rowe.

Rowe's face darkened, eyeing the leather. He gave a subtle shake of his head and Justin shrugged, then dropped the belt and went to work on the rest of his clothes.

"We should talk some, don't you think?" Rowe said, raising an eyebrow then aiming a pointed glance Dani's way.

Justin kept his expression neutral and his gaze aimed at his zipper, which he was drawing down. "Dani, you need to talk about this first?"

She didn't blurt an answer like she usually did when she was flustered. He raised his head.

Dani's mouth opened and her tongue wet her upper lip. "Um...guess not."

Rowe's lips firmed, and he patted the mattress beside him. "Come here, sweetheart."

Dani skimmed across the floor and climbed fully clothed onto the mattress.

Coming to his knees, Rowe slid a hand beneath his pillow, pulling out two condoms. "We'll take care of you tonight."

"I know," she said softly. "I'm not afraid."

Rowe bracketed her cheeks and bent to kiss her mouth.

Dani sighed and opened for him, meeting his kiss.

Justin felt uneasy. Like a voyeur watching the two of them share the intimate moment. When they drew apart, Rowe pressed his forehead against hers...then both heads turned toward Justin.

He stiffened, feeling for a moment like they'd passed another secret message and were studying him together. Justin shrugged off his shirt and pushed down his pants. When he stepped out of his clothing, he stood with his hands braced on his hips, watching them both while suspicion caused the hairs on his arms to lift.

"She has too many clothes on," he ground out, knowing he sounded like a dumbass. But *goddamn*, they seemed to draw strength from each other.

Determination gleamed in Rowe's light blue eyes. "Dani's not a whore, Justin. And she's a little nervous."

Well, so was he, but he'd be damned if he let either one of them know it.

Justin crawled onto the tall king-sized bed, stopping next to the couple in the center who still faced each other. This close, he could breathe in the scent of Dani's pussy, the come still clinging to her skin. Rowe had to smell it too.

Skin stretched tight across Rowe's cheeks, his jaw firmed. The dusting of whiskers added an outlaw appearance that, for once, Justin didn't find funny. Rowe's edgy glance also took him aback. He'd always known how to handle Rowe, knew how to seduce him. With the woman between them, Rowe seemed to draw his masculinity more tightly around himself, reacting like a man protecting his woman.

Oddly, the subtle change from vulnerability and need to strength made Justin's body grow even more rigid. A surge of adrenaline, white hot and acrid inside his mouth, had him wanting to compete with Rowe, face off against an adversary over the right to claim the woman.

But if he took the scenario a step further in him mind, he knew he didn't want Rowe going anywhere afterward. He wanted to pound at his ass, brand him with the knowledge he'd never take the lead, never have more of Dani than he'd allow.

Justin drew in a deep, sharp breath, not liking the feelings Rowe aroused in him—lust, jealousy, a need to dominate that was miles beyond the sexual games they'd played.

What did that say about himself and the kind of man he was?

Ruthlessly, he turned his attention to Dani, who watched him from behind a carefully blank expression. Not something he'd accept either. "I want her naked and on her back, Rowe. I want her spread."

Dani's eyes widened and her small pink tongue wet her bottom lip. Justin remembered the feel of her mouth sucking his cock, and his dick jerked.

"Dani's not a dog," Rowe said, his voice deepening, the words spoken slowy. "She's not a bitch you can jerk on the lead and make her do whatever you want."

Justin knew Rowe was cautioning him, telling him to gentle up, but he didn't know how. He acted on instinct, and right now everything inside him told him to take them both to the mattress, make them both submit.

Justin swallowed. "I think I'm in trouble here," he whispered.

Rowe's gaze raked over him, then softened on his face. He gave him a little nod. "You trust me?"

Hell no. But he trusted himself even less. "Yeah."

"Lie down."

Justin ground his jaws together, but the pair parted and he slid between them, turning to lie on his back with the two of them staring down at him.

Dani's gaze clung to his cock. The hunger in her stare had him fighting the urge to growl and rise up to crawl all over her.

Rowe reached beneath the pillows and slid something else down.

Justin turned his head and snorted. The fuzzy cuffs from the cabin. "You expect those to hold me?"

"Yeah, I do."

And then, Justin understood. They wanted his surrender. His willing surrender.

Rowe slipped the cuffs around his wrists.

Justin curled his fists. "All right, you have me here. What are you going to do now?"

Rowe smiled and raised his head to catch Dani's glance. Her green eyes sparkled with mischief. This time, Justin didn't bother suppressing a deep rumble of frustration.

Dani bent and pressed her lips against his. "We're doing this for you, Justin."

"You think I want to be the one on the bottom?"

Her smile sank a dimple deep in one cheek. "Nope. You're gonna hate it."

Dani sat and tugged off her boots, tossing them across the room. She made a show of wrestling off her clothing, giving them sly peeks to let them know that she knew she had their rapt attention.

When she was finally nude, Rowe's hand cupped the back of Dani's head, and he pulled her long blonde hair, drawing her up. Then meeting over Justin's body, the two kissed. Rowe's hands cupped her shoulders, then stroked downward, moving in to palm her breasts.

Dani moaned and leaned closer, her knees snuggling close to Justin's side.

Rowe trailed kisses down her neck, to the top of her small breasts. Then he scooped up a nipple with his mouth and suckled hard.

Dani's hands clutched Rowe's light brown hair; her head fell back.

If his hands had been free, Justin would have reached up to slide his fingers into her cunt and see how wet the other man made her, but in the end he didn't need to touch. Her scent ripened, her nipples spiked. Her lids lowered and kiss-softened lips rounded around soft, jagged gasps.

His cock ached. The accidental brushes of their thighs

against the tip as they surged closer nearly killed him. But he wasn't going to beg. Neither was he going to jerk the chains holding him to free himself. He felt too edgy, too feral, and while he might have been willing and eager to let loose with violence on Rowe, he didn't want to frighten Dani.

Instead, he grew increasingly rigid and desperate for relief.

Rowe lifted his head and pressed a quick kiss against Dani's forehead. "Come here," he growled.

Dani climbed eagerly over Justin. Rowe scooted backwards, arranging her for his pleasure, laying her down perpendicular to Justin's body, her head resting on his belly. Rowe parted her thighs then thrust his arms beneath her knees. "Put me inside you."

Rowe was using the voice—Justin's tone and uninflected commands.

Dani turned to glance at Justin. Her eyes were a little wild, but her head turned back to Rowe and she reached down and grasped his shaft, placing the tip of him against her entrance.

Rowe stroked forward. "Watch me fuck you."

The command was meant for Dani, but Justin couldn't look away. Rowe's cock thrust in, then came back, glistening with her juices then sank inside again.

Justin knew what her heat felt like, consuming him, sucking him in, but watching also put other images in his mind, of Rowe's arrow-shaped tip breaching his ass and stroking straight inside.

Justin grunted and raised his knees, letting his belly sink to cup the back of Dani's head. His cock grazed her cheek and she turned toward it. He couldn't see it, but he felt the brush of her wet tongue against his blunt head, felt her mouth fasten around it, and he held himself still to prevent slipping from her hot, wet mouth.

Rowe's strokes quickened, jerking Dani up and down. Her lips suctioned harder to keep her grip around him. Dani's breasts quivered with the ferocity of Rowe's motions, her body flushed with heat, and she raised her legs, toes pointing outward while Rowe moved closer on his knees and hammered her pussy.

The lush, wet sounds grew sharper, wetter, and Dani's belly curved, her knees bent and she drew her legs upward. She wanted more, wanted the cock slamming into her to come deeper.

Watching, aching, Justin couldn't help but stare at the couple's groins as they slapped together noisily. God, would they ever just finish it?

Dani gave a muffled cry against his cockhead, her teeth tightened and Justin cursed, but her body curled into itself, and he knew from the choked cries vibrating against him that she was coming hard.

Rowe pulled out abruptly and ringed his cock with one hand at the base. His chest billowed, glistened with sweat.

Dani's tongue swept over Justin's crown then her mouth withdrew. Her head turned toward Rowe. "What do you want?" she rasped.

"Depends on our friend here," he said, his gaze slowly lifting to Justin.

And Justin knew what Rowe wanted. Knew how he wanted to finish himself off. "No," Justin said, the word coming in a quick, emphatic gust.

"He's not ready, Rowe." Dani's voice was pitched low. The throaty texture nearly had Justin begging for her to swallow down his cock. Her hand smoothed over her belly, sweeping up to squeeze her own breast then downward. Her fingers skimmed her folds.

Justin dropped his head against the pillow and closed his eyes tight. *Jesus Christ*, he wanted to fist his hands around the chains and rip them from the bedpost. His body was primed, aroused like never before. He wasn't one to postpone his own pleasure, but he recognized that when his release came it would be cataclysmic.

And he wasn't sure which partner would give him the greatest pleasure—not at that moment. With Dani's fingers teasing him with the moist sounds she coaxed from between her legs, and Rowe's thick, reddened cock, held tightly in his own grip, Justin didn't want to choose. He just wanted release.

"Whatever..." he whispered and closed his eyes.

The cuffs opened. Bodies moved on the mattress. Then hands rolled him over. Soft kisses trailed from his neck to his ass. A slender hand slipped between his thighs and he spread them, giving Dani access to massage his balls.

"Come up on your knees." Rowe's voice was tight, grinding.

Justin blew out a deep breath and did as ordered, already feeling relief by the change of position. Dani came down beside him. Her soft hair brushed his belly as she slid under him. She ringed his cock and licked it up and down like an ice cream cone.

While she held off his orgasm, Rowe kneed Justin's inner thighs, forcing them to widen. A tongue tracked down the crease of his ass, and Justin buried his face against the mattress. This wasn't happening. He wasn't letting this happen. Not in front of Dani.

But she didn't seem alarmed or put off. Her hungry little mouth glided open-lipped, up and down his shaft.

A tongue swept over his asshole, and Justin instinctively tightened, drawing it inward.

Laughter, deep and filled with gravelly amusement, gusted against him. "How many times did I let you have my ass? I loved it. So will you."

"This isn't something I do."

"It wasn't something I ever wanted, not until you." Rowe's fingers pressed against the sides of his opening, a tongue dipped inside and swirled.

Not something Justin had ever dared.

God, when they were done with him he was going to fuck them both raw.

The tongue withdrew. Moisture landed on his hole and fingers swirled in it, then digits thrust inside.

Justin couldn't help the groan that slipped out.

Laughter beneath and behind him made him grit his teeth. He wouldn't give them the satisfaction of letting them know just how far outside his comfort zone they'd pushed him.

But the fingers stretching him curved and prodded, touching the little gland he'd never had stimulated. If Dani hadn't been stubbornly gripping his cock, his come would have splashed against the bedding in an instant. Instead, his legs quivered, his belly jumped.

Dani moved deeper beneath him, her lips surrounded his head and she suckled him.

The fingers withdrew and Justin knew what was coming next. He rolled his head. *No, no, no.* But Rowe's perfect arrow head prodded him softly, then pushed forward.

The moisture and the heat softened the grip of his tight little ring, and Rowe penetrated him, sliding inward in short little thrusts that burned and ached and felt so goddamn good Justin felt the carefully constructed walls around his sexuality crumble.

Rowe thrust in and out and at last, Justin understood how Dani must feel—powerless, overwhelmed, excited and beyond all coherent thought except for the need to feel the next deep stroke.

"Not 'til I'm ready, Dani," Rowe gritted out.

Her murmur vibrated around Justin's cock, and he couldn't help the little pulse he gave, no matter that it seemed to excite Rowe even more. Rowe's fingers dug into his hips, and he slammed hard against his ass, driving himself deeper and deeper.

The burning ache didn't relent; the skin clothing his cock felt tight and ready to split. Rowe hammered on, thrusting, his belly slapping against Justin's ass. The sounds adding to the excitement humming in his ears.

"Now, baby, now!" Rowe shouted and then liquid heat spilled inside Justin, and he realized instantly they'd forgotten the condoms, but he couldn't care. The sensations filling him were too strong. Rowe stroked and Justin rocked counter to him, prolonging his orgasm.

Then Dani swallowed more of his length, her tongue swirling over the sides of his shaft, and her fingers eased their pressure around him.

Justin shouted and lunged his hips, pushing into her throat, ignoring the choking sounds and Rowe's muffled groan as he took his cock along with the swift short jerks.

When he'd emptied his balls, Justin hung on his arms while Rowe gently withdrew and Dani scooted from underneath him.

Hands turned him, urging him down on the mattress. Dani slid over him. Her face nuzzled his chest, just above his heart.

Chapter Seven

Justin wrapped his arms around her. He sought Rowe's gaze but the other man was already backing off the mattress and padding toward the bathroom. He closed the door quietly and Justin's jaws scraped shut.

Rowe had fucked him. Made him tremble. Dani had witnessed it.

He rolled over, trapping her beneath him. He used his knees to roughly spread her thighs, then slid a hand between them and gripped his half-softened cock and inserted the head into her pussy.

"Don't think I can, Justin," she moaned. "Hell, you can't."

"Give me a minute." He lay over her chest, not caring he was too heavy. He needed to be inside her.

"Afraid?" she asked softly, her arms sweeping around his back.

He was, but he wasn't letting his pride bleed all over her. He'd fuck her hard, make her forget. Force himself to forget— his embarrassment, his lack of control...how damn good it had been.

His cock, surrounded by steamy heat, slowly filled, and he flexed his hips to thrust inside her.

Dani groaned. "God, you two will kill me." But her fingernails dug into his shoulders and scraped down either side of his spine.

Justin shuddered. "Can't take it? Or maybe you don't want

the both of us?"

Dani drew a short, deep breath. Her mouth tightened and her eyes narrowed on his expression. "What are you asking?"

"You gonna choose?"

Her head tilted as she studied him. "Do you want me to?" Her fingers gentled as they swirled over his back. "Would that make this easier for you, baby? Is this too much for you?"

"Think I'm afraid?"

Dani placed a palm along one side of his face and stared into his eyes. "Yeah, I do," she whispered. "I felt you quiver. I heard you gasp and moan and grind your teeth. You wanted it so bad, and you hated that you did. Why?"

"I'm not like that," he gritted out.

"And yet, you seduced Rowe."

"I didn't think..." He grimaced, unable to complete the thought aloud, then ground his cock hard into Dani.

"What didn't you think?" she gasped. "That you'd care about him? You thought it was just sex, right? What about me? Are you fucking me because I'm a willing pussy?"

"Stop it, Dani." He powered into her again, wanting to shut her up.

Her feet smacked the back of his calves, and she began to wriggle beneath him, pushing at his chest to make him stop. "No! I want to know. Am I the one who ought to walk away?"

Her struggles, the tears welling in her eyes, froze him. He hadn't meant to hurt her, not really. Hadn't meant to force her. He rested his forehead on the pillow beside her while he got control of his anger. Then he turned to whisper in her ear. "This can't work without you."

Her breaths held a ragged edge that cut him to the bone. "Because I'm the smokescreen to the rest of the world? Afraid everyone will figure out you're bi-curious?"

"I don't give a fuck what anyone else thinks," he growled softly.

"But you can't get your own head around it, can you?" A deep sigh rifled his hair. "I'm tired of talking, Justin. Just give it to me the way I like it."

He stayed silent then his temper spiked again. He was angry with her. With Rowe. With his own hungry cock. He came up on his arms and stroked hard, pounding into her. Hurting her, he knew because she turned her face away.

Justin pulled out and flipped her, bringing her to her knees. "Don't move."

He glanced at his belt on the carpet, but her skin was more tender than Rowe's. His hand then. He cupped his palm and swatted her buttocks, several times in succession, watching them jiggle and the flesh turn pink.

Dani glanced over her shoulder at him, a mulish expression on her face.

He swatted her again, holding her gaze.

She narrowed her eyes, challenging him. "Think that will get me off?"

He rolled and shoved his legs over the side of the bed, stomping toward the belt. He folded it double, hoping the extra layer would blunt the sting, then stalked back to the bed.

Her green eyes widened, but she didn't make a move to escape. She turned her head sharply and reached up to grip the headboard, which arched her back and lifted her bottom higher.

Justin wanted to rub his lips all over her ass, cuddle her, worship her with his mouth. She was perfect. Defiant, obedient, beautiful. *Loving.*

She cared about him. Loved Rowe. Was willing to risk her brother's disapproval, her town's respect. And for what? For her, it wasn't just about the sex. Never had been. So why was she here?

Could he hope that someday she might feel an ounce of the affection she lavished on Rowe?

For now he'd give her what she wanted. Stripe her until her flesh burned, her pussy melted, and she came apart. Then he'd fuck her hard. Ride her like a man. Face to face. And he wouldn't rush getting up afterward, however hard it would be. He'd let her see what he felt.

He gave her soft skin a last caress, then lifted the belt and swatted her.

A soft gasp escaped her. Her fingers gripped the edge of the headboard tighter.

The leather sang against her skin, left pink welts that crisscrossed her pale buttocks. Her body shivered and she moaned, but never once did she ask him to stop.

Gauging her readiness by the fluid skimming down one thigh, he dropped the belt and cupped his hand again, this time taking careful aim at her pussy. He spanked it, and Dani bounced against his palm, pushing against it, begging silently for more.

But he didn't want to finish her this way. He leaned over her trembling back and pried her fingers from the headboard and brought her up.

Dani sat against his thighs while he soothed her belly and breasts with gentle caresses. Then he lifted her, turned her around and urged her to the mattress where he stretched over her, covering her shoulder to toe.

His warm, wet palms cupped her cheeks. His thumbs wiped the tears leaking from her eyes. He didn't know why she wanted this, didn't know why he was so eager to mark her, but they were bound by the need. That had to be enough for now.

Her legs spread under him, and he nested his cock between her legs and flexed his buttocks, sinking into her lush heat. With his forehead against hers, he watched her eyes flutter open.

"I want your arms around me," he rasped.

She did so instantly, wrapping herself tightly around him. Then he loved her, pressed so close he couldn't drive deep, but loving the softness underneath him, the heat that bound them together, the tender, loving embrace as she clung to him and stroked his back.

She tilted her head and pressed her mouth to his, and Justin kissed her back, not opening his lips to invade her mouth but giving her a sweet, soft brush of his mouth before he pulled his head back. "I love you, Dani."

Embarrassment warmed his cheeks. He hadn't meant to blurt it out like that. Hadn't meant to expose so much. But the soft, sweet smile stretching her lush mouth told him he'd made her happy.

He sighed, relieved he'd done it. At last.

A cough sounded from beside the bed. Dani and Justin turned to watch as Rowe sat on the bed. "Not so bad, is it? Trusting someone with your heart?"

Justin felt the last of his fears melt away. Rowe's crooked grin spoke of his own happiness.

Justin rolled to the side, bringing Dani between them. But he slid her thigh over his, unwilling to lose the connection.

Rowe stretched out behind her and draped his arm over her hip.

His hand cupped her buttock.

Air hissed between her teeth.

"Ouch?" Rowe winced in sympathy.

Dani giggled, and then bit her lip, looking over her shoulder to give Rowe a sheepish smile.

Justin arched an eyebrow at Rowe then bent to bury his lips in the corner of her neck while Rowe planted moist kisses along the back of her shoulder.

But when the two men lifted their heads, it felt just as natural, just as fulfilling, to seal their lips together over the body shivering with soft, feminine laughter.

Justin bit Rowe's lower lip, and then sucked it into his mouth, loving the sound of the helpless moan he forced. He pulled his cock free from Dani and rolled her to her back, then released Rowe's mouth. "I think I'd like to watch," he whispered. "This time."

A week later, Dani stood humming as she chopped lettuce, tomatoes, onions and red bell peppers and tossed them together. The back door was open, just the screen door keeping the bugs out. The aroma of steaks cooking on the grill made her mouth water.

She grinned, knowing that even though she'd prepared several side dishes while the men watched meat roast on a grill, *they* were the ones responsible for dinner.

She shook her head, wondering how she'd ever get credit for a meal without screaming with so much testosterone warring for supremacy.

Not that she really minded and wasn't completely amused by the way the two men competed to please her.

No, she couldn't mind too much when the result was a body that ached deliciously from their fierce "attentions". Even if she could use a little more sleep.

After the evening at Lafferty's, they'd elected to meet at the Ayers ranch house each night. Some evenings she'd wait until after she'd eaten dinner with Cutter, but his disapproving silences depressed her. She'd hoped that he'd relent, but Cutter was stubborn.

And rather than rub salt into a wound, she never slept over with the men. After they'd enjoyed themselves, whether in bed or cuddled together on the couch watching a movie, she'd head home to her lonely bed out of respect for her brother—but damn if that wasn't getting old.

She knew where she wanted to be. Here. With Justin and Rowe. Cutter needed to let go.

Justin entered the kitchen, holding a platter of sizzling steaks. His sharp gaze narrowed on her expression. "Why the long face, sweetheart? We take too long grilling the steaks?"

She forced a smile and shook her head. "Everything's ready. Just need to put that platter and this salad on the table and we're good to go."

Rowe stepped around Justin, and his eyebrows lowered. "Not so fast." He lifted his chin to Justin, who set the platter on the counter, then both men came close.

Two sets of hands slid around her waist, and Dani sighed and hung her head because she couldn't make up her mind which chest she wanted to lean against. "This is hard."

A curled finger lifted her chin. Rowe's blue eyes raked her face. "This all coming too fast? Wanna slow down?"

"Want one of us to take a step back, Dani-girl?"

The tension in Justin's rumbling voice had her sighing again. She really didn't want to worry the guys with her issues. They were still coming to grips with their own regarding their three-way relationship.

Dani stepped back to have both men's faces in her view and said, "I don't want to leave tonight. I don't want to ever go to sleep again without you both beside me."

Rowe reached over and slid a lock of her hair behind one ear. "Are you sure? We know how you feel about your brother. We can wait."

"I can't," she said, giving them a small, tight smile. "He won't ever approve, and I don't really need it. Whether he cuts me out of his life, well, it will be up to him. He's the one who'll be lonely."

Justin blew out a deep breath and stepped toward her, his hands gripping her waist and lifting her off her feet to bring her close.

Dani wrapped her arms around his shoulders, hooked her legs around his waist and smiled over his shoulder at Rowe.

Rowe's eyebrows waggled. "I think we'll have to nuke the steaks later."

Justin had read his mind, because he was already striding toward the kitchen door.

Dani's smile stretched, and she leaned her cheek against Justin's. "But you both worked so hard to cook for me."

Justin squeezed her. "Damn straight. And I had them spiced just right."

"I knew when to take 'em off the grill." Rowe's huge grin said he knew their claims were a sham.

Dani loved the way the two men had bonded. Just as she and Rowe could communicate with just a look, so now could Justin and Rowe—at least when it came to pleasuring her.

Justin strode into the darkened bedroom and sat her on

the edge of the bed. Rowe turned on the overhead lamp and both bedside lamps. The men liked to watch, however much she might prefer a little shadow to hide her flaws.

But she had to admit, it was a huge turn-on seeing the two of them stripping naked and striding straight for her, both their expressions hungry and sharp-edged.

Rowe's beard was a little scruffier, making him look more like a pirate now than a saddle tramp with a devilish glint in his blue eyes.

Justin still looked like sex—dark, smoldering eyes and feral tension riding his bronze face and body.

Her body quivered even before they reached for her and undressed her. Every inch of skin they bared received a wet kiss. When she was nude, Justin urged her toward the center of the bed and pushed her down. Two hungry mouths suckled her breasts.

Dani moaned as hands smoothed over her belly. Justin parted her folds, while Rowe's slick fingers slid inside her. She raised her knees and pumped her hips, fucking his fingers, squeezing around the digits as her nipples tightened beneath the flick of their tongues.

She stared at the ceiling and knew without a shred of doubt that she belonged here, with both of them, and that they'd be happy together.

Justin and Rowe lifted their heads and shared a long, sensually charged look.

Her heart fluttered, knowing whatever they planned to do would shock and delight her. She surrendered, offering no resistance as they turned her to her side.

Rowe lay down and slipped an arm beneath her, pulling her over him. "Take me inside you, baby."

She reached between their bodies, grasped his cock in her hand, pointed the tip at her entrance and sank.

Rowe groaned beneath her. Justin's hands glided down her back, cupped her bottom then came up again, pushing her gently forward.

Rowe grasped her hips and held her pinned to his body as Justin left the bed and opened a bedside drawer.

She started to lift her head to follow him, but Rowe tsked and reached up to kiss her.

Dani felt the thrust of his tongue and ground down along his shaft. But his fingers bit into her ass, a silent warning she obeyed.

The bed dipped beside them. Justin crawled behind her and shoved Rowe's legs wider to make room. Then he cupped her ass again and parted her cheeks.

Dani gasped as something cool and slick rubbed against her back entrance. "You're not."

"I am," Justin insisted, just a hint of command in his voice. Enough to tell her he wanted this, wanted her surrender, but that he'd allow her the choice.

Dani groaned and hid her face against Rowe's shoulder.

Both men chuckled.

Rowe combed her hair with his fingers. "You know how much we enjoy it. Don't you think you'd like to give it a test run?"

"I'm already filled to capacity," she groused.

"Thanks for that," Rowe said, sounding proud.

Justin grunted. One fingertip circled on her tiny hole. "Want me to stop, Dani-girl?"

Dani growled, then without lifting her face, gave him a muffled, "Make me."

Justin gave another chuckle, this one tight and pained. The finger swirled again then slipped inside.

Air hissed between her teeth. The tiny muscles gripping the finger burned, but not uncomfortably. Both men had teased her there, stroked fingers inside her when they made love to her, sometimes two or three. She realized they'd been prepping her all along for this.

"Fuck, she's tight," Justin said, his voice deepening.

"Have to relax," Rowe whispered.

She laughed. "Impossible."

The finger stroked inside, deepening, and her pussy convulsed around Rowe's cock. "Can't come yet."

"The thought of it..." she began.

"Yeah, the first time Justin had me, I didn't have time to get used to it. He wrestled me to the floor and had his wicked way with me."

"Wish I could have watched."

Rowe kissed her cheek. "Better get on with it, Justin. She's wet. She won't last very long."

A second, then a third finger thrust inside and Dani panted, rolling her face on Rowe's chest. "Please, please," she whispered.

The fingers pulled free, and then the soft, blunt head of Justin's cock pressed against her entrance.

Dani tensed, but Rowe crooned into her ear; his hands smoothed down her back and up, soothing her.

Justin pulled back then pushed again, this time, using a small side-to-side motion that eased him into her. When the tip of his cock was inside, he pushed a little deeper.

A low, agonized groan sounded behind her.

Dani knew how Justin felt, but she hadn't the breath to make a sound. The pressure and heat were consuming her, and her thighs and belly were tightening. "Justin...oh God..."

"Dani...gotta move..." Justin ground out behind her.

"Do it!" Her pussy rippled, sucking at Rowe's cock, clenching around him as Justin began to thrust inside her, rocking her forward and back on Rowe.

Rowe's arms closed around her, his body trembling beneath her.

Justin's hands clamped hard on her hips and stroked deeper, faster, until her back bowed and she cried out.

The explosion caused her whole body to vibrate, both entrances to pulse. While she drifted back Rowe groaned beneath her and Justin shouted, hammering harder, faster.

Dani melted against Rowe and laid her face on his sweaty chest. Justin collapsed on top of her, each deep, ragged breath pressing her down harder against Rowe.

"Can't fall asleep, you two," Rowe said softly.

She lifted her head and turned it to catch Justin's tired, one-sided smile. "Guess I better move first."

He pulled slowly away and Rowe and Dani sighed. She snuggled closer to Rowe's chest and must have dozed, because the next thing she knew a soft, warm cloth was washing her between her legs.

Rowe rolled to his side and gave her a quick kiss, then climbed out of bed with more energy than a man had a right to after what she'd been through. Dani lay on her stomach, her head cradled on her crossed arms.

Large, warm palms landed on her shoulders and began to rub.

"Mmmm...I don't have to stay awake, do I?"

"Not unless you change your mind about going home," Justin said quietly.

Dani blew out a breath and turned, meeting his steady gaze. He sat on the edge of the bed. His face was expressionless, his eyes alert.

And she knew what he was thinking. Would she choose to stay? Had she meant it when she said she loved him?

Dani sat up and wrapped her arms around his waist and moaned. "Think we can talk after I've had some sleep? You wore me out."

Justin's hand cradled her head, and he tilted it back. "Sleep as long as you like. We'll be here when you wake up."

She gave him a smile and closed her eyes. Justin laid her back and pulled the sheets up. His footsteps padded away, toward the bathroom, to Rowe. She was too tired to be curious about what they had to say. Settling down in the center of the bed, she knew she'd made the right choice.

Rowe dried his belly with a nubby towel and watched Justin staring at his own reflection in the mirror. Justin's jaw looked carved in granite. His dark eyes appeared haunted—not a look Rowe had ever seen the cowboy wear.

"Dani gone?" Rowe asked quietly.

"No, sleeping." Justin's gaze lifted to Rowe's in the mirror. "She wants to stay the night."

Rowe sighed. "Big brother's not gonna be happy."

Justin's hands tightened around the edge of the counter. "We can't keep playing games here. We have to do right by her."

"And that would be?" he asked, although he had a feeling he knew where this was leading.

"You gotta marry her." Justin pushed away from the counter and turned. He set his butt against it and folded his arms across his chest. "Once Cutter's satisfied, things will settle down. I don't want Dani pulled apart."

Rowe nodded and slung the towel over the top of the shower rail. "How do you feel about that? Me marrying her?"

Justin shrugged, but the tension in his shoulders belied the casual gesture. "Always knew it had to happen."

Rowe canted his head to stare into Justin's blank gaze. "Do you think things will change? Between all of us?"

"Nothing lasts forever."

"You don't think we can make this work?"

"You two marrying makes sense. You both run in the same crowd. No one would bat an eye."

Rowe didn't like that Justin had ignored his question. "Justin, me putting a ring on her finger doesn't spell the end of us."

Justin's eyes narrowed, and his gaze flickered over Rowe's nude body. "Worried I'll get bored with you after you and Dani become official?"

"Should I be? There some other guy you wanna fuck?"

Justin unfolded in an instant. His hands shot out, gripped the bony notches of Rowe's hips, and shoved him against the cool tiled wall. "You know damn well I've never fucked another man," Justin growled.

Excitement quivered through Rowe. The edge of violence in

his lover's voice, the hard bite of his fingers and the thrust of his thickening cock dispelled any doubts Rowe had about where Justin's affections lay.

Justin Cruz was caught—and didn't much like admitting how off-balance and out of control the thought of Dani marrying Rowe made him feel. And Rowe would lay odds Justin didn't know which side of the equation bothered him most. He was worried about being left out.

Any doubts Rowe might have felt about whether Justin was committed melted away. He lifted his hands and thrust his fingers through Justin's thick, warm hair. Leaning forward, he glided his lips over Justin's, opening his mouth to accept the firm thrust of the man's tongue.

His cock throbbed, filling quickly as Justin groaned and deepened the kiss, sucking against his lips as he thrust wildly inside.

Justin slipped a hand between their bodies and cupped Rowe's balls, massaging them, then moved upward to wrap his strong hand around Rowe's dick. He tugged it, squeezing and pulling until Rowe broke the kiss and leaned his head against the tile. "I'd never leave you," he gasped. "Not for Dani. Not for anyone."

Justin's lips twisted. "I won't fucking let you."

Rowe smiled. Let Justin think he was in charge. Let him believe he could take control. Rowe gave it to him, willingly. "Tell me what you want," he said softly.

Justin's hands smoothed upward then cupped Rowe's shoulders, gripping him hard as he shoved him to his knees.

Rowe hid a smile as he kissed Justin's taut belly and nuzzled through the crisp hairs surrounding his proud, straining flesh. He didn't bother with teasing him, and instead opened his mouth, sucking the crown between his lips.

Justin cupped his cheeks, tilted Rowe's head the way he wanted it, and stroked forward, sinking into his eager mouth.

The musky taste of sex and sweat burst on Rowe's tongue and he suctioned hard, drawing in the flavors as his hands caressed Justin's ass.

"Fuck! Take it, take all of it!" Justin growled.

Rowe groaned and widened his jaws, breathing through his nose and swallowing to take Justin deeper.

The tremor that shivered beneath Rowe's palms worked its way up and down Justin's strong frame.

His breaths hitched, his growls softened into choppy, sobbing moans, and still he plowed deep into Rowe's mouth, thrusting wildly.

Tears burned Rowe's eyes and he shut them, accepting the intimacy of the moment, knowing Justin was past caring about his pride, had forgotten to mask his vulnerability or his deep need.

Rowe welcomed the moment, falling deeper in love with Justin. Justin might still want to fight his attraction when the passion waned, might want to name it something crass and safe, but Rowe knew better. Justin was scared but too ensnared to run.

When Justin's come spilled down his throat, Rowe swallowed, drinking him down, loving him with his mouth and tongue until Justin trembled inside his embrace. He pushed up, gliding along Justin's sweating skin, and wrapped his arms around him. "I promise you," he whispered into Justin's ear, "I love you. We love you. That won't ever change."

Dani covered her mouth as her jaws stretched around a wide yawn.

Justin's lips twitched. From across the kitchen, he lifted his coffee cup, a silent reminder that more sleep wasn't part of the plan. Dressed only in his blue jeans, the top button open, all he had to do was breathe to turn her on.

Both men were similarly attired. And they'd allowed her only a T-shirt, wanting easy access, but needing her "interestin' parts" covered so they could get through breakfast without having to clear the table.

All in all, Dani had never felt happier, if a little tired. The men had stamina she envied.

Dawn had come and gone unnoticed. The ranch hands hadn't come knocking. Maybe word had already started to spread, because her car was still parked in front of the house. Whatever the reason, they were all too happy, too sated to give a damn.

She might be a little less than fresh, and her "interestin' parts", as Justin would say, were a little raw, but she was satisfied the three of them had come to an understanding. Justin loved them both. Had admitted it aloud. They'd returned the sentiment, over and over—whispering, shouting, moaning around their avowals.

A door crashed in the distance, and both men stiffened as heavy footsteps thudded toward the kitchen door. Dani had only a second to pull down the hem of her shirt when the door swung open and Cutter stormed inside. His gaze slammed into hers then rose to Rowe's who sat opposite of her at the table. His shoulders relaxed...marginally, but then Justin cleared his throat.

Slowly, Cutter turned his head, his gaze raking over Justin. A flush of anger blazed across his cheeks. "Dani, get dressed. We're leaving."

Dani set her cup on the table and rose. She walked slowly toward her brother, her stomach trembling. This wasn't how she'd wanted to tell him, but she wasn't about to live her life to make him happy.

"I don't want any fighting in my home," she said softly.

Cutter's eyebrows lowered, confusion warring with his anger in the glare he pinned her with. "I expect a ring."

Dani's glance cut to Rowe, whose lips pursed. Then to Justin, whose expression grew carefully blank.

Rowe cleared his throat, drawing her attention back. His expression was tight, his jaw clamping hard. He drew a deep breath then released it and closed his eyes for a second. When he opened them again his gaze shot to Justin then back to her. He gave her a nod.

And because they'd known each other so long, thought like

one person, she understood. Rowe might *want* to be the one, but Justin *needed* this. They'd teach him what love meant. She turned to her brother and smiled. "I'm marrying Justin, Cutter. Get used to it."

Justin's dark brow arched, but a smile began to stretch his lips. He dropped his gaze to his coffee cup.

"It's not what I wanted for you," Cutter muttered.

"But I'm happy. And I'm sure."

Cutter's jaw tightened, but his fists uncurled at his sides. "I don't approve."

He nearly strangled on the words and Dani took pity. "You don't have to. But don't worry about me. Justin...and Rowe...are what I want."

Cutter's eyes closed briefly. When they opened, he couldn't meet her gaze, but he nodded and turned on his heels, leaving as quickly as he'd arrived.

When the door swung shut behind him, Dani sagged.

Strong arms enfolded her from behind. Bronzed arms. Justin. Dani turned inside his embrace and pressed her wet cheek against his chest.

"You should have chosen Rowe," he said gruffly. "Everyone knows he's a better man."

"Rowe and I chose you," she said, snuffling. His heartbeat, strong and steady, reassured her.

"I'll make all the arrangements," Rowe said quietly.

"My brother will damn well give us the biggest wedding this county has ever seen," Dani said, pulling away from Justin because she wanted to see both her men.

Rowe had left the table and stood beside them. "You planning on giving everybody somethin' to talk about?"

"You mean beside the fact I'm marrying the town's bad boy?" Dani grinned, feeling all her worries melt away beneath Rowe's lopsided grin. "We're gonna have to work on learning a six-legged waltz."

Justin's laughter shook his chest.

The surprising sound of it, deep-timbred and free, lightened her heart. When Justin pulled her and Rowe into his embrace, they smiled across his broad chest. They'd done the right thing.

Sure, there were details of their arrangement to work out. But she knew she wanted Rowe's child first. His reward for his unselfish act. Somehow, she knew Justin would be all right with that. In just a few years, they'd have more love surrounding them than any three people could ever hope to achieve.

Dani mouthed the words, "I love you."

Rowe smiled and gave them back.

Justin hugged them harder. "You know I want me some of that too."

Dani ducked under Justin's arms and pinched his side, then dashed out of the kitchen toward the bedroom. The sound of the men, jostling each other against the corridor's walls as they followed, had her giggling. When an arm caught her around the waist and she was flung over a sturdy shoulder, Rowe's by the shape of the ass she was staring at, she erupted in peals of laughter.

She lifted her head and met Justin's cat-like smile as he stalked after them both. Lord, could a girl get any luckier than this?

Then Justin arched those bold, sleek eyebrows, and Dani felt a frisson of feminine alarm. No matter how many years they all shared, she knew she'd always feel like this. Desired, unbearably excited, loved—and by the only two men who could complete her.

Dangling over Rowe's shoulder, she reached out a hand.

Justin lifted it and kissed her palm. "Don't think I'm gonna go light on either of you, baby."

"Cowboy, I'm countin' on it."

Unforgiven

Chapter One

Cutter Standifer stuck his finger inside the collar of his dress shirt and tugged. Damn thing felt tight. And every time he glanced at the bride and *grooms*, it just got tighter.

His little sister had wanted to be married in the sunshine, so they'd chosen the lawn on the south side of the house in front of his mother's rose garden. He'd had landscapers working around the clock to clean up the overgrown flower beds. No one would find fault with the yard, the house or with the celebration he'd paid for. However, if they didn't finish up quick, everyone's Sunday-best clothing would be drenched in perspiration.

June in West Texas was hot as hell even though they'd scheduled the ceremony for just before noon.

If his mother had been here, she'd have approved his preparations. He'd done his duty. Dani looked prettier than the pink and yellow roses blooming in the background. She wore their mother's white wedding dress, which had only needed a few tucks around the waist to fit and left too much of her tanned shoulders and chest bare for his liking. She'd twisted her long blonde hair up into some kind of knot that made her neck and shoulders look feminine, fragile and innocent. No one looking at her now, with her green eyes soft and bright with unshed tears and her lips curved into a wide smile, would know she was anything but fragile. And she damned sure wasn't innocent.

Cutter jerked when the people seated around him erupted

in a loud cheer.

The *official* groom bent Dani over his arm and kissed her like he wasn't going to stop until her stays popped and he had her naked and under him. The crowd enjoyed his enthusiasm.

Cutter's stomach clenched and he looked away. Not until the bridal couple had trailed down the aisle toward the house and the reception did he stir.

And then he moved like an old man, taking his time following the wedding guests inside, listening as music poured out the door onto the wrap-around porch.

Reluctantly, he reminded himself his duty wasn't done quite yet. He had a party to oversee. Just a couple more hours and he could close the doors on the last guest and settle down to getting stinking drunk.

He wondered if anyone else who'd been watching had caught on to the fact the best man had looked every bit as happy as the bastard who'd placed the ring on his kid sister's finger. Rowe Ayers, the best man, had beamed every time he looked at Dani—and at Justin Cruz.

As Cutter stepped into the ballroom, he caught sight of the threesome again and his stomach churned with disgust. Rowe was with the bridal couple, still smiling. First at Dani, and then at Justin.

What the fuck did that mean? Cutter didn't really want to know. The thought of his sister, sandwiched between those two bastards was bad enough. The thought that maybe there was something happening between the two men... Well, it just wasn't something he could let himself think about and not lose his breakfast.

Add to the facts that Justin Cruz looked like the cat that swallowed the canary and Cutter felt like his head was ready to explode.

The pulse at his temple hammered. His face was hot. His muscles tensed for a fight. Just one little word from the wrong person...

"Well, will you lookie there," Wade Luckadoo muttered next to him, holding a Shiner Bock beer in one large fist. "They sure look cozy. Wonder if they plan to dance the first waltz in a goddamn conga line."

Cutter clamped his jaw tight. So maybe he'd been thinking the exact damn thing, but Wade wasn't going to get away with slandering his sister. "You wanna step outside?"

Wade's eyebrows shot up. His hands lifted, holding the beer high. "Cutter, dammit, I didn't mean a thing by it. You know me'n my mouth."

Cutter sighed. He'd really hoped Wade would oblige him with a fight. They were evenly matched and Wade never held a grudge after every time Cutter had tried to kick his ass.

"Still, they did make quite a commotion at the saloon, cozying up together on the dance floor. Didn't seem to mind what anyone was seein'."

"Wade..." Cutter let his tone slide into a sharp-edged warning.

Wade shrugged. "Just sayin' they look happy. Wish't I was that goddamn happy."

Cutter saw red. He reached over for the beer in Wade's hand, and Wade surrendered it cheerfully and began rolling up his shirt sleeves. "Just remember, I'm doin' you a favor. Saw the way you looked at Cruz all thru the ceremony. If that horny bastard had married my little sis, I'd be ready to spit nails too."

Cutter set down the Shiner on the reception table and shrugged out of his tuxedo jacket, then slowly rolled up the sleeves of his pristine white shirt. The tux was only pennies on top of the cash he'd laid out for his sister's sham of a wedding. Dirtying it up a bit would give him some satisfaction. Wiping the growing grin off of Wade's face would give him even more.

"Outside?" Wade offered.

Cutter cut a quick glance around the room and saw Justin leading Dani out on the dance floor. "Act casual. Don't want her to know." But with the number of glances swinging between the couple cozying up for their wedding dance and the two men stalking toward the door, there wasn't much of a chance all hell wasn't about to break loose.

Texans liked a little drama at a wedding. The fact Dani was marrying the town's biggest bad boy had been enough to ensure every invitation she'd mailed had been RSVPed with an enthusiastic yes.

Now Cutter was going to give them another spectacle to keep them talking for years.

Maybe if he hadn't chugged one beer after the other before the ceremony, trying to cool his temper, he wouldn't be so eager to make sure everyone knew he wasn't all right with things. More importantly, from his point of view, he didn't want anyone paying too close attention to the fact the best man was just as touchy-feely with the bride as the groom.

He was doing this for Dani's sake, he told himself.

Wade pushed through the back door, his booted heels pounding on the planked porch. Before he took the first step down toward the dirt, he turned.

Cutter didn't give him any warning. His fist clipped the other man's jaw, sending him backward.

Wade missed every step on his way down. He sat in the dust, shaking his head, and then worked his jaw side to side. "You're madder than I thought," he murmured.

"It's not entirely you," Cutter ground out.

"Didn't think it was." Wade grinned and came to his knees, then ungracefully stood. He swayed only once, before bringing up his fists. "You see Katie?"

Cutter narrowed his eyes to angry slits and swung again.

This time, Wade ducked under the fist, bobbing up with a wide grin. "Sure looks pretty in that little blue dress. Wonder if she's even wearin' any underwear."

Cutter growled and ducked his shoulders, raising his fists higher and aiming at the spot on Wade's jaw he knew would end his chattering. Speculating about his sister's marriage was one thing. Mentioning Katie Grissom's name in his presence was the last straw. She hadn't been invited to the wedding. She was the last person in Texas who should be there. Wade knew it too.

His friend must have read the tightening fury in his expression, because his grin faded and his gaze narrowed like he was finally going to take the fight seriously. They both had similar builds which made them frequent sparring partners, neither liking to pick on a man less able to stand up to him.

Now that Wade seemed ready to get serious about his ass-whooping, Cutter took deep, even breaths and settled into a fighter's stance, letting his knees relax a bit as he bobbed side to side, looking for an opening to punch Wade with a wicked right hook.

But Wade ducked, coming up under Cutter's arms, and slammed both sides of his ribs with bone-crunching digs.

Cutter backed up and wheezed, shaking his head to clear it of some of the anger. He'd never win if he went at Wade like an angry bull.

Behind them, footsteps creaked on the wooden porch as more and more of the wedding guests pushed outside to see what all the fuss was about. Whispers and soft laughter, punctuated by groans every time a punch landed, grew behind them until bets began to be shouted over the crowd.

Cutter realized he didn't care whether he won or lost, just that Wade keep hammering away at him, because each blow distracted him from the pain he felt inside.

He'd failed his parents. Failed to keep Dani safe. Failed to protect her honor. She'd let Justin seduce her pants off, and then let Rowe convince her that their nasty little threesome could work. And no matter how many times he'd tried to broach the conversation, tell her all the reasons it could never work, shouldn't work, he hadn't been able to convince her.

This was a lesson she'd have to learn on her own. But he'd had to lay out consequences that had hurt them both. He withheld her portion of her inheritance, as was his right according to their parents' will.

They'd envisioned her being vulnerable to fortune-hunters like Cruz, but thank God, they'd never worried about her fucking around with two men. Living with both in sin. Sullying their family name.

For the first time, Cutter was fiercely glad his parents weren't there to see her wedding day. He'd done his best, tried to talk sense to her. But when she'd remained stubborn, he'd given her the wedding their mother would have wanted.

Dani had been a vision in white. Tiny sprigs of pink flowers formed a crown on her head, and the pink roses she'd carried in her arms had matched the soft, happy color in her cheeks.

All the while he'd walked her up the aisle, his heart pounding hard against his chest, his stomach churning, he hadn't missed the looks the two men at the end of the aisle had given her—like they couldn't wait to muss up every inch of her body.

"Don't look now," Wade mumbled. "Your old girlfriend stepped outside. And I'm a hunerd percent sure she's not wearin' any bra."

Cutter balled his fists and lunged, swinging wide.

Wade stepped out of the way and laughed, then landed another one-two flurry against Cutter's ribs.

Cutter felt Wade's knuckles slam hard and took another wheezing breath, but couldn't resist darting a glance toward the crowd lining up along the rails of the veranda.

He saw a glimpse of royal blue silk, a slender figure standing on tip-toe to see over the shoulder of another spectator. She'd dared show up today of all days?

Hell, he already had good reasons to vent a little fury, but now he wanted blood. He ignored the slam against his jaw and spread his arms wide, launching himself at Wade with a loud roar and taking him to the dirt where they rolled, digging fists into each other's sides.

One punch clipped his chin, and Cutter blinked, feeling dizzy.

Wade rolled him to his back.

Cutter dug his booted heels into the ground and bucked, turning them both again. This time, his fist connected with Wade's glass jaw and the man deflated underneath him, his arms falling to his sides.

"Uncle?" Wade slurred.

Cutter grabbed his collar in one hand and lifted Wade's head and shoulders, drawing back his arm to land a final blow and wipe the tired smirk off his friend's face.

But strong fingers wrapped around his wrist and held him. He glanced over his shoulder, ready to tear into whoever had the nerve to interfere, and found Justin Cruz glaring down.

"Dani's pissed," Justin said under his breath. "You startin' a fight at her wedding."

"Dani'll just have to get over it. I have."

Justin dropped his wrist and shrugged. "All I promised to do was try."

Cutter turned his attention back to Wade, but didn't see the broad fist arcing his way until it landed on his cheek. He slid off Wade's waist and lay on his back in the dust, shaking his head and cupping his tenderized face.

Wade leaned up on an elbow. "We through?"

Cutter gave him a grimace. "You sucker-punched me."

"So what? Call it a draw?"

Cutter growled but nodded, then slowly sat up.

Again, his glance cut toward the crowd beginning to fall away now that the excitement had ended. He caught a glimpse of Katie's little backside twitching as she hurried away.

What the hell was she doing here? And why stay to watch the fight?

Had she been worried about him? Did she even give a shit anymore what happened to him? Or was she here because of Justin?

The thought that she might still be carrying a torch for his brother-in-law ate a hole in his gut.

"Better get cleaned up before Dani sees us," Wade said, crawling to his knees.

Cutter snorted then dragged himself up, pushing up from Wade's shoulder and offering the other man a hand. With their arms slung over each other's shoulders they stumbled toward the steps.

Katie hurried back toward the ballroom to get lost in the crowd, knowing Cutter would come crashing through the door at any moment now the fight was over. And what had that been about?

That he wasn't happy about Dani's choice in men was apparent to anyone with eyes, but fighting still seemed an excessive reaction. Even for Cutter.

The fact she'd caught his glare a couple of times when he'd panned the people gathering at the rails hadn't meant a thing. He hadn't been looking for her unless it was to wonder what she was doing here.

She'd crashed the wedding. Not because of Justin. They were long over. And she was happy for him, *the bastard*. Justin had used her like he had every girl who'd ever had the misfortune to stroll across his path.

Not that she could hold a grudge against the man. She'd fallen for the sultry heat in his eyes and had wanted to use him to force Cutter to piss or get off the pot so far as their own casual relationship was concerned. She hadn't planned to let things go that far, but she'd been drawn by the unexpected heat and undeniable aura of command that Justin had turned on her.

Never had a man gotten to her so quickly, not even Cutter, whom she'd loved.

She'd never forget the morning after she'd succumbed. The doorbell had rung, and she'd opened it, still bleary-eyed and aching from Justin's loving, to find Cutter on her stoop, a smile on his face and his cowboy hat in his hand. His eyes had raked her once, and a frown settled between his dark brown eyes. His gaze had lifted, going to the footsteps padding her way.

He'd turned quickly on his heels and stomped off the porch. She'd glanced back to find Justin behind her, buttoning his jeans.

"Friend of yours?" he'd drawled.

But he'd known about her and Cutter and the fact they'd been dating for months. Everyone knew.

And everyone had quickly discovered why Cutter had dropped her like a rock after that day because someone saw her leave Justin at his truck, which he'd left parked the previous night at the saloon.

She'd been ruined, marked as just another of Justin's easy lays. After he'd stopped calling her, other men had tried to fill in his shoes, but she'd been burned already and her heart hadn't survived the aftermath of her mistake.

To this day, she kept to herself, didn't date. Speculation had died down when everyone began to wonder who Justin's next conquest would be.

Not until she'd seen the announcement of Justin's wedding and the fact it would be held at the Standifer ranch had she let herself think about everything she'd lost. The impulse had been too irresistible to slip into the house, to see how Justin and Dani—and *and apparently Rowe*—were doing, but especially for a chance to watch Cutter.

She'd arrived late and sat to the side behind tall urns filled with lilies during the ceremony. She'd run to the bathroom when the band struck the first note in the ballroom in the old house. Not until she was sure everyone was deep into their drinks had she started to mingle, always with an eye for where Cutter was.

When she'd seen him and Wade head out the door, glowering at each other and rolling up their sleeves, she hadn't been able to resist joining the throng pushing through the doors to watch the fight.

She'd kept behind everyone, standing on tiptoe to catch a glimpse.

Cutter's back had been to her for most of the fight and she'd drunk in the sight of his broad shoulders and thick arms and thighs as his muscles tensed. Watching the two men go at it like latter-day gladiators had sent a thrill of heat through her body unlike anything she'd felt in a long, long time.

When Cutter's glance had panned the porch and honed in on her, she'd taken a step back, hoping he didn't know it was her because she didn't want to leave just yet.

Weddings were always roller coasters. Happy, tense times for the participants; poignant reminders to observers. She'd clutched a tissue in her hand throughout the ceremony, envying the smiles the bride and groom and best man had shared.

All the while she couldn't help thinking that she might have been the one up there, standing exactly where Dani stood, gazing into Cutter's eyes as he slipped a ring on her finger—if only she hadn't strayed.

Infidelity wasn't something Cutter would ever forgive. She couldn't forgive herself. So she'd been a little tipsy. She'd been more than a little frustrated with how slowly Cutter had taken his courtship. Grown angrier the more she drank that fateful night with the fact he held the reins in their relationship and didn't seem to notice she wasn't happy with the pace.

Justin hadn't had to work all that hard to get into her bed. But even before he'd rolled off her, she'd known she'd just made the biggest mistake of her life.

Katie slipped from the ballroom, and headed down the hallway toward the living room and the front door. She'd tortured herself long enough with regrets. It was time to go home.

Just as she stepped into the living room, an arm reached around the corner, fingers closed around her wrist and whipped her toward a massive chest. The scent of spicy cologne, dust and male sweat assailed her, and she knew who held her inside his tight grip even before she raised her eyes.

Cutter tsked. "Katie Grissom. Funny, I know you weren't on the list of invitees."

Reluctantly, Katie lifted her gaze from the open collar of his shirt to meet his cognac-colored gaze. The color had always seemed so warm, so inviting, but now with angry color in his cheeks, his narrowed eyes made her heart kick into a panicked flutter.

She licked her lips. "Maybe I'm a guest."

"Then where's your date? Maybe I should return you to his side." His narrowed gaze and the bruising on his cheek and jaw lent him a sinister air. "Just to make sure you don't forget who you came with."

Katie pulled on her hand, attempting to break his hold, but he was stronger, more determined to keep her captive than she was to escape. One side of his mouth drew up in a nasty smirk.

She stopped fighting and blew out a frustrated breath. "All right, so I crashed your party alone. I was just on my way out."

Cutter's face hardened and his thighs crowded against hers. "Why are you here, Katie? Did you miss Justin?"

Her body betrayed her, heat softening her core. Could he feel her belly quivering against his? She shook her head. "No, I'm happy for him. Although I really think Dani deserves better."

He grunted, and then pressed her wrists against her lower back, bringing her closer still.

Katie wished she hadn't had the wicked urge to go completely commando when she'd dressed. There was no way Cutter missed the fact her nipples were tight and digging into his chest.

"Miss me?" he whispered.

Katie opened her mouth to tell him to go to hell, but the anger in his taut expression halted her. Did she want him mad enough to goose walk her to the door or just mad enough to make him let loose some of the feral tension vibrating through his body?

Isn't this exactly what she'd wanted when she'd donned the little dress this morning, forgoing every scrap of underwear for a lavish coat of lotion to make sure every curve glided beneath the scrape of a callused palm?

She licked her lips and tilted her hips—just enough to brush her belly against the thickening ridge of his cock. Oh yeah, she'd felt it.

His darkening glance said he had too.

"Guess you did," he growled. "Or were you being that particular when you got dressed?"

His words stung, but her body trembled from sensory overload. Cutter was too much man for her to make the smart choice and shove away from him.

Katie dropped her gaze and tugged one hand free to slip the buttons of his shirt open, one by one. When the opening exposed his bronzed chest and crisp, brown curls, she slid inside it and smoothed her palm over his hot, sweaty skin. "I've always been...particular."

His chest expanded, and then he dragged her hand away, bringing it behind her back to shackle both inside one large fist. "Looks like you've got a choice," he whispered.

"Doesn't seem that way to me," she said just as softly, tugging at her hands—more for show, because she didn't really want to be free.

His face bent toward hers, and her lips parted. But instead of the kiss she craved, he nuzzled into her hair beside her ear. "You know where the door is. You decide one way—don't let it slam you in the ass."

Katie shuddered as he inhaled along her cheek, like an animal scenting prey. "Or?" she managed to force through her tight throat.

He straightened and his glance cut to the stairway leading to the upper floor and the bedrooms.

Her eyes widened. "But you have guests."

"Who are busy sucking down alcohol at the moment. They won't miss me."

Cutter turned her in his arms and jerked her closer, pressing every inch of himself against her backside. His free hand skimmed up the hem of her short dress, sliding up her thigh to the curve of her bare bottom where his hand paused.

She stood still while his body tightened even more against her and his hand slipped forward, over the top of her thigh before gliding right between her legs.

His breath hissed between his teeth even as his fingers slid over her smooth pussy and into moisture.

Katie didn't care that at any moment someone might walk down the hallway and see them like this, with his hand under her skirt, her pussy exposed. She braced apart her legs and let her back bow around her bound hands to lay her shoulders against his chest.

His strong, thick fingers traced the waxed outer folds, then tucked between them to skim over the sensitive inner lips. A single digit dipped inside her entrance and swirled.

Her legs trembled, her knees nearly buckling beneath her.

His hand withdrew from beneath her skirt, and Cutter loosened his grip on her wrists, freeing her, and stepped back. "Choose," he said, in an even voice.

Katie glanced over her shoulder, thinking fast. She knew this wasn't the answer to all their problems, but she wasn't backing down from the challenge in his rigid face. If she ever hoped for another chance...this was it.

She rubbed her wrists, stiffened her spine, then turned in her high-heeled sandals and sauntered toward the stairs.

Chapter Two

Cutter followed the slow, sexy roll of Katie's round hips all the way up the staircase. By the time her little fuck-me heels snicked on the wooden floors of the hallway above, his body was as hard as a brick wall, his cock surging against the front of his trousers.

While he climbed, he eyed every inch of her frame, from the thick red curls that fell mid-way down her back, the gentle slope of her shoulders, the indent of her narrow waist, the lush swell of her ass and finally, to the long stretch of sleek legs he knew were stronger than they appeared. His hands itched to claim every inch of her, but he curled his fists, ruthlessly reminding himself this wasn't about pleasure.

Having her here at his mercy, at last, seemed to heighten every one of his predatory senses. Damn, he could smell her, even from this far away. The crisp, feminine mixture of perfume and musk drew him like a bloodhound to a fresh trail.

His fingers were still damp from her arousal, but he resisted the urge to bring them to his mouth and taste her. He wouldn't be weakened by his own desire.

He didn't know what her game was, but she'd accepted his invitation. Too bad for her he didn't plan to do more than ease his own lust and kick her to the door. She didn't deserve any more consideration than that. Revenge and an easing of his temper were his only goals.

She paused at the first doorway and cast a questioning

glance his way.

He shook his head and waited for her to continue down, past the next and the next bedroom. At the end of the hallway, she didn't give him another look, but turned the doorknob and stepped inside, pulling up the hem of her short dress even before he managed to close the door behind them.

So she was eager. Again, he didn't care. Only *his* urgency, *his* lust mattered.

She'd betrayed him, and done it with the one man he'd never forgive her for. The year-old memory of Justin's narrow-eyed triumph when he'd strode up behind Katie, stuffing his cock back into his blue jeans, had been enough to kill their relationship forever.

But if she wanted to give him a little release, who was he to turn her down? Any cunt would do.

The dress slithered upward in a soft rasp over her slender body, baring her bottom and slender waist. She tossed it toward the arm chair next to the bed and climbed onto the mattress, giving him a luscious view of her ass.

He ripped open his shirt, listening as the remaining buttons pinged on the wood floor. His belt was open, the top button of his trousers gone before she reached the center of the bed and lay down. Rolling to her back, she lifted her legs, pulling them together and to the side so that her pussy was hidden, leaving only the sweet curve of her thigh and buttock exposed.

His gaze raked her chest, lifting an eyebrow at the way she covered her breasts with her hands. But it wasn't out of shyness. She squeezed them and closed her eyes, her mouth opening around a little moan.

Fuck. She'd been sexy as hell when he'd been seeing her, but in a shy, kittenish way. This Katie had learned a thing or two about how to arouse a man. She tugged her nipples and a soft gasp escaped her rounded mouth.

His own mouth watered. His cock jerked, thick and insistent. He kicked off his shoes, thrust down his pants and boxers and stepped out of them. Cutter pulled open the drawer of his bedside table and plucked out a condom. With precision, he tore open the packet and palmed the latex circle. Knowing she watched, he slowly cloaked his cock, giving himself a single, hard-fisted stroke before he followed her onto the mattress. He grasped that sweetly curved thigh and turned her hips, both hands opening her as he came down over her, and thrust his cock straight into her center.

Katie didn't seem to mind he'd skipped any preliminaries, but then again, she was already wet, already squeezing around him, her silken walls sucking him into her. When she tried to wrap her legs around him, he thrust his arms under her knees and pushed up her thighs, holding them opened for him to slam unimpeded into her juicy cunt.

He knelt in the center of his bed and banged her, without grinding once against her sensitive clit. When she slipped her hands between her legs, he shook his head and stopped stroking, waiting for the moment when she got his message.

Her hazel eyes widened, understanding now that this was going to be all about him or he was through.

Her mouth opened, but she ground her jaws shut and turned her face against the coverlet.

Cutter closed his eyes, let his head fall back and shut out the sight of her, concentrated only on the feel of a wet pussy surrounding him, trying not to care whose body he sank inside as he thrust again and again.

Nearly mindless, swollen and edging toward release, he didn't care how quick he came. It had been too damn long. He'd run through half a dozen one-night stands in the month following her betrayal, but nothing since, because they hadn't approached the memories he had of what it felt like to slide inside her wet, tight pussy. They hadn't smelled the same, hadn't felt as soft...hadn't felt right. And he damn sure hadn't wanted to talk to them, not like he used to with Katie.

He'd missed her and hated her for it. However, he wasn't the one who'd strayed. So why the hell was he feeling guilty now? He thrust harder, deeper, until the pressure in his balls exploded and he couldn't think, could only fulfill the primal instinct to pour his seed into her. He stroked more slowly, savoring the steady pulses as he emptied himself.

When he opened his eyes, he gazed down. Katie's head was still turned, her belly quivering. Again, her hands covered her breasts—this time to hide.

He knew because her knees pressed inward against his arms, trying to close. He dropped them and scooted back on the mattress, watching as she closed her legs and turned on her side, facing away.

As his breaths evened and the heat of his anger cooled, something lodged inside his chest, heavy and nearly choking the back of his throat. He'd never been this cold with a woman, this cruel. Even if she deserved the edge of his anger, she hadn't deserved to be used like this.

But what could he say and not make things worse? No way would he comfort her. She'd get mixed signals, and he didn't want her to think they ever had a chance at resuming their relationship. They were done.

A knock sounded on the door and it swung open. "Cutter, you in here? Dani's ready to toss the bouquet—"

Cutter aimed a glare at Rowe, whose eyes widened on Katie. "Tell her I'm on my way."

The door closed quietly, and Cutter backed off the mattress, his glance falling away from Katie, who still hadn't moved. His clothes were a crumpled, dirty mess, so he slid open his closet doors and pulled out another crisp shirt and dark trousers. Then he headed to the bathroom without a word to the woman who lay as still as a statue in the center of his bed.

Stupid, stupid, stupid! Katie couldn't still the self-recriminations that echoed in her head. Her breaths came in sharp, jagged sobs, but she held back her tears. She'd never cry over Cutter Standifer again. She'd been a fool. He'd taken what she'd offered, and so much more. Her pride lay in tatters. Her soul felt as bruised and tender as her sex.

From the moment she'd woken that morning and stared at the wedding announcement clipping she'd stuck under a magnet on her refrigerator door, she'd had this feeling stirring inside her. Something warm, something hopeful, like she had to give it one more try to make things right.

What had she been hoping for? She'd half expected him to give her a cold stare then ignore her like he had every time they met by accident in town. She'd hoped he'd at least offer her a polite greeting, a chance for her step closer and apologize, because the guilt had haunted her for so long.

Instead, he'd used her like a whore. And she'd allowed it—because she felt she owed him something for her betrayal.

But they were even now. And he'd made it all too clear this was the only thing they'd ever have. Katie heard the bathroom door open and close, heard his footsteps walk around the room, back to the closet, to the door.

"Stay here." Then the door closed, and she opened her eyes to make sure she was alone.

Only then did she sit up and take stock. The wedding party was gathering on the porch below. This time laughter told her the bride and groom were getting ready to leave.

Loud shouts of encouragement, howls of laughter—and she knew the bouquet had been tossed into the arms of some other girl.

Katie crawled off the mattress feeling drained, and went into the bathroom to wash away moisture dripping down her thighs.

Thank god someone had thought to use a condom. She hadn't needed the pill in a long, long time.

She dressed, wishing she had more to wear than the thin silk dress. Had everyone known she was naked underneath it? That morning she'd only cared that Cutter noticed.

She slipped on her sandals and hurried out the door. She'd sneak out the back and get to her car before anyone even knew she'd left. Cutter wouldn't care she hadn't obeyed. He'd just be relieved he didn't have to look at her again.

Cutter watched the trail of dust the little red Mustang

kicked up as Katie pulled away from the pasture they'd roped off for a makeshift parking lot. No one else noticed. All eyes were on the bridal couple who laughed as Justin's old pickup, waxed to an impudent shine, pulled up with ribbons tied to the antenna mast and cans clattering behind it.

Rowe stepped out of the cab, held the door for Justin to slide inside, and clapped his shoulder. Then he ran around the front of the truck and held the door for Dani, whom he kissed on the cheek and gave a wink.

No doubt he'd return to the party with the rest of the guests and dance with a string of ladies, just long enough so no one would remark when he slipped out the door to join Dani and Justin as they packed for their trip to Mexico.

Cutter's fists curled, but he couldn't work up the deep, disappointed anger he'd held close to his chest in the weeks since Dani had announced she'd marry Justin and live with the two men on Rowe's ranch.

She'd made her bed. He hoped like hell she'd be happy, because he'd have to kill two men if they failed her.

When the pickup drew away, he forced a smile to his lips and accepted the congratulations from his friends for a great wedding. Even Wade came up and slung an arm around his shoulder. "Gonna be lonely in this house now, ain't it?"

Cutter shoved him back and gave him a pained grin. "I like it quiet."

"And you always look like a wounded dog." Wade lifted one rusty brown brow. "Where'd Katie run off to?"

Cutter cursed under his breath and stalked off, Wade's wry chuckles following him up the stairs.

He'd finished with Katie. Gotten her out of his system for good this time.

So why couldn't he shake the picture of her body curled in on itself and her shattered expression as he'd left her alone in his bedroom?

Shame crept across his cheeks, heating his skin. A cold, hard knot settled in his belly. What he needed to do was forget.

And he knew just the way to do it. He turned back to Wade and tilted his head toward the front door of his great big house. "Let me get you a drink. And then maybe I'll wipe that grin right off your face for good."

Cutter took another long draw of his beer and slammed the bottle back down on the table. Wade had wandered off, following the curling finger of a certain blonde he'd been seeing, and leaving Cutter alone to stew in his own juices.

Cutter grimaced and took another pull of his beer. The Katie he thought he'd known would never have been that bold. Back in the day, she might have met his gaze across the dance floor and given him a shy smile. An invitation he would have been helpless to refuse.

She'd moved to Two Mule while Dani was in Austin at school and opened a small diner. He'd been curious about anyone foolhardy enough to start a business in a town where nothing ever changed and nothing new ever succeeded. They'd all underestimated her cooking and her quiet charm. Like all the single men in the county, he'd showered and shaved, polished his best boots and headed to Katie's Diner every chance he got.

At first, he'd been content to watch her fend off the invitations of every other guy with a steady smile that soothed the disappointment. She'd been determined to make a success of her venture. When it appeared she'd weathered the lessening in traffic after the honeymoon period, she'd relaxed, hired more help and settled in, getting to know the town folk.

She hadn't dated much. After she'd finally accepted his invitation, she hadn't dated anyone else at all. He'd thought his claim was struck. And he'd begun a slow courtship, doing everything right, he'd thought. After the first date, he'd left her with a kiss. When she'd had him over for dinner, he'd kept his hands on all the safe places—her back, the tops of her hips. They'd watched a movie in the dark, and they'd kissed. He'd remained in blue-ball hell for weeks until one night she'd cornered him on her couch, sliding a knee over his lap and settling down, a stubborn tilt to her chin.

"Are you attracted to me at all?"

Cutter had swallowed, wondering if it was a trick question. The proof of his feelings was awakening, responding predictably to the weight and heat of her open thighs. "Baby, you know I am."

"Then is there something wrong with you? Something you're not telling me. Because if there's a problem—"

He hadn't been able to help the smile that tugged at his lips.

She'd slapped his shoulder. "Don't make fun of me. I'm serious. I've all but laid it on a platter for you."

"I'm a careful man, Katie. I don't want either of us to make a mistake."

"You this careful with all the girls you date?"

He hadn't answered her question. Maybe he should have. Instead, he'd slipped his hand behind her neck and brought her head close. With his mouth only an inch away from hers, he'd whispered. "Tell me to leave if you don't want me in your bed, Katie."

Her response had been a quick press of her lips against his, and then all talking had been over.

He'd made quick work of her blouse, skimming it over her head. His hands shook with his eagerness. Her body trembled against his. Lying her down on the sofa, he'd taken his time, careful not to overwhelm her, careful to find every place on her body that made her moan or quiver, starting with her mouth and slowly working downward.

By the time he'd stroked lips, tongue and fingers down her neck to the tops of her breasts, she'd arched her back to press eagerly into his palm. Latching onto a distended nipple, he'd pulled it into his mouth, gently laving the pink tip with his tongue, circling over and over until her fingers had dug into his scalp and urged him lower.

Hurried kisses glided along her abdomen, and he paused to

push into her belly button and treated it like the precious place between her legs, circling, stroking inward, until she'd keened between tightly clenched jaws and widened her legs, cupping his shoulders with her knees and writhing in slow undulations that lifted her damp, musky scent. And he'd been lost.

As much time as he'd taken to get her to that point, he couldn't get his pants off fast enough. He shoved them past his hips, donned a condom and knelt on the floor. He tugged her upward, guided her hips over him with his hands, trying to remember not to dig his fingers too deep into her soft bottom, but needing her slick sex to glide down his cock because he didn't know how much longer he could hold back.

She'd gripped his shoulders hard, her eyes wide and a little wild. Her breasts had shivered in front of his lips and he kissed her nipples again, giving each a quick suckle, before wrapping his arms around her back and bringing her down.

Katie's inner walls had clutched him in creamy heat, rippling up and down his shaft as he urged her to take him, groaning when she began to glide up and down, slowly at first, and then desperately fast, breathless gasps gusting against his face.

She'd been so beautiful. Her red hair floating up and down with her helpless movements, her hazel gaze locked with his, until her pussy clamped hard around his cock and her eyes squeezed shut.

She hadn't moaned or cried out, but he could feel her come apart, rapid little squeezes rippling along his shaft, her fingernails biting into his shoulders.

He'd kissed her shoulder. "It's okay to make some noise."

She'd grunted but shook her head, the frown drawn between her eyebrows not worrying him a bit, because he knew she was still deep inside her orgasm. The pulses tugging at him, the slick wash of excitement that lubricated his shaft, had pulled him straight into an orgasm so strong, he'd groaned and pumped upward, spearing into her while she'd watched him with her wild eyes.

After that night, he'd taken a step back. He didn't know

why. Maybe that little hint of sensual ferocity she'd displayed had taken him aback. He wasn't sure he really knew her. He didn't know if he could please her. He'd set her on a pedestal and it had tilted, toppling his preconceptions of what he wanted in a wife and a helpmate. He'd wanted someone like his mother. Someone who could cook. Someone predictable, who'd be there when he needed her, but would be content with what he gave her—children, a nice home, a proud name.

Cutter had known she was confused, even hurt by his withdrawal, but he thought they'd come far enough that she'd give him time to think and get comfortable with the idea that this sensual creature could be his.

In the end, she'd shown her true colors, and he told himself again and again that he was glad he hadn't made the mistake of asking her to marry him.

A chair scraped beside him, and he turned, frowning as Rowe settled in the seat beside him.

Rowe cleared his throat. "It's not any of my business..."

"Damn straight, it's not."

"Look, I couldn't help noticing, something wasn't right... Up there." Rowe glanced away, then his cheeks billowed as he blew out a deep breath. "Did you hurt Katie?"

Had he hurt her? Probably not the way the bastard meant. "Mind your own damn business."

Rowe speared him with a glance. "She looked ready to cry."

Cutter wondered if Rowe knew how close he was to kissing the floor. "She didn't say no, if that's what has you worried."

"Katie's good people. I know all about the mistake she made. But she's suffered."

Cutter arched a brow. "That's supposed to mean something to me?"

"You two were pretty close."

"I'm not the bad guy here."

Rowe nodded then looked out on the dance floor. "Justin regrets ever going near her. You've been decent to him about the wedding."

"No I haven't. My sister doesn't get a thing beyond this party from me."

"Dani doesn't need anything else, but she was happy you stood up for her. Justin wanted me to tell you something...about Katie."

Cutter's fingers squeezed around the slick beer bottle. "I don't want to hear a goddamn thing about her, especially if it's coming from him."

"He's not proud of what happened. He'd stopped by the saloon and found Katie crying. She tried to mop up and make a joke about it. But she was hurting. He invited her for a drink."

Cutter lowered his brows and aimed a furious glare his way. "Rowe, we've known each other a long time, but you aren't a friend. Walk away now."

Rowe gave him a tight smile. "Fact is, I don't care if you take a swing at me. Dani wants you happy. Justin and I want peace between us. You're gonna listen here, or we can take it outside where I'll have to shout it at you."

Cutter set the bottle on the table beside him, and eased his fingers from it. The sooner Rowe had his say, the sooner he could get drunk. "Finish it."

"It's true. Justin greased the gears, got her a little drunk and pouring out her heart on his shoulder, and when she finally got mad, he turned it. Made her want a little revenge. He took her to bed."

Cutter curled his fists and began to rise.

Rowe pressed down on his shoulder. "I'm almost done. Just thought you should know. It was just the one time. She didn't return his calls afterward. Told him to go to hell when he stopped by her cafe. She regretted it. It was a moment of weakness. She was vulnerable to Justin, and he knows how to exploit weakness."

Cutter's lips lifted in a snarl. "And yet you just gave away the girl you love. To him. Don't you think he manipulated you just a little bit as well?"

Rowe grunted. "Yeah, I'm sure he did." He turned to Cutter,

his expression softening. "But the secret is, he loves me. I know that creeps you out, but he loves us both. He's not going anywhere." Rowe stood and glanced down at Cutter, his expression softening. "What you have to figure out is whether you're happy alone. Would you rather hold onto your anger for the rest of your life and never know what you might have had with her?" Rowe faced the ballroom and lifted his chin. "Thanks for the wedding, but I have a plane to catch."

Cutter grimaced. "Don't think I'll ever get used to it—you two—and Dani."

"Oh, I think you'll come around. But we do have a lot to prove to you, and you need to get your head in a better place. Talk to her."

Cutter shook his head and lifted his beer. The last thing he wanted to do was talk to Katie. He'd shown her exactly where she stood with him. Besides, she'd probably just slam the door in his face.

Still, he couldn't forget how she'd looked when she'd moved to embrace him with her legs, her face softened, color blooming in her cheeks, and her gaze glossy and hopeful—until he'd rejected her.

He'd never thought of himself as a particularly hard man. Was he becoming his father? He'd been tough as nails. Admired by all, but relentless when it came to instilling certain values and an old-fashioned work ethic. He'd wanted to be sure he left the ranch in worthy hands.

Well, the ranch was still on solid ground when others were faltering with the economic turndown. Cutter wasn't in hock to his eyeballs, had the cash to spend on shipping in hay to weather another drought.

So he had the burden of running the ranch squarely on his own two shoulders. He'd hoped Dani would bring them a partner, that she'd at least take over the office management to free him up to do what he liked best. Ride herd.

Dani might have been willing to fill that role if he hadn't been so hard-nosed about her marriage. He might still find his own partner, but he hadn't found a woman smart enough, strong enough to take on the job of a rancher's wife. He'd thought for while that it might be Katie, but she'd proven to have feet of clay.

She'd let that bastard Cruz romance his way into her bed and there was no way he'd ever trust her.

But it had felt good sliding inside her again—warm, wet, snug. She'd always felt just right lying inside his arms. Maybe she'd be willing to be fuck buddies. It wasn't as if she was too particular about whom she slept with.

Maybe he could start with an apology. Not that he'd really mean it. But if it meant he might get some sweet release, with a woman he knew was compatible with him in at least one way...well, why the hell not?

He set down his beer and nodded to the caterer. She could see to satisfying his guests' needs. He'd paid enough to ensure that.

He touched his pockets, glad he'd swiped the keys from his dresser and headed for the door.

Chapter Three

Katie didn't know why she'd decided to open the diner today. She'd posted a note earlier that morning to let customers know that she'd be closed. She could have stayed home, drawn the blinds and wallowed all day in self-pity.

But she'd been restless. After she'd showered Cutter's scent from her skin and tossed the blue dress into the trash, she'd automatically donned her jeans and *Katie's Diner* T-shirt and headed out the door.

She'd let the staff go for the day. So she was the sole waitress, cashier and cook. Not that she'd been busy since she'd flipped the *Open* sign. Her only customer so far was Ole Win, whom she'd told yesterday not to come, but maybe the habit was too ingrained. He came every day, ordered the same meal, then read his paper while he downed a pot of coffee, which she kept fresh.

Already he'd told her another one of his stories about the old days in Two Mule, before the roads were paved, when men still tied horses to a hitching rail in front of the saloon.

Not that she minded the chatter. She enjoyed his stories most days, but today her mind wandered, back to the wedding and that awful moment when Cutter had thrust inside her a little too hard and fast and made it crystal clear she'd never have a chance at earning a place back in his life.

Not that he'd hurt her physically, not really. Her body had been primed, her pussy melting and caressing his length the whole time he'd fucked her.

She wouldn't allow herself to use a prettier description for what he'd done, what she'd invited. She'd had the crazy notion that if she could get them in the same room, stripped of clothing and old resentments that maybe he'd give her a second chance.

Cutter wasn't willing. He'd only taken what she'd offered. Without strings.

She couldn't feel ashamed about what she'd allowed to happen because she'd needed so badly to touch him. However, now, she thought that maybe she was ready to let go.

The bell above the door chimed and she glanced over her shoulder then did a double-take because Cutter was striding through the door, his hard gaze pinning her like a butterfly to a display board.

Katie stiffened and cast a quick glance toward Win, who'd perked up in his chair and was following Cutter's progress as he made his way toward her. No doubt even the old codger was aware of the rumors that surrounded her and Cutter's demise as a couple. Now the old tattletale would have another story to add to his arsenal.

"We have to talk."

Katie gave Cutter her back and swiped a table she'd already cleaned, determined to ignore the heat she felt prickle up and down her spine. "You already made your point," she muttered. "There's nothing left to discuss."

"Let's not do this here," he said, laying his hand over hers and the soggy dishcloth.

She slipped her hand from underneath his and pressed it against her stomach before turning, then took a step backward because she hadn't realized he'd come so close.

His thighs rubbed up against her, and she drew a deep breath, leaning back to prevent his chest from touching hers.

Too late. Her breasts were already aching, her nipples spiking against her bra. Thank God she wore an apron or he'd know her body was a lot happier than she was to see him here.

His fingers latched around her wrist, and he tugged her behind him, heading toward the kitchen door.

"Let go. This is getting old, Cutter. You can't drag me around like a dog on a leash."

"Bitch on a leash," he murmured.

"What did you just say?"

He halted and faced her, standing so close again, his warm breaths washed over her face. "Dammit, Katie, don't fight me. All I want to do is talk and I don't want an audience."

Maybe he'd come to apologize, but his thighs rubbed hers again, and she felt his cock, thickening under his jeans.

She glared, and then peeked around his shoulder at Ole Win, who was pretending to read his paper, but glancing their way over the top of his reading glasses. "In the kitchen then, but make this quick."

He followed her, so close he bumped her backside when she paused to lift the counter ledge. The kitchen door swung and Cutter pushed her forward, toward the walk-in freezer in the back.

At least the cold would keep their clothes in place and the conversation short. She opened it and swung around as he followed her inside, ducking because he was taller than the ceiling height.

Frozen puffs of breath, short and fast, gave away her agitation. "Can we get this over with?"

Cutter raked a hand through his short-cropped hair. "Why'd you leave in such a hurry?"

Katie planted her hands on her hips. "We were through."

"Maybe I wasn't."

"So sad," she said, in a singsong tone.

His gaze narrowed. "You seein' anyone?"

"You think I'd have let you do that if I was?" Then she had the grace to blush. She'd done just that to him

His eyelids lowered as he looked down her body. Then he came closer. "Just makin' sure I'm not stepping on anyone else's toes."

"Why the hell should it matter to you? Gonna ask me on a date?" she said, raising her chin.

"Not exactly." He bent over her, his hand slipped beneath her hair. His palm was warm against her cooling neck.

Katie lifted a hand to his chest to push him away, but he was as immoveable as solid rock.

"I'm thinking we should see each other," he said, his sliding toward a sexy growl. "Every now and then."

Her eyes widened. A lead weight settled in her middle, but lower, her body began a slow burn. "You're saying we should fuck. Tell me, are you thinking you could just drop by whenever you're horny?"

"Yeah."

"And what about me? What about when I'm horny?"

One corner of his mouth quirked. "You wantin' rights too?"

"I'd be stupid if I let it be all about you and your needs again."

"Mad 'cause I didn't finish it for you?"

She'd been devastated, but all those weepy moments were past. Anger flared, hot enough to melt the ice coating the walls. Did he honestly think she was such a slut she'd go for a proposition like this?

Then again, she'd never gotten what she wanted, sexually, from Cutter Standifer. When they'd dated, he'd been painfully remote. Even after they'd finally gotten naked. Today, he'd been ruthlessly cruel.

But if he wanted something from her now... Well, wasn't she in a position to bargain for more? Did she want to risk her heart with him again? If he was even contemplating having an affair with her, did that mean that somewhere deep inside him, he still cared?

God, she was pathetic. The cruel twist of his mouth didn't betray a single ounce of pity or affection. Still, her body reacted, predictably, to his presence.

Her pussy still ached from his earlier forceful thrusts. Unabated arousal had kept her edgy, angry. From just the memory of his invasion, her body had remained primed, her clit swollen, her nipples tight and hard. Even now, moisture seeped into her panties.

Could she do this? Begin a strictly sexual relationship without losing herself and her self-respect? She still wanted him. And didn't she deserve pleasure for herself?

Katie lifted her chin and kept her gaze locked with his. "If I do this, you won't be the only one getting what you want."

Cutter's eyes crinkled at the corners. The beginnings of a smile.

She glared, resisting the urge to lean into him and surrender, because her body was melting despite the frigid air surrounding them. "Things won't be like they were before."

"I'm not offering to go back. This time, I'm not in it for the long haul."

His honesty hurt, but she appreciated it just the same. She lowered the hand she'd braced against his chest. "No lies. No games. Nothing but pleasure between us. For as long as we both want this."

He nodded, his hips surging toward hers, his cock pressing against her belly. "Agreed. No promises. But...you will only sleep with me. No boyfriends. For as long as this lasts."

"I'll want the same from you. No other women."

His face hardened. "I don't fuck around."

Her gaze fell away. "Can we not rehash old news? We can pretend to be polite."

"People are gonna talk. We can't keep this secret...our seeing each other again."

"Afraid they'll think you're a fool?"

"I don't give a fuck what they think. But you have a business to run...friends who might get curious."

Katie shrugged. "I'll say we're taking it slow. Just dating again."

"Fine." Cutter slid a hand behind her, cupping her bottom. "Can you close up?"

"I just opened the diner. I'm not gonna kick Win out."

Cutter's mouth tightened. The hand behind her neck tugged her hair.

He hadn't kissed her before at the wedding. She hadn't realized it until she'd showered and then she'd nearly cried, because she'd wanted a little tenderness, a little consideration.

His mouth hovered above hers now, and then his lips rubbed. She wasn't letting him set the pace again. She caught his lower lip with her teeth and bit gently.

Cutter froze. Then his hips surged again. Both hands clamped around her bottom, cupping her buttocks, then lifted her.

She wrapped her legs around his waist then let go of his lip.

His head slanted and she opened her mouth to suction against his until he thrust his tongue into her mouth and they pressed closer, chests hardening, mouths devouring.

Cutter pulled back his head. "I want you."

Katie's breaths came in short, excited gasps. "Can't...not now. Stay. I'll make you something to eat."

Cutter rested his forehead against hers. "When he leaves, you'll turn the sign around. I might not wait to get you home."

Katie felt her first smile of the day tease the corners of her lips. "Gonna christen my restaurant?"

"Never done it here?"

She shook her head. The only men she'd "done" in Two Mule were him and Justin. Both in her home. Come to think of it, she'd never had Cutter in her bed. A chill bit her spine and she shivered.

"Cold?" he whispered against her lips.

She nodded.

He ground his clothed cock against her sex. "Fix me something to eat." He held her while she dropped her legs and stood on her own.

She swayed and he chuckled. His hands caressed her ass and squeezed, his cheek rubbed against hers. "Something fast."

"Ole Win?"

"He's old. Not stupid."

Katie made Cutter a patty melt, which he wolfed down with fries. All the while she moved behind the counter, his gaze never left her body.

She felt self-conscious, awkward, because her hips felt fluid, rolled with a little extra wiggle she couldn't help. Her sex was swollen and wet, and her breaths wouldn't even out, staying short and shallow, which kept her slightly dizzy and on the verge of nervous laughter.

Ole Win still hadn't budged, but he'd dropped any pretense of reading his paper. His attention hopped from Katie to Cutter and back, as though watching his favorite soap opera.

Katie poured Cutter a cup of coffee and slid it across the counter. His hand captured her wrist, and his thumb rubbed against her thudding pulse.

Ole Win cleared his throat. "Think I'll mosey along. See you tomorrow, Katie."

She didn't look his way, caught by the heat building in Cutter's expression. "See ya, Winston."

The door closed and Cutter stood. "Your keys."

She reached for her purse beneath the counter and tossed them.

He caught them and turned on his heels, striding quickly to the door. He locked it, turned the sign, then took the time to turn the blinds and shut off the view of the street outside.

When he turned, she was already pulling her apron over her head and wiping her sweaty hands against her sides.

Cutter's face was set, hard. His eyelids drooped as he halted opposite the counter from her. "Climb up."

Her heart accelerated, heat filling her cheeks. "What?"

"Climb up on the counter. I'm hungry."

Katie blinked, but hopped onto the counter and swung her legs to his side, facing him.

Cutter pulled her closer, stepping between her thighs.

"It's a little high," she said, suddenly breathless.

"Not for what I have in mind." Cutter's jaw tightened, and

229

he gripped her waist then slid up her T-shirt.

Katie lifted her arms and let him drag away the shirt. She started trembling, even before he unsnapped her bra and pulled it, crushing it in his fist as he drew it away.

Katie dropped her arms at her sides, letting Cutter stare at her breasts.

Her nipples tightened, spiking hard.

Cutter reached up and her mouth dropped open, expecting him to cup her, tease her aching tips, but he pressed between them, forcing her backward. She lay back and braced herself on her elbows to watch as he unsnapped her jeans.

Cutter bent and his tongue licked the vee of skin he exposed as he slowly slid down her zipper.

"Cutter, please," she moaned. Not again. Not slow. Her pussy pulsed, liquid spilling from inside her. She needed his cock, needed it fast.

"Please what, Katie?" he said, nuzzling her lower belly while he gripped her waistband in both hands and dragged down her clothing.

She lifted her bottom, letting him peel down the rough denim and her cotton panties. His face centered between her closed thighs and his tongue slid along the closed seam of her sex, the tip touching her hardened clit.

Katie cried out, her body vibrating. "Please. Get my clothes off now. Fuck me, Cutter."

He lifted his head. "My turn, first."

Katie moaned and reclined on the counter, knowing he wasn't going to give her what she needed, not yet. God, it was just like before. He'd tortured her. Taking her slowly in excruciating increments.

He pulled her pants down further, just past her knees. His hands landed on her thighs, his fingers dug gently into her flesh. "Part your legs."

Katie whimpered at the note of command in his voice, something she'd never heard from him before. Something Justin had done, which had completely demolished any reservations she'd had about having sex with him.

His thumb slid into the top of her folds, pressing on her hooded clit, then lifted the thin hood to expose the rigid knot.

As cool air brushed over the hot pleasure center, Katie's breath hitched.

He bent again, his gaze rising to hers then closed his lips around her clit and sucked hard.

Katie's knees jerked upward then opened, giving him more room. His deep, humorless chuckle vibrated against her, adding to the sensations already stealing her mind.

He'd never gone down on her, never even touched her there, except to slide his cock inside her. She'd wondered if after that first time, he hadn't liked something about her—her scent, the sight of her smooth sex...

She'd felt unfeminine, rejected. Justin had renewed her confidence, praising her body, her "sweet, sweet pussy" as he'd gone down on her. She'd hated herself for needing him, hated that he was the one who'd given her what she needed, and then she'd hated Cutter because he'd made her vulnerable to a user like Justin.

However, now she didn't doubt his attraction. He suctioned her, glided his tongue over her folds, delving between to consume the fluids seeping from deep inside her.

His fingers played, circling her entrance, and then thrusting inward. "I won't stop until you scream, so you better not hold back." His voice was tight, harsh.

Katie's belly quivered and jumped. Her head thrashed on the countertop. The rhythmic pull of his lips, the increasing depths of his thrusts, built tension in her core that curled so tightly she knew when it unwound, she'd lose it.

Cutter paused with his fingers deep inside her, then drew his lips away from his teeth and gently bit her clitoris.

Katie jerked, her back bowed hard, lifting off the counter, and she splintered into a million pieces.

Even to her own ears, her cry was ragged, a desolate note fading slowly in the stillness that followed. Katie sagged against the counter and stared at the fluorescent light, buzzing on the ceiling.

Cutter tugged off her boots, stripped her jeans and panties the rest of the way off, then opened his pants and shoved them just past his backside.

When he held out his hand to her, she didn't hesitate, letting him bring her upright. He cupped her buttocks and lifted her from the counter.

Katie wrapped her arms around his shoulders and held her breath as he lowered her. His cock nudged between her folds, and impossibly, her pussy spasmed, making a wet sound as it welcomed the blunt, round cap entering her.

Cutter's strong shoulders flexed beneath her palms, and she reveled in the show of strength as he lowered her slowly, sliding her pussy down his cock, then lifted her. He showed no signs of strain as he repeated the action, although his jaw tightened and red flared in his cheeks.

"This how you want it?" he asked.

"Thought this was your turn," she said breathlessly.

"Changed my mind."

"Then I want it fast," she said, biting her lower lip, then gasping as he moved her hips in circles. "Hard. I want it hard."

"Think you can come again?"

She blinked. Not something she'd ever experienced before—multiple orgasms. But maybe the fact her arousal had stretched over the whole damn day made her more sensitive, more responsive than usual. Sensual tension curled around her core again. She nodded slowly, and then dug her fingers into his shoulders as he turned and strode to the nearest table.

He began to lay her down and she reached out and swiped the condiments and napkin holder to the floor.

Cutter laughed, the sound low and wicked. Her pussy convulsed around him, moisture spilling to coat his shaft as he leaned over her.

This time he didn't seem to mind as she wound her legs around his waist. She relaxed against the cool wood as he pumped into her—short, forceful thrusts that rattled the table and shoved it across the linoleum floor.

Katie tilted her hips, helping him deepen his thrusts. Cutter grunted and came up, gripping the sides of the table, his chest just above hers. He glanced down their bodies to where they were both naked. Then his narrowed glance swept back up. "You on the pill?"

She considered lying to ease his mind, but sucked in a deep breath and shook her head.

His jaw ground shut, his lips thinned, but he didn't stop stroking. "You'll let me know. If something happens."

"Sure," she lied, surprised he hadn't stopped cold. Cutter was anything but careless. Maybe he didn't believe that she hadn't needed the pill in the months since they'd split.

But why didn't she insist on protection? Katie pushed the thought aside, unwilling to answer that question, even to herself. If she turned up pregnant, the last thing she'd want was a reluctant Cutter offering her help. "Gonna keep talking? Because I'm just about out of breath."

Cutter's lips curved and he flexed his buttocks, hammering into her pussy in hard, short thrusts that built friction all along her channel walls. Katie felt the tension curling around her core and eased her legs higher up his back.

Cutter's eyes closed and Katie drank in the sight of him, straining over her, his thickly muscled arms and chest tensing, his hands tightening their grip on the edges of the table. Glancing down between them, she watched in fascination as he cock pistoned into her, moisture shining all along his reddened shaft. She'd never watched a man fuck her before. The motion was so fluid, so graceful and rhythmic.

When she glanced up, his eyes were open again, watching her and heat filled her cheeks. "I've never watched."

Something crossed his face, an expression so fleeting she couldn't tell if it was regret or disbelief, but she didn't have time to ponder it, because he straightened, letting go of the table and standing with his feet braced, continued to pump inside her.

Now nothing impeded either of their views. But she had

nothing to hold onto and her hands skimmed restlessly along the table top as her breaths grew shorter, and the tension wound tighter.

Cutter lifted his hand and stuck two fingers into his mouth. He rubbed a thumb over the top of her sex, skimmed over her hooded clit, and then pushed it up to expose the swollen knot.

Katie's breath hitched. Her eyelids fell to half-mast, but she kept right on watching as he brought those two moistened fingertips down and swirled them gently over her clitoris.

Her legs jerked convulsively around him. Her back arched off the table.

Cutter groaned and pounded harder, rubbing in circles and pressing harder, then pinching her clit.

That was all it took, Katie gasped, her hands landing on her breasts and squeezing them hard while his cock slammed into her.

"Jesus... Fuck..."

Katie felt the same way, wanted to shout, but she bit her lips and held back her cries, closing her eyes tightly and turning her head side to side until the convulsions rippling up and down her channel slowed.

When Cutter's hands uncrossed her legs behind him and he stepped back, severing the connection, only then did she open her eyes.

His attention was on his slick cock.

But she didn't move, although her back ached from resting on the hard surface, and her body was fully exposed while he was tucking in his shirt and buckling his belt.

He glanced her way, then picked up napkins from the countertop and stood in front of her again, a frown bisecting his dark brows.

His fingers crumpled the napkin, and he took a breath then stroked her folds and inner thighs, gentle strokes that nonetheless excited her sex because the fibers were a little coarse and her clit and vagina were raw and sensitized. She gasped and bit her lip, but her pussy clasped and opened, making another of those embarrassingly wet, succulent sounds.

His eyes darkened, and his breaths quickened. "There are thousand ways I want to take you, Katie." His voice was husky as he rimmed her with the paper again.

Katie widened the legs dangling from the table. "Maybe I'll let you try every one of them."

Chapter Four

There'd been no maybes about it, Cutter mused as he pulled into her driveway one evening a week later. Katie had game. She'd surrendered everything to him. Accommodated his every whim—*enthusiastically.*

Which had him wondering if things would have turned out differently between them the first time if he'd given her a hint how willing he was to experiment.

Last night they'd lain stretched across her bed, his head between her legs, her lips wrapped around his cock. When he'd exploded, he'd tried to withdraw, but she'd squeezed his balls in warning and sucked his cock, swallowing his come, then lazily lapped around the cap like it was an ice cream cone. She'd reached down and pulled his hair, reminding him he still had work to do, and he'd finished her, although he'd been so wrung out all he wanted to do was drag her down beside him, wrap his arms around her and doze.

But Katie never let him rest. It was as if she wanted to cram as many experiences in as she could. Was she afraid he'd end it before she was sated?

He was a long way from being done with her.

It should have worried him. And sometimes, he did hesitate. Even this morning, when he'd been riding a four-wheeler along the fence line, he'd halted on a hilltop where he knew the signal was strong and hit redial on his cell phone. When he'd realized how naturally that had come, he'd thumbed the off switch and stared at the phone.

She'd been the last person he called. He opened his sent messages and realized most of them were to her. And for what? To make a date. To talk about what they wanted for dinner. To tell her to take down her patio umbrella because a thunderstorm was coming and he didn't want it blown away. Things a man who was in a relationship would do. Things he'd done with her before. And he'd easily fallen back into the same pattern.

He hadn't called her back and fell into a black mood which followed him like a dark cloud all afternoon, wishing he could call and cancel, but knowing he wouldn't. Blood thrummed all day through his body, kept his dick thick and hot from just the memory of how her mouth had looked stretched around it as she'd sucked.

The dark mood still held him in its grip. He'd driven out of Two Mule and followed the interstate to an Adult Superstore a couple of exits down. The items he'd bought were in a brown paper bag on the seat next to him. Katie's eagerness to experiment had to have its limits. And Cutter planned to find them tonight.

He'd always considered himself a meat and potatoes kind of guy. Preferring plain food to spicy. The same with his sex. But Katie challenged him. He hated feeling like he had to compete, but he knew Justin's reputation and wanted to make sure he obliterated his memory. Whatever the other man had done to get to her, he'd discover it and make damn sure she knew who the better man was.

Her front door opened and he cut off the engine and climbed down from his truck. The wind whipped up, gusting and catching the screen door, making it bang against the wall.

He climbed the steps, eyeing the little T-shirt that stretched across her breasts. Her nipples were round little pebbles under the soft cotton. Her legs were bare beneath skimpy shorts, and he knew she'd left off any underwear because that was what he preferred. And she always accommodated his preferences.

Her gaze travelled over him then snagged on the paper bag

he held in one fist. "A present for me?"

"It's for me."

Katie licked her lips then her mouth stretched into smile. How could her expression be so open, so happy when he knew he looked as dark as the thunderclouds filling the evening sky?

He closed the door behind him and dropped the bag on a table next to the door. "I want you naked."

She wrinkled her nose at him. "No, 'how was your day'? Or even a mention of the weather?"

"I'm not in the mood for small talk."

"I can see that."

He arched an eyebrow and she rolled her eyes, but grabbed the hem of her soft pink tee and pulled it over her head, then shoved down her shorts and kicked them away. "That better?"

Cutter's gaze trailed down her body, pausing to note the tightness of her small, rose-colored nipples. He'd bet money if she opened her thighs, he'd see moisture glazing her pale skin. "Bend over the arm of the sofa."

"You're in a hurry." There was a tight, expectant quality to her voice.

Was she getting worked up about his intentions? "I'm waiting."

Katie gave a nervous laugh then strode toward the sofa, color washing her cheeks and chest. But she bent over the sofa arm.

Cutter reached for the bag and the items he'd already unwrapped. He took the tube of lubricant, uncapped it and squeezed it onto his forefinger. Then he stepped close to Katie and smoothed a palm over her ass. "You said you might let me take you any way I wanted..."

"Guess it depends on what you have in mind," she said sounding breathless.

"You can make me stop any time you want."

"But you'll walk, won't you?"

He might—but not before he'd eased the lust pulsing in his dick. Katie didn't have to know that. He traced a finger down the crevice dividing her buttocks.

She gasped and her bottom tightened, but she didn't offer a complaint.

He parted her and brought the lubricant-covered finger to the small furled opening he'd only teased before.

A low moan slipped from her lips and she laughed nervously again. "I hope you know I've never..."

"Glad to hear it," he bit out. "But it doesn't mean I'm gonna stop."

"*Jesus.*"

He rubbed the lube in circles, pressing against her, and then pushed his fingertip inside her.

Her muscles tightened around him, squeezing as they tried to eject him.

"You have to relax because I'm just getting started."

"Cutter, I don't know if I can," she whispered.

"Is it painful?"

"It burns."

"Can you take it?" He stroked deeper, just past the last knuckle.

"*Jesus.*"

Cutter pushed deeper and rotated his finger, easing into her, stretching her. His dick jerked, pressing hard against the front of his jeans, but he was a long way from being able to ease that ache.

He pulled out his finger and reached for the other item he'd purchased. He squeezed lube onto the end of the plug and smeared it down the length of the slender column. "I'm going to place something inside you. Take deep breaths and relax...as much as you can."

Her head lowered to the leather sofa and she widened her stance, giving him silent permission to proceed.

Cutter's lips twitched and he set the tip of the butt plug against her asshole and pushed it gently inside.

The slender tip didn't hurt that bad, easing into her. Katie sighed in relief as he slowly pushed inside her. However, the deeper it entered, the wider it grew and the delicate muscles surrounding her entrance burned. "Wait!"

"Is it too much? Shall I stop?"

And let him call it quits? He'd been testing her all week, pushing past every inhibition she'd ever had. However, this was too much—too invasive and embarrassing. But he'd warned her of the consequence if she balked. "Just give me a second."

Katie turned her face, laying one hot cheek against cool leather and closing her eyes. She concentrated on loosening the tension around the slick plug he'd inserted. "All right. I'm okay now."

The plug pushed deeper, the shaft of it widening more, stretching her uncomfortably, but she wasn't really in pain. Whatever lubricant he'd used seemed to numb her a little, just enough so that she could take it. The plug broadened again as it pushed deeper then narrowed in circumference. She drew a deep sigh of relief as he stopped pushing.

"You can get up now."

"What?" she asked, trying to clear her mind of the sudden rush of lust that flooded her pussy.

"I'm done. You'll wear that tonight. Now, what's for dinner?"

Katie rose gingerly from the sofa arm and pushed back her hair before glancing at Cutter. He was still completely dressed, but his features were tight, his gaze narrowed as he watched her expression.

She tilted her chin and even though she didn't want to turn and give him a view of her bottom with the plug settled snugly at her back entrance, she did anyway, walking slowly toward the kitchen.

But she felt its thickness with every step and realized that while he'd been pushing into her ass, her sex had become swollen and fluid dripped down her thighs.

And the bastard had to know it too. She hoped like hell he was as uncomfortable and hot as she was.

They ate the meal she'd prepared, meatloaf and scalloped potatoes. A fresh apple pie sat cooling on the counter top, but Cutter was eager to continue with the new game.

Katie had squirmed on her seat throughout the entire meal, whether from the plug or embarrassment that she sat naked while he hadn't removed any clothing, he didn't know.

But the color in her cheeks and the desperation evident in the way she kept biting her lower lip was doing a number on his control. His cock was so swollen and hard it felt like the skin surrounding it was stretched to the limit.

He stood and began to undress next to the table while her eyes grew wide.

When he was nude, he walked to the apple pie and cut himself a slice, carrying to the table. "Can I get you one?" he asked, holding it like a pizza slice and taking a bite.

"I'm full," she muttered.

"Yes, you are," he drawled. "Does it hurt?"

"Let's not talk about it. Just finish your pie."

It was the first time she'd shown him any irritation, and Cutter grinned. He strode toward her and knelt, then turned her chair to face him. "Come on. Take a bite."

He held up the pie, and she glared but opened her mouth obediently and took a small bite.

He finished off the rest, licked his fingertips, and then leaned close.

Katie's mouth opened, but he ducked and latched onto a nipple chewing gently on the tip. "Prefer cherries to apples, anyway," he murmured.

"You finished eating?" she asked, gasping.

"Funny, I'm still hungry." He rose and held out his hand.

Katie eyed it with suspicion but laid her palm against his, and he squeezed and tugged her upward. When she was chest to chest with him, he enfolded her in his arms and reached around to cup her bottom. He nudged the base of the plug and felt her breath gust against his shoulder. He smiled again.

"Cutter?"

"Yes, baby?"

"I don't think I can take much more."

The tension in her soft voice was everything he could have wanted. "Go on back to the bed. I'll be there in a minute. I'm just gonna put the dishes in the sink."

"You can leave them."

He gave her a quick stare, the same look he'd used to halt any arguments over the past few days.

She clamped her mouth shut and walked away.

Cutter couldn't help watching the sway of her hips and the glint of the base of the rubbery plug peeking from between her buttocks.

He made quick work of the dishes, palmed the last item from the paper bag, then walked slowly down the hall, making as much noise as possible, because he knew she was impatient, and he wanted her to know he didn't care.

She'd pulled the covers off the bed and lay in the center of the white sheets on her side, facing him, one arm over her belly, the other curled beneath her head.

Cutter walked to the bed and plucked the pillows from top of the bed and laid them down, one atop the other. "Lie over this."

Katie groaned. "I didn't know you were a sadist."

"There're lots of things you don't know about me."

She skimmed his face, then sat up and climbed over the pillows, arranging herself so that her bottom was lifted and her knees parted.

Her inner folds and entrance were a deep, dark pink and slick. Cutter set the vibrator on the bed behind her and pulled on the base of the plug.

Katie dragged air into her lungs, not releasing the breath until he'd pulled the plug free.

"Don't get too comfortable."

"There's no way you can come inside me...there," she

mumbled.

"Not planning on it...tonight. You're still pretty tight. But I have something I think you're ready to enjoy."

She leaned up on her arms and started to turn her head.

"No peeking." Cutter picked up the slender dildo and lubed the end, then circled the tip around her tiny hole and slowly pushed. He flicked the switch near the base and Katie jerked as it began to hum.

"No, no, no...," she groaned as the vibrations, gentle at first, revved up.

Cutter's chuckle was deep and dirty. The dildo slid deeper, and then he moved between her legs. He traced the edges of her folds with his fingers and moisture spilled from inside her, coating her sex and his hand.

"Damn," he whispered. His breath cooled the liquid trailing down one thigh. His tongue curled around her sex, following the path his fingers had taken then dipping inside.

The small muscles encircling the dildo clutched it hard, trying to eject it, but he covered the base and pressed it deeper while a callused thumb grazed the sensitive skin of her perineum.

Katie's desperate moan and the subtle shiver that wracked her slender frame had him growling behind her, and he shifted again. This time she cried in relief when the blunt round head of his cock nudged between her lips.

He liked the way her pussy looked, clasping around him like a mouth, making moist, lewd sounds that tightened his balls.

He pulsed forward, swaying, dragging his cockhead around her entrance, wetting it. Then he sank deeper and swirled again as he came out, a reverse screwing that made her tremble and drove him crazy because he wanted to plunge deep and hard inside her.

Her back sank and her chest rubbed on the comforter. She writhed like a wild thing and he flicked the switch again, taking the vibrations a notch higher.

Katie gave a thin wail and came up on her arms, pushing back against him, trying to take him deeper, rocking on his cock, tugging on him with her tight little cunt lips until he couldn't stand it a second longer.

Both hands landed on the notches of her hips and he slammed forward, ramming against the base of the dildo with each sharp thrust.

"Yes!" she cried out, lunging backward, fighting his grip because he held her firm, controlled the tight, sharp thrusts that churned in the silky fluid flooding her channel.

Cutter's balls tightened. He gritted his teeth, fighting the urge to come because the sensations were too amazing, and he wanted to stay there longer. Wanted to feel the clench of her cunt, the hum vibrating through her sugar walls, and her silky heat surrounding him. Already her excitement produced a steady flow of moisture, leaking out to wet the base of his cock and lower belly.

The sounds they made together only fanned the flames. Lush, suctioning clasps and sharp, wet slaps as his belly and thighs slammed against her bottom.

But he wasn't Superman, and she was quickly coming apart. Katie's whole body shuddered and short ragged whimpers filled the room.

Cutter leaned closer, shortened his thrusts and reached to grab one corner of her shoulder and wrap the other fist in her hair.

Her head came back with an agonized groan and he hammered her. His balls burst, come jetted deep inside her, and again, he wondered, fleetingly, why the hell he'd forgone the condom.

But her body bowed, her pussy convulsed around him, squeezing in strong, rhythmic pulses that milked his cock until he slowed behind her, shuddering.

Slowly, he unwound his fist from her hair then gathered her up, sitting her on his lap with his dick still deep inside her, savoring the gentling of the contractions and the heat that slicked their skin.

He dragged in a deep breath and lowered his head, gliding his lips from the rounded curve of her shoulder to her neck.

Katie reached behind her, cupped the back of his head and turned her face toward his.

Cutter kissed her like he never had before. *Voraciously.* Plundering her mouth with his tongue, sucking her bottom lip between his teeth and biting, then covering her mouth to rub his lips in drugging circles.

Katie kissed him back then broke away. She rested her head on his shoulder while her breaths rattled in her chest. "I think the vibrator has to go."

Cutter smiled, liking the wry humor in her voice and felt relief that she was recovering. He'd thought to push her past her comfort zone, but Katie was strong, willful, and unwilling to back down from a challenge.

"Bend over the pillows again and I'll take it out."

"Both—take them both out." She leaned over the pillows again.

"Sore?" he asked, smoothing his hands over her soft ass.

"Shut up, Cutter. Just do it before you see my bottom blushing."

"It's already pink. Like I spanked it."

Her pussy tightened around him and Cutter grinned.

"God, this is more embarrassing than when you stuck it inside me."

"My dick or the dildo?"

Katie gave a short shocked laugh. "I'm going to kill you."

"Embarrassed because you're not aroused now?"

"Yeah, because you can see everything and all I can do is lie here like a blow-up doll."

He flicked the switch to off. Her body relaxed and she gave a soft moan. Reluctantly, he withdrew his cock, which felt chilled when the air hit it. Then he slowly pulled out the dildo and backed off the bed to head to the bathroom. When he reached the door, he glanced over his shoulder.

Katie was still hunched over the pillows, but her gaze

followed him.

"Join me in the shower?"

A quick smile turned up the corners of her mouth and she sat up, raising her arms above her head.

Cutter watched the lengthening of her torso, the shiver of her round breasts, and felt his cock jerk in reaction to her sexy movements.

She rubbed her hair and grimaced.

"Did I pull too hard?"

Katie gave him a saucy grin. "Just hard enough, cowboy."

Chapter Five

Katie untied the apron from her waist and lifted it over her head. "See you tomorrow," she called over her shoulder as she grabbed her purse from under the cash register and headed for the door.

Ole Win glanced up over the top of his reading glasses as she drew alongside him. "Glad to see you and Cutter got things worked out," he murmured.

Katie hesitated, then pasted on a smile and pushed through the door into the bright sunshine. She and Cutter didn't have anything worked out between them. They existed in a kind of limbo where the only things they talked about were unimportant or strictly about sex.

Not once had they broached the subject of her affair with Justin. It loomed between them, growing larger and uglier the longer they ignored it.

At least from her point of view. And she'd become a coward, unwilling to rock the boat because her time with Cutter was precious.

As she walked along the sidewalk toward the grocery store, the sunshine which usually buoyed her spirits, beat down on her unprotected head. Perspiration broke on her forehead and upper lip and her stomach churned.

When she reached the grocery, the air-conditioned air relieved her for moment, but then a strong wave of nausea hit her. She clamped her hand over her mouth and rushed toward the back of the store and the restrooms.

She made it through the door, punched open the stall and bent. Breakfast and lunch landed in the toilet bowl. When the urge to retch eased, she sighed, hanging above the rim of the toilet with a hand braced against the stall and the other against her knee.

A paper towel entered her line of vision and she grabbed for it, wiping her mouth before she glanced over her shoulder.

The room tilted and an arm slipped around her waist. "Easy now. No quick moves," came a feminine voice.

Katie blinked and turned slowly. Dani Standifer stood beside her, and then reached past her to flush the toilet. "Let's get you cleaned up."

Katie let the younger woman lead her to the sink and stood docilely while Dani wet more paper towels and washed her face. "Rinse your mouth. You'll feel like a new person."

Katie cupped her hands beneath the faucet and did just that, then swallowed a small, cool sip. When she glanced up in the mirror, Dani was smiling softly behind her.

"My brother know?"

"Know what?"

Dani tilted her head. "You don't have a clue, do you?"

"What are you talking about?"

Dani shook her head, a rueful smile curving her mouth. She took Katie's hand and pulled her out of the restroom, then purposefully dragged her down an aisle. She stopped in front of a shelf of pregnancy kits and Katie swallowed hard.

"We'll share," Dani said. "There're two in the box. Wait right here while I pay."

There was no way Katie was going to be spotted standing in front of the pregnancy tests. By dinnertime, the whole damn town would think that she'd been knocked up. And there was just no way that could be true.

She closed her eyes. Stupid, stupid. Of course, she'd known she could get pregnant. Neither of them had mentioned using a condom, and she'd thought that maybe Cutter thought she'd been lying when she told him she wasn't on the pill, because why else would he go uncloaked whenever they made love?

It wasn't because he hoped to trap her. But what was her motive? Katie didn't want to examine it too closely because she thought she knew.

Dani found her in the candy aisle, looking at chocolate, which was her comfort food. "Come on," she said, grabbing her hand again and pulling her toward the restroom. "No time like now to find out for sure." She sounded excited, even happy.

Katie wanted to throw up again.

In minutes, she found herself sitting in the stall next to Dani's peeing onto a wand.

The toilet in the next stall flushed, feet appeared beneath the bottom of her stall door. "No stalling. I'm dying to see."

Katie cleaned up and flushed her toilet, holding out her wand in front of her when she opened the door. Not the least shy, Dani grabbed it and laid it on the side of the sink beside hers and pulled out the instruction pamphlet inside the box. "It says wait three minutes."

"I'm not pregnant," Katie said grumpily. And she promised herself if that were true, she'd buy a crate of Trojans, and to hell with the games she and Cutter played.

"Okay, so that's the purple control band. If we get a second band in the window we're going to have babies!" Dani's eyes glittered, her cheeks were a healthy, glowing pink. If anyone looked pregnant, it was her.

Katie studied her own reflection. Dark circles beneath her eyes, green-toned skin. She looked like she had the flu.

"Oh my god!" Dani squealed, then grabbed both of Katie's hands and hopped up and down. "Oh my God!"

Katie didn't bother asking her why she was excited. Her stomach roiled and she tugged her hands from Dani's and rushed to the toilet again.

When she'd emptied her stomach completely, she hung over the toilet with her eyes closed, feeling ready to cry.

"You're not happy," Dani said softly behind her.

Katie snorted and straightened. "If there was a second goddamn purple band, then the answer would be yes."

"Do you think Cutter won't do right by you?"

Katie turned and firmed her lips. "I don't want Cutter to feel like he has to *do* anything. That's not our agreement."

One of Dani's pale brows lifted. "Agreement?"

"Long story. Not pretty. Can we cease with the questions? I need to sit down and I prefer someplace that doesn't smell like vomit."

Dani tucked her hand inside her arm and pulled her out of the restroom. "I suppose your restaurant is out of the question too?"

"I'd rather the whole world didn't know right this minute."

"Your house isn't far. Shall we head that way?"

Katie shook her head. "No, Cutter might show up early, and I don't want to talk to him yet."

"That settles it. We'll go out to my ranch. He'll never think to look there. And he's not likely to drop by. We aren't talking these days."

Dani led her to her car. Katie didn't really want company, would have preferred to go to her own place and crawl into bed. But Cutter had his own key now and the last thing she wanted was to fall beneath his discerning stare. The man knew everything about her body, read her moods—even if he didn't care about her heart.

"Tell me about this agreement," Dani said as the car left the town's city limit.

"I don't think Cutter would want me to."

"Who else are you going to talk to, Katie?" Dani asked, worry settling a crease between her pale brows. "I'm his sister. I know how hard-headed that man can be. And I know all about you and Justin. I'm assuming he figures somewhere in your problem with Cutter. So far as my brother is concerned, every problem boils down to my husband."

Katie turned to stare at Dani's profile. Other than the

stubborn, square chin there wasn't much of family resemblance between Dani and her brother. "If you know about me and Justin, why are you talking to me?"

Dani shot her a quick glance. "Oh, don't think for a moment that I'm not jealous as hell of every woman who's slept with him, but I know how persuasive he can be. How irresistible he is. I don't blame you. And I know he regrets ever taking you to bed. He did it for all the wrong reasons."

"I did it because I thought your brother didn't find me sexy," Katie murmured.

Dani's lips twitched. "Gawd, you're stupid."

"Thanks."

"Justin went after you out of frustration over me. He thought he didn't have a chance in hell of ever getting close to me because Cutter would never approve of him as a beau. Not very smart, but when it comes to emotions, men don't look too deep. It was all about revenge."

"Nice to know he cared so much about me."

"He likes you, but the fact you were seeing Cutter made you all the more attractive as a target." Dani shrugged. "Never said my man was perfect. But he is changing. That's what guys do when they fall in love. They try harder to figure us women out."

They turned off the main road onto caliche road, bumped over an iron cattle guard set over a culvert and through the gates of the Ayers ranch.

Katie straightened in her seat. "Cutter didn't seem too happy about your marriage."

"He was ready to spit nails. He was there when I proposed to Justin."

"You proposed?"

Dani gave her a mischievous smile. "It was a spur of the moment thing. Cutter walked into Rowe's kitchen and found the three of us nearly naked and looking like we'd spent a night doing...well, exactly what we'd been doing...and he said he expected a ring. He thought for sure Rowe would step up, but I chose Justin. It didn't really matter which man married me. We're all committed. That bother you?"

Katie shook her head about the woman's openness over her unconventional relationship "No, I envy you having someone who loves you. Two someones seems...selfish."

Dani grinned and cut the motor. "Come on in. I'll make a pot of tea and find some crackers. Then you're going to tell me all your secrets since you know all of mine."

Katie followed Dani inside and settled at the kitchen table while Dani prepared a tray which she sat in the center of the table.

"Now, tell me about this agreement," Dani said, taking a seat, one leg bent beneath her and the other dangling.

As Katie unloaded about everything that had transpired since Dani's wedding, the blonde's expressions changed.

When Katie told her about how he'd gotten her up the stairs during the reception, Dani's lips curved and her eyes danced.

When she came to the part where they'd both agreed to become fuck buddies, her eyebrows drew closer and her gaze softened. "You're in a bad place. You've given him everything he wanted without making him work for a thing. He has no motivation to change."

"I knew we didn't have a future. I never got from Cutter what I wanted the first time around—satisfaction. I told myself that's all I was in it for."

Dani snorted. "You might sell that to Cutter, but I'm a woman. And I know how far we'll go for love. You are still in love with him, aren't you?"

Katie stared at her tea cup and let out a deep, dejected breath. "I never stopped. I knew as soon as Justin...finished...that I'd made a huge mistake."

"That's a hard one to overcome," Dani said softly. "Cutter's a black and white kind of man. He won't forgive infidelity easily. But you have a weapon now. One you can use if you really want him. But you can't let him make this another agreement. You have to hold out, make it hard for him—force him to change his mind."

Katie lifted her gaze, knowing tears were welling, but too unhappy to care that Cutter's sister could see. "What if I don't think he's wrong to distrust me? Even hate me a little."

Dani reached over and placed her hand atop Katie's and gave it a squeeze. "Katie, you made a mistake. You regret it. Have you ever told him you're sorry?"

"He won't talk about it. Neither will I."

"It's got to happen. Eventually. You can't carry it around or it'll fester."

"We're talking like Cutter would even need to have a relationship with me to be a part of this child's life. He doesn't. I'd share, with or without us being a couple."

Dani lifted her hand and tucked a lock of Katie's hair behind her ear then settled back in her chair. Her steady gaze held Katie's for a long moment. "If you don't think you're deserving of more, don't you think your child is?"

Katie swallowed the lump lodged at the back of her throat. "I don't know if I could live with him and not be with him, you know what I mean? I can get pretty ugly too when I'm hurt."

"You have to tell him about the baby. Start there. But don't you dare let him plan this whole thing out. Don't let him take control, because he will, and then he'll insulate himself from hurt, from any chance of growing to love you again. He did that to me after our parents died. Shut me out in the cold."

"What about you? You have this baby, his niece or nephew, don't you think it's time for y'all to put aside your resentments too?"

Dani nodded and shoved back her chair. "Yeah, I do. And I think I'll start right now." She got up from the table and headed for the phone.

"What are you doing?"

"Cutter needs to know where you are," Dani said over her shoulder. "It's a great time for me to give him my news."

"Before the guys know?"

Dani wrinkled her nose. "The guys know. They're the ones who told me to go get the kit."

"How'd they figure it out?"

"My boobs got tender right away, and when my period didn't come... Rowe guessed and talked to Justin about it. They thought it was pretty damn funny I was the last to know."

"Do you mind my asking...do you know which one's the father?"

Dani's lips twisted into a wry grin. "Well, unless there was a condom malfunction, this baby's Rowe's. Justin married me. I promised the first kid would be Rowe's."

Katie raised her eyebrows, impressed by how nonchalantly the threesome treated the issue. "Sounds fair."

"Don't get me wrong. Justin's jealous, but we've figured out productive ways for him to channel it." She waggled her eyebrows and smiled. "I promise you don't want to know how."

Katie returned her smile then drew a deep breath when Dani pressed a speed dial number.

"Cutter, it's Dani. Katie's over here at the ranch with me, without a car. Can you drop by to pick her up?" She hung up the phone. "I left him a message. Shouldn't take him too long to check. He's never without his cell."

"Then why didn't he pick up?"

"He doesn't like talking to me. He's still angry. But he's about to get over it."

Katie felt her stomach tighten at the thought of facing Cutter so soon. "Don't mention a thing about me. *Please.* I'd like a little time to think about it, and about what I want."

Dani nodded. After that, the women drank their tea in silence, which suited Katie just fine. She had plenty to mull over.

In the distance a door slammed. "Gawd, this feels like déjà vu," Dani muttered.

Heavy footfalls trailed through the house. The kitchen door swung open and Cutter strode inside, his gaze landing on Katie and narrowing before he turned to his sister. "Dani, what's this all about?"

Dani's eyes rounded innocently. "Why's this thing gotta be about anything? Two girls can't meet for a gossip?"

A muscle flexed along the edge of his jaw. "Katie, you ready to go?"

Katie swung her gaze toward Dani.

"Not gonna ask what we were talking about?" Dani said slowly, folding her arms over her chest.

"No."

Dani's chin shot up. "I'm pregnant, Cutter."

Cutter's breath caught and his expression turned darker. "Who's the daddy? Do you even know?"

"I'm pretty sure it's Rowe."

His chest rose then he let his breath out. He raked a hand through his hair. Tension eased from his jaw. "You feelin' all right? Do you need anything?"

Dani gave him a soft smile. "I need a hug...from my big brother."

Cutter's back stiffened, but Dani's hopeful expression must have done a number on his stubborn stance. He strode forward and Dani unfolded her arms to slip them around his waist. She hugged Cutter close.

Katie sighed with relief, glad the two of them were talking now.

Cutter's eyes closed for a moment. "I want you happy," he said, his voice thick. "You know that, right?"

"I am, Cutter. I swear it." She eased back in his embrace and stared into his face "But I need you in this baby's life. Can you do that for me?"

His expression only slightly less dour, Cutter met her steady gaze. "I don't know. To be honest, I'm still mad as hell."

"Will you try to get over it? We're all family now."

Cutter issued a short, filthy curse, then shook his head. "Jesus, did you have to marry *him*?"

"It was the right choice. I know you don't understand, but you don't really have to. All I want from you is for you to be there for me and my baby. You've got less than nine months to make peace with Justin and Rowe. Please try."

Cutter didn't answer, but he kissed her forehead and set her away from him. "I can't promise I'll ever be their best buddies. But I won't take a swing at them."

Dani wrinkled her nose at him. "That's a start. I'd like you to come to dinner here. Bring Katie. I like her."

"Katie might be busy," Cutter said, his tone dead even.

Katie glanced away. He still meant to keep their relationship compartmentalized. She wasn't good enough to bring around family.

Dani gave her a wink. "Well, if you can free some time in your busy schedule, we'd love to have you."

Katie nodded, but gathered her purse and headed for the door, Cutter on her heels.

Minutes later as they pulled out onto the ranch road, which was more of a graveled path, Cutter gave her a glare. "How'd you wind up at Dani's without your car?"

"We met in town and started talking," she said, trying to keep her tone light because she hated lying to him. "She invited me out. I think she's a little lonely for girl talk."

"She made her bed."

"Are you happy...about the baby?"

Cutter's chest expanded around a deep breath. "She isn't thinking very far ahead. What happens when the kid goes to school? What happens when they have the next one? Whose name will the children bear?"

"They have time to work it out."

"It's not fair to the kid."

"Maybe people will be more accepting than you think."

"In this county? But it's not my problem. And I'm not going to hold it against the child. He'll have Standifer blood."

"Will you love him?"

He gave her a quick questioning glance. "You think I'm such a hardass I can't?"

She shrugged and looked out the passenger side window.

"Just making conversation."

"Dani ask you to feel me out?"

"No, but she does hope you'll cut her and the fellas some slack—for the sake of the baby and because she misses you."

"She say that?"

Katie shrugged. "She didn't have to."

"I'm through talking about her. You're coming home with me."

Katie felt a wave of melancholy wash over her. Cutter would set aside his dislike of Dani's situation to do right by her baby. When he discovered her own pregnancy, he'd do whatever he thought was needed, maybe even marry her, to protect his own child.

Not the way she'd wanted to slip back into his life for good. If he asked and she said yes, then Dani was a hundred percent correct. He'd provide for her and the child, but he'd never have to face the issues that still haunted them. She'd never have his whole heart, and she wasn't going to settle for less.

But she didn't have to face that hurdle now. Not just yet.

He pulled up beside the house, and she didn't wait for him. She opened her door and slid from her seat, not looking back as she headed directly inside.

The house was empty and shadows inside were lengthening from the setting sun.

Cutter's footsteps clipped across the oak floor as he followed her into the living room and straight up the stairs. She went to the room at the end of the hall, already unbuttoning her shirt.

Cutter closed the door behind them and strode toward the dresser, emptying his pockets and dropping his watch into a tray on top. He walked to the bed and sat on the edge to pull off his boots.

They undressed without exchanging words, like people who'd been married for years who were only going through the motions. Only she knew as soon as he lowered himself over her, the quiet restraint would end.

Skin to skin, they couldn't pretend they didn't burn for each other. She'd convinced herself over the weeks they'd been seeing each other that it meant something. Maybe she'd only been fooling herself.

She pulled back the covers and tossed them toward the end of the bed, then slid across the cool sheets and lay diagonally on the mattress.

Cutter's gaze drifted over her body, his expression set. What the hell was he thinking? Was he only anticipating how good it would feel once he slid inside her? She was. But she was also thinking that maybe, this should be the last time she let him have her like this. Without commitment. Without discussing what lay between them.

Cutter climbed onto the mattress and right over her, settling down on top of her. At last, his cool demeanor slipped. Heat blazed in his brown eyes. His nostrils flared. His mouth curved slightly, and he dipped his head and nibbled on the lobe of one ear.

Katie shivered and wrapped her arms around him. She'd show him one last time how much she loved him even if she could never say it out loud. She spread her legs beneath him, lifting her knees to hug the sides of his hips.

Cutter started to scoot down, dragging his mouth over her shoulder, and she knew he'd tease her breasts, glide his tongue and lips down her belly and eat her out, but she wanted him inside her. *Now.* She dug her hands into his hair and pulled, and leaned up to suck his bottom lip between hers and bit.

His chuckle was warm, filling her mouth with his sweet breath.

She let him go and slanted her face to kiss him. She circled her head, rubbing his mouth and stroking her tongue inside.

His dueled with hers, then he growled. His cock prodded between her legs and she tilted her hips to receive him.

He lifted his head. "In a hurry?" he rasped.

"I've been thinking about this all day. Can't wait."

He rolled his buttocks, digging his cock into her, but only a couple of inches, just enough to sink the tip inside.

She squeezed around him, and then undulated underneath him, urging him to turn to his back by pulling his hair. When she had him there, she straightened and brought her knees on either side of him. She placed her hands on his chest as she began to rise and fall, taking him inside her in greedy thrusts that soon had her sliding down his full length until she ground against the base of his cock.

Her breaths deepened, shortened.

His hands cupped her breasts, and his fingers plucked at her nipples until they spiked.

She held his gaze and fucked him, rocking up and down, taking him deeper, faster, until his hands glided on the sweat slicking her breasts and belly.

He gripped her waist, lifting her, but she fought his hold, unwilling to let him take her beneath him again. She shook her head and glared, slamming onto him, fucking him hard then leaning down to brace her hands on either side of his shoulders so that she could rub her aching nipples against his chest.

His hands cupped her buttocks and squeezed, parted them and she flung back her head. Her hair stuck to her shoulders, her breaths were jagged, but she couldn't stop, didn't want to give up control.

A finger slid between her buttocks and rubbed over her small, tight hole and she bit her lip, pausing to savor the tip as it sank inside her. He'd taught her to crave that.

"Want more?" he said licking the sweat from her neck.

She knew what he was asking. Something she'd resisted until this day. The anal play with the plug had continued a time or two, but she'd hadn't been ready, hadn't thought she could want it. But suddenly, with his thick finger thrusting inside her, she wanted the pain, wanted the discomfort, wanted something stinging and burning to match the ache building inside her chest and lodging next to her heart.

She nodded quickly and the corners of his mouth kicked up. A wicked, dark glint entered his eyes.

He could think he'd triumphed all he wanted. She didn't really care. She straightened and climbed off his hips. He jerked upright, and crawled behind her, pressing between her shoulders until she bent and braced her hands on the mattress.

He arranged her bottom at his preferred height, nudging her thighs apart to just the right width, then he spread her cheeks.

A thick drop of moisture landed in the crease and he rubbed it over her tiny, sensitive hole. This time she didn't squirm with embarrassment. Her breaths hitched and she quivered. Her back sank and her bottom lifted to his touch.

Cutter's low, dirty laugh sounded behind her and then his cock was sliding in her crease, rocking up and down. He was huge, swollen, the ridge around the tip scraping deliciously up and down, and then he pointed his cock right at her hole, and she drew a deep breath.

"Don't tense up," he said, his words guttural and tight.

Her head sagged between her shoulders and she concentrated, easing the instinctive grip of the muscles until he pushed and he was inside.

She moaned at the sudden, burning stretch.

He froze behind her, his fingers digging hard into her ass. "*Fuck, baby,*" he groaned. "S'goddamn tight."

He didn't move for long seconds, holding himself still, but she didn't want him to go easy, to take her gently. She wanted to hurt, wanted to feel the pinch and heat. She gathered strength in her thighs and pulsed backward, trying to take him deeper.

"Easy, easy," he hissed between his teeth.

She reached with one hand between her legs, curling her stomach until she caught his balls. She massaged them gently, tugging on them, caressing them, until a shudder passed through him and into her.

She squeezed her ass around his cock, then curled farther and rubbed his balls, pulling him toward her.

A gust of pained laughter preceded his gentle thrust

forward. "Let go, Katie."

Katie shook her hair back. "Not until you give me what I want."

"You're not ready."

She shot him a glare over her shoulder. "Says who?"

His dark brows lowered. His chin jutted stubbornly. "I don't want to hurt you."

But he already had. If this was the last time they'd be together, she wanted it to be memorable. "Just fuck me, Cutter. Make me like it."

Chapter Six

Cutter's cock was ready to explode. Still, she didn't know what she asked of him. "Let go of my balls, Katie."

Katie's grip on his sac eased then her fingers slipped away.

Back in control again, he bent over her back, kissed her shoulder and then smoothed a hand over her hip and around her belly, diving between her legs where he thrust three fingers inside her pussy.

She was wet and her cunt spasmed around him. Satisfied she really was ready for more, he thrust his cock and his fingers inside her, working her, stroking gently into her ass and hoping like hell he'd come soon because he wanted to slam violently inside her, but he didn't want to hurt her.

He thumbed her clit and found it distended and exposed. He rasped it with the callused pad again then squeezed it. She jerked, her back sank and her shoulders rose. She rubbed her head against his shoulder, bucked her hips and came unglued.

She came hard. He knew because rhythmic convulsions surrounded his shaft and digits, milking him. Fighting his own blinding excitement, he continued to play with her, waiting until the rippling shivers waned.

Freed at last from his responsibility to see to her pleasure first, he let go. His balls exploded and come jetted inside her.

Cutter's rubbed his forehead on her shoulder and thrust, jerking inside her. Her body quivered and rocked...the motions slowing, slowing...until she stilled except for the trembling, and the only thing keeping her from tumbling to the bed was his hard cock and the fingers still stuffed inside her pussy.

Katie sucked in deep, ragged gulps of air. Her arms collapsed and her head fell to the bed.

Cutter pulled his hand from between her legs and slowly withdrew his cock.

With his own lust sated, Cutter turned his attention back to Katie. Her body still trembled, her breaths were jagged, noisy gasps.

He pushed her, rolling her to her back, then lifted her thighs over his shoulders and lay down, supporting his torso on his elbows.

Her hand slipped between her legs, covering her pussy. "No more. I need to bathe."

Cutter licked the tops of her fingers, then slipped his tongue between them and stroked up and down the seams. "Katie, don't deny me. I won't believe you're shy. Not with me."

"Please, I need a moment."

Her tone, aching and shattered, left him feeling powerful and oddly guilty. He kissed her knuckles, one by one. "Take away your hand, baby."

Katie's fingers pulled back, resting on her mons, as though she felt the need to keep them ready to protect herself again.

Cutter breathed in her scent—sweat, musk, a hint of a floral soap. He followed a sudden impulse and rolled his face in her moist center, coating his cheeks and tongue with her fluids. Then his lips made a more targeted foray, suckling her smooth outer labia, then nibbling at the pink inner lips. While he teased her sex with kisses, he snuck fingers into her entrance, thrusting them gently inside and swirling, twisting them in and out.

Both hands clutched his head and held him above her sex, and he chuckled, pleased she'd surrendered everything again. To show his approval, he latched onto her clitoris and pumped his fingers faster.

Katie's belly quivered, her thighs jerked, her buttocks lifted off the bed to pulse her pussy against his mouth.

Cutter sucked on her clit, clasping it harder, and rubbed his tongue over the hardening tip. When her buttocks lifted higher, he bit down, gently.

Katie, always so reluctant to give him sound, arched off the bed and screamed.

He released her clit, licked it to soothe the ache and slowly pulled his fingers free. Then he came up on his knees beside her and rolled her to her belly again.

"Stay here," he said, forcing his voice not to shake because he felt as wiped as she did.

He padded to the bathroom and soaked a washcloth in warm water and a squirt of soap, then cleansed himself. He tossed it in the hamper, wet another and headed back to the bed.

He halted beside it, and stared down. Katie's head lay on her folded arms, her face turned away. The silent sobs that shook her back made him hesitate.

Had he hurt her after all? Or was this something else? She'd been acting strange, a little remote, since he'd escorted her from Dani's kitchen.

Was she having second thoughts about their arrangement?

He shouldn't have cared. He'd known this wasn't going to last forever. Someday soon, he'd have to break it off anyway because she couldn't have a permanent place in his life.

But please don't let it be today.

He sat on the edge of the bed and washed her gently with the warm, wet cloth. The thing he ought to do was ask her what was wrong, but he didn't think he could handle the answer. Not if she wanted to talk to him about Justin and their impossible future.

Instead, he headed back to the bathroom to get rid of the cloth, then washed his hands and splashed cool water over his face. Anything to stall.

Staring at himself in the mirror, he read the tension in his jaw, saw a shadow of a deeper, darker emotion lurking in his gaze. Katie got to him in so many ways, but he'd been ruthless—with her, with himself. He couldn't let himself love her again if he couldn't trust her. And how the hell could he ever forget the sight of Justin's smirk as he'd padded up behind Katie, zipping up his goddamn jeans.

No, he'd never be able to forget. Forgiving didn't seem as hard now as that.

He broke with his own gaze and pushed away from the counter.

Back inside the bedroom, he approached the bed. Katie lay on her side, her back to him, the sheet pulled up and tucked beneath her arm. He lifted the corner and crawled in behind her.

He'd intended to lie back, close his eyes and rest to get ready for the next round because he was greedy and wanted more and more. Somehow he'd fill his need for her, reach the end of the attraction that flared as bright as the Texas sun every time they touched.

However, once he lay beside her, he couldn't resist the urge to scoot closer. He came up behind her and pressed his lips against her shoulder. Then he wrapped an arm around her waist and pulled her closer until her back warmed his belly.

He placed his hand over the one she had resting on her stomach. Katie's breath caught.

Cutter closed his eyes. "What's wrong?" he found himself asking even though he'd promised himself he wouldn't.

"This arrangement we have," she whispered, "It's over."

Cutter froze.

"I'm not sorry for it. I mean...about agreeing to it. But we weren't smart. You see I was at Dani's because she and I had things to talk about. A secret to share."

Cutter realized his fingers were wrapped tightly around hers, and he eased his grip. His jaws were another matter. They ached from the tension that kept them grinding his teeth hard. "What secret?" he finally forced out.

"I'm pregnant." She gave a short laugh that sounded more

like a sob. "Funny, isn't it?"

Cutter heard the words, but it took a moment for them to sink in. His reaction once he got his head wrapped around the fact wasn't what he would have expected. There was no anger. No self-recrimination. All along, part of him had been hoping.

If she carried his child, he'd never have to let her go. "You'll marry me."

"No, I won't," she whispered. She moved away, and keeping her back to him, sat on the edge of the bed. "I need you take me home now."

He sat up, staring at her rigid back, anger rising swiftly. "Katie, we're not done here."

"Yes. We are." She stood and slowly walked around the room, gathering her clothing from the floor. Then she went into the bathroom, leaving him staring at the door as it closed.

What the hell had just happened?

She was pregnant with his child. He'd proposed. Why would she refuse?

Confused and irritable, Cutter dressed then waited impatiently for the door to open again so that he could continue the discussion.

However, when Katie did come out, her chin was tilted high. He knew better than to argue with a woman when her back was up. She'd come down off her high horse when she had a chance to think it through. His offer was the only thing that made sense.

Throughout the drive to her house, he watched her from the corner of his eye. But Katie's rigid posture never relaxed and she didn't look his way once. He chose a safe subject. "Have you been to a doctor?"

"Not yet. Dani and I used a pregnancy kit she bought to test."

So that's what this afternoon's gossip session had been all about. She'd lied.

"I want to be there when you see him."

"The doctor?"

He nodded and gripped the wheel tighter. "I'm gonna be part of his life. He's a Standifer."

"I would never keep a child from you. But you're getting ahead of yourself. It might be a girl."

He grunted. A girl. With red hair and wild streak a mile long, no doubt. Maybe she could be home-schooled and save him some gray hairs.

"Would you mind if it's a girl?" Katie asked, her tone indicating she was worried.

"A boy's easier."

"You think?"

Now that they were talking, he breathed easier. "You don't have to worry about boys coming home pregnant."

Katie's jaw dropped and her gaze narrowed. "You know, I did tell you I wasn't on the pill."

"Still, you didn't ask me to wear a condom, did you?" he said, aiming a glare her way.

"It takes two to make a baby," she grumbled. "You weren't exactly the safety patrol."

Cutter relaxed against the seat, enjoying her flare of temper. It sure as hell beat the cold shoulder she'd given him before, and with them, anger always lead to a meltdown of another sort. His heartbeats began a slow, purposeful thrum.

He pulled into her driveway and turned in his seat to talk, but she was already jerking on the door handle.

Katie slipped to the ground and stomped toward the door.

Cutter cursed under his breath, determined to follow her, but then hesitated. That's exactly what she expected him to do. He slammed the truck into reverse and pulled sedately out of her driveway, leaving Katie staring after him from her porch.

He smiled as he pulled away. He'd let her stew a while. Maybe she'd have a good cry too. When he came back, she'd be ready to talk some sense.

A knock sounded on the front door. Katie pulled the stopper from the bottom of the sink and peeled off her plastic gloves. Cutter hadn't held out long.

She'd used the time to fix a light meal, something that she hoped she'd keep down this time. And she'd thought long and hard about what he'd said. How he'd said it. Maybe Dani was wrong.

Cutter hadn't been angry when he'd found out they were going to have a baby, but he also hadn't been gloating. And there'd been real caring in his gruff voice when he'd asked her what was wrong. Could she really be this in love with the man if he didn't love her back? Even just a little?

The knocking sounded again. "Coming," she called out. She set her face into noncommittal lines and swung the door open. Only it wasn't Cutter standing on her porch. "Justin, what the hell are you doing here?"

Justin Cruz's dark, brooding glance swept over her. A muscle flexed along his jaw, and then his gaze dropped away. "Dani told us everything."

Katie firmed her lips. "I still don't get why you're here."

"I made a mess of things between you and Cutter. I want to make it right."

Katie shook her head. "Take care of yourself. Whatever's between the two of you, you work on that. I'll take care of my own problems."

"Dani said he's stubborn. That he won't easily forgive. I could talk to him."

"Talk to him?" she scoffed. "If he won't listen to me, *and he's sleeping with me*, why the hell do you think he'll hear you out?"

Justin shuffled his feet. "We're family now. Related by marriage and blood."

"You need to leave. He left in a huff. Knowing him, he'll be back any minute and the last thing I need is for him to find you here again."

Justin reached out and covered the hand gripping the edge

of the screen door. "We're here for you, however this works out."

Tears stung her eyes and she nodded her head. "Leave. Please?"

An engine gunned in the distance and both of them turned to see Cutter's big black truck screaming down the road.

Her stomach sank. This was so much like that other time, both her and Justin looking guilty as hell and Cutter's face as dark as a thundercloud as he parked the truck at an angle, blocking Justin's exit.

Cutter's door slammed and he stomped toward them, his gaze slicing from her to Justin, where it stayed.

Justin held up his hands. "This isn't whatever you think this looks like."

"Oh yeah?" Cutter raised an eyebrow. "What is it then? You hear she's pregnant and suddenly you give a shit?"

"Cutter," Katie broke in. "I asked him to leave."

"Katie, you get back in the house. Justin and I are gonna have a chat."

However, Cutter was rolling up his sleeves.

Justin sighed and turned to Katie. "Get inside. Close the door. And keep away from the window."

Men. Katie blew out a deep breath. "This is my house. *My fucking porch.* You two aren't gonna brawl here. There's been enough talk. Enough scandal."

Justin gripped her shoulders and turned her, pushing her gently through the door.

"You shouldn't have done that," she whispered, catching Cutter's tightening features.

"Cutter's got some things to get off his chest. I'm gonna oblige him."

"Fine," she said, catching the edge of the door, "But if either of you think I'm going to talk to you after this, you've got another think comin'." She closed the door, shutting out the sight of the two men stepping off the porch, and leaned against the door.

At the first slamming fist, she sobbed and ran for the

bathroom to empty her stomach.

"I have to say, you've got some nerve showin' up here," Cutter growled.

Justin circled him, his fists raised, his expression neutral. "I don't want to fight you. Truth is, Dani'll kick my ass for being here."

"You shouldn't have come anywhere near Katie. You fucked her up once; I won't let you do it again."

"About that…"

Cutter swung, but Justin ducked beneath the blow. "Don't go there," Cutter ground out. "Not if you don't wanna eat dinner through a goddamn straw for the rest of your life."

"You'll have to shut me up first." Justin ducked again and punched Cutter's ribs.

Cutter's breath left in an agonized grunt. "Quit dancin' and fight."

Justin stepped out of range of Cutter's furious jabs.

"I've loved Dani since she was young thing. Never thought I had a chance. Not with you keepin' watch over her. I knew I wasn't good enough."

"Damn straight." Cutter barreled in, feinted to the right and slammed Justin's jaw with his left.

Justin stepped back and wiped blood from his lip with the back of his hand, stared at the blood and grimaced. "Katie's fall was my fault from beginning to end. I wanted revenge—against you. Not my proudest moment. And I'm truly sorry."

Cutter gritted his teeth. "I don't want apologies. I want you the fuck out of our lives."

Justin's features darkened. His jaw grew taut. "It's not happening. Dani's my wife. She's gonna have more kids. Some'll be mine. You have to get past this."

"I don't have to get past a damn thing." Cutter tightened his fists and crouched lower, determined to end the fight now.

"Dani wants you in our lives. I'll do whatever it takes to make that happen. If it means letting you use me for a

punching bag to get rid of the bile you have stored up, so be it."
Justin dropped his hands by his sides.

Cutter screwed his face up, rage building. "Put up your fists.

Justin took a deep breath which he blew out as he straightened.

Cutter pulled back his fist, sure Justin would have to protect himself—even if only out of instinct. He swung and struck Justin on the cheek.

Justin's head jerked back and he fell like a ragdoll to the ground.

Cutter kept his arms high, hovering over Justin, hoping he'd open his eyes and get back on his feet. He wasn't nearly done. Wanted the bastard to fight him like a man.

Behind him a door creaked and crashed; footsteps raced toward the two men.

Katie fell to her knees beside Justin and cradled his face between her hands. "Justin, you stupid, stupid man. Open your eyes."

Cutter's hands dropped. His anger bled out as he watched the tears tracking down Katie's face. He backed away and turned, heading toward his truck.

"Where do you think you're going? You have to help me get him inside."

Cutter stiffened, but didn't turn. "I'm done."

"You can be done after you help me get him inside. You're responsible for this. Your sister won't be happy if he doesn't wake up."

Cutter shut his eyes briefly then faced her. He closed his heart, closed off the emotions boiling inside him. He strode toward them, bent and grabbed Justin's arm to jerk him upright. Then he pulled him over his shoulder in a fireman's carry and trailed behind Katie into her house.

"Put him on the couch." She reached for the phone. "I'm calling Dani. You go get a wet towel from the kitchen. He's bleeding all over my couch."

Cutter grunted, but did as she said, listening with only half his attention as Katie made the call.

When he returned with a wet cloth, she took it from him and sat beside Justin and washed his face. "If he doesn't wake up quick, we'll have to call an ambulance."

Justin's hand shot up and grabbed her wrist. "Don't need an ambulance," he slurred. "Feels like I ran into a goddamn sledgehammer."

Katie sighed and placed her hand alongside his undamaged cheek. "What were you thinking, letting him use you like a punching bag?"

"That I deserved it," he whispered.

Katie's eyes filled, and Cutter turned away from the two of them to gaze out the window. He didn't like the emotions simmering inside him—shame being the one that climbed to the top. He'd wanted to kill Justin to remove him from his life—from Katie's and Dani's lives.

"I'll be outside," he said, and let himself out the front door. He didn't go far because his legs felt weak, so he sat heavily on the steps. A cold hollow feeling settled in his gut and he started to shake.

Cutter stared at his hands, at the bruises on his knuckles. He'd wanted to kill Justin. But when the other man had fallen, he'd thought he'd succeeded and he'd felt sick to his stomach.

For as long as he lived, he'd remember all expression leaving Justin's face as he fell backward. It surpassed the other memory, the one that had allowed him to nurse his anger, the one that had driven a spike between him and Katie.

Katie had been wrong. But he hadn't been blameless either. He'd been remote, pushed her away when she'd needed him to assure her he cared. He'd given Justin the perfect in.

Justin had been wrong to use Katie for his own pleasure and for revenge against him. But he'd never have had a chance at her if Cutter had treated Katie the way she'd deserved in the first place.

Remorse surpassed shame, and his shoulders fell. He

wouldn't be surprised if Katie decided he wasn't fit to have a place in their child's life. He'd been a hard, cruel bastard.

Rowe's truck pulled in behind his. Dani slipped from the cab before Rowe cut the engine. Cutter couldn't meet her gaze as she raced up the steps and entered the house, but he heard her cry of dismay and winced.

"You've done it now," Rowe muttered.

Cutter curled his fingers into fists then dropped them to his knees. "He shouldn't have been here."

"You're right. But I doubt he came for the reason you think."

Cutter hung his head. "How do I make this right?"

"You really want to?" Rowe's voice held an edge of anger, but a deeper streak of exasperation. "Or do you want to keep carrying around your anger?"

"Katie...she won't marry me."

"You thought it had something to do with Justin?"

"Not really. But when I saw them standing there together. I lost it."

Rowe pressed a hand to his shoulder and settled on the step next to him.

"Congratulations, by the way," Cutter muttered.

"Same to you." Rowe's gaze swung toward him. "We're both gonna be fathers. Justin's gonna be your kid's uncle. Don't you think it's time to let go?"

Cutter nodded. "I want to."

"Can you forgive Katie? Can you get past the fact she cheated? Some men couldn't."

Cutter's gaze lifted to the wide, cloudless sky. That's what it all boiled down to—the one thing that he couldn't seem to get past. If he didn't figure out how to let go, he'd lose her. And suddenly, he knew he'd be hurt worse if he let her slip away. "I love her. I have to try."

"You ever tell her that?"

"I didn't know it myself. Not until Justin hit the ground, and I thought I'd killed him. I wanted to take it back. I didn't want her to look at me like I was some kind of monster. I don't want to be that man."

"Don't go anywhere. We'll clear out and give you a chance to talk with Katie."

"What do I say? I've stopped her cold every time she tried."

Rowe squinted as he raised his glance to the sun as it flared at the horizon. Then he aimed a steady glare at Cutter. "You start with 'I'm sorry'."

Cutter nodded and ground his jaw tight, afraid like he'd never been before in his life. Not even when his parents had died and the responsibility for the ranch and raising Dani fell on his shoulders. He'd done his duty then, but this time, he knew happiness would never be his without Katie.

Katie watched Justin stumble out of the house, his arm draped over Rowe's shoulders for support. Dani gave her a worried look.

"You go on." Katie picked up the soiled towel and worked at a spot of blood on her sofa, but the more she rubbed, the larger it got. "Dammit."

"I'll replace it," came a low, growling murmur.

She didn't turn toward Cutter, afraid if she did she'd launch herself at him and beat her fists against his chest. "Don't bother. I don't want anything from you."

"Katie, I'm sorry."

"I know. But it's not enough."

"Do you want me to leave?"

She opened her mouth to tell him yes, but her throat closed. She nodded and kept her face turned so he wouldn't see the tears leaking down her face.

A deep sigh sounded behind her, footsteps shuffled toward the door. She waited but Cutter didn't open it.

She glanced over her shoulder. His hand was on the knob, his head was bent, his shoulders drooping. She'd never seen Cutter anything but strong and the sight tore at her heart. "Did you really think I wanted him?"

"No."

"Then why?"

"He hurt us," he whispered.

Katie felt a wash of cool relief pass over her. The sorrow in his voice was everything she could have hoped for. Cutter wasn't cold or withdrawn. And he wasn't angry anymore. She rose on shaking limbs and walked slowly toward him. When she stood directly behind him, his breath caught.

Katie lifted her arms and wrapped them around his waist and pressed her cheek against his strong back. "I love you, Cutter Standifer. I've only ever loved you."

A deep inhalation expanded his chest and belly. "Katie, I can change. I'd like to try."

"I don't need you to change. I just need you to be with me. To not shut me out. I love you, and I won't ever let you down again."

"I can't promise I won't. I have a temper."

"I won't give you any reason to lose it again."

His hands closed over hers and he squeezed. "I want to marry you; I want to be a good husband, a good father."

"You will be. And I'll marry you. But I have to know...will you ever love me back?"

Cutter lifted her hands and turned inside her embrace.

She didn't know she'd been crying until his thumbs swept the moisture from face. "Look at me, baby."

Katie pressed her lips together, blinked away the tears and slowly lifted her face.

Cutter shook his head and pushed her gently back, then he sank onto one knee and drew one of her hands inside his. "I have to do this thing right. Will you marry me, Katie Grissom? I love you and I want to spend the rest of our lives proving it to you."

Katie felt a smile pull at her lips. "I can think of few ways you can start."

Cutter blinked and his face lost its fierce tension. When he met her gaze, his eyes shone with tears. "Gimme a list. I'll start right now."

Cutter thought heaven must be filled with simple pleasures. Katie's head, nestled on his shoulder as she slept was one of them. He could get used to this, crave it like a drug, make it a habit he'd never want to break. He didn't for a minute think that all their problems were behind them. He still had peace to make with Dani and her men. Much as it stuck in his craw, he'd do his best to accept Justin within the circle of his family.

His respect for Justin had grown the moment the man had lowered his fists. Only a man in love would sacrifice so much.

Katie stirred, her legs nudging his as she stretched. When her eyes opened, he smiled. "You been waitin' on me to wake up?"

"Yeah. Wanted to make sure you were rested."

She gave him a wicked grin. "Am I gonna need it?"

Cutter didn't answer her with words; he rolled with her, stopping when he had her under him. "Take me inside you."

"You always know just what to say to get me in the mood."

He grunted, pleased she was teasing him again. Cutter slipped his arms beneath her, and cupped her ass. Then he flexed his hips and drove inside her.

Katie's breath left her in a harsh gasp.

"Too fast?"

"Perfect," she whispered. "You overwhelm me. If you haven't figured it out. I love that about you."

He remembered a time when he'd thought he had to go slow with her, and he grimaced. "Guess I'm slow learner."

"That's okay. I'm not." She undulated beneath him, rocking her hips upward to take him deeper. Her legs opened wider, her knees rose and snuggled against his hips.

"Do I have to be gentle now?"

"Not for a few more months."

"Good," he growled and plunged inside her. Katie's warm,

wet depths caressed every inch he thrust inside her. "You feel so damn good."

Katie nuzzled his shoulder then bit gently into his skin. "When I'm here, you covering me from head to foot, I feel small, really feminine, you know?"

"Do I scare you?"

"When your face hardens into granite, yeah you do. Because I know you're close to losing it. I like that I do that to you."

"Baby…baby, *fuck*," he chanted, thrusting faster.

Her legs wrapped around his waist; her feet rested on his buttocks. He liked the weight, liked being locked to her body. Silky liquid slicked his cock as he drove into her again and again.

Katie's head turned side to side as her eyelids slid closed. Her mouth opened around a throaty groan.

Cutter bent and smoothed his lips over the tender skin beneath her jaw then suctioned. She'd have a mark, something she'd scold him for, but anyone looking at her would know she'd been branded.

Soon enough she'd wear a brand everyone could see in the swell of her belly where their child rested beneath her heart. Warmth filled his chest as he stared down at her, watching the soft color flood her cheeks, the sweat break on her forehead, and her mouth gasp around her labored breaths.

He pushed up, lifting his chest from hers.

Katie's eyes slowly opened and her gaze locked with his. "I want it all, Cutter. Don't you dare hold back. I'm not fragile." She placed her hands on his chest and gently raked her nails through his hair.

Her encouragement was just enough to send him over the edge. He gathered his knees beneath him and increased the speed and depth of his thrusts, hammering toward her core.

With her back arching, her nails digging into his spine, and her eyes losing focus, he felt powerful, masculine and complete.

Cutter was a simple man—a meat and potatoes kind of

guy. And the simple pleasure of watching Katie's face as she shuddered toward her orgasm would be enough to keep him content for the rest of his life.

About the Author

Until recently, award-winning erotica and romance author Delilah Devlin lived in South Texas at the intersection of two dry creeks, surrounded by sexy cowboys in Wranglers. These days, she's missing the wide-open skies and starry nights but loving her dark forest in Central Arkansas, with its eccentric characters and isolation—the better to feed her hungry muse! For Delilah, the greatest sin is driving between the lines, because it's comfortable and safe. Her personal journey has taken her through one war and many countries, cultures, jobs, and relationships to bring her to the place where she is now— writing sexy adventures that hold more than a kernel of autobiography and often share a common thread of self-discovery and transformation.

To learn more about Delilah Devlin, please visit www.delilahdevlin.com. Send an email to delilah@delilahdevlin.com or join her Yahoo! group to enter in the fun with other readers as well as Delilah: DelilahsDiary@yahoogroups.com

GREAT cheap FUN

Discover eBooks!

THE FASTEST WAY TO GET THE HOTTEST NAMES

Get your favorite authors on your favorite reader, long before they're out in print! Ebooks from Samhain go wherever you go, and work with whatever you carry—Palm, PDF, Mobi, and more.

samhain
publishing Ltd

LaVergne, TN USA
05 November 2010
203721LV00002B/1/P